# PHANTOM OF EXECUTION ROCKS

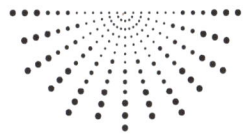

## MJ MILLER

PENDANT COVE BOOKS

Copyright © 2020 by MJ Miller

All rights reserved.

No part of this book may be reproduced in any form or by any electronic or mechanical means, including information storage and retrieval systems, without written permission from the author, except for the use of brief quotations in a book review.

This is a work of fiction. Names, characters, places, and incidents either are the products of the author's imagination or are used fictitiously. Any resemblance to actual persons, living or dead, businesses, companies, events, or locales is entirely coincidental.

*For Eric. 4 down, 96 to go.*

Few will have the greatness to bend history itself; but each of us can work to change a small portion of events, and in the total of all those acts will be written the history of this generation.

— ROBERT KENNEDY

# CHAPTER ONE

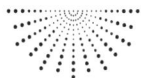

She could do this. Of course she could. Luce looked back towards the line of cars parked in the driveway. She'd told her sister no party. Not this year. But Annie didn't listen. She never does. Just plaster on a big smile and walk right in like she owns the place. That's all. So what if she's miserable. So what if that asshole detective with the burning eyes is there. So what if she's in no mood to celebrate. Suck it up, Luce, she told herself. Suck it up. Do it for Annie.

With a deep breath, she straightened her posture and smoothed out her skirt. She double-checked that she was presentable. And with as big a happy face as she could muster, walked in, feigned surprise at the resounding cheers, and headed straight for the wet bar in the sunken living room.

"Happy Birthday, Sis!" Annie threw her arms around her sister from behind, hugging her fiercely. Shaking her head and chuckling, Luce relaxed and smiled sincerely this time, turning to face her younger sister. Who she noticed with envy still looked like a twenty-something in her mid-thirties. The freckled faced youthful abandon had never left. Annie was the joyful one. Always had been. A dreamer who somehow always knew life had something wonderful in store. Luce envied that joy. Even tried to absorb some of it hoping it might rub off on her.

"Did I not tell you no party?" she asked, eyebrows raised.

"Yeah, but you say that every year. And I needed to do something nice for you. You know, after all the chaos I've caused. Please be happy. Please?"

"For you, I'll be happy, Annie. OK?" Luce sighed, smiled, and looked around. The same familiar faces all headed towards her.

The woman of the hour. Only she didn't want to be. She wanted to sit outside with a large glass of wine and wallow in self-pity. Last time all of them had been together, it was to witness Chris, her future brother-in-law, profess his undying love for Annie, after 15 years of mistakes and missed opportunities. It was an amazing moment for Annie. But bittersweet for Luce. She wanted that for herself, who wouldn't? Only that wasn't her style. Luce's love life was more serial dating than romance. Swipe left, swipe right, toss the phone across the room. With one tragic exception, her longest relationship was a long-ago summer fling with a lifeguard who took her virginity and gave her chickenpox.

She felt a familiar tingle and closed her eyes briefly. Preparing herself.

"Happy Birthday, Luce."

That voice. OMG, that voice. Deep. Sexy. And could only belong to one guy.

"Thanks," she nodded, trying to maintain her cool demeanor. Detective Andy Holman was a walking, talking, breathing sex god. Tall, broad shoulders, light sun-kissed hair, and brilliant dark eyes. If only he wasn't so smug and arrogant, she might... nope, she thought, not going there.

She tried to maintain eye contact. Tried to steady her gaze. And was failing miserably. He smiled at her as if he knew what she was thinking. They hadn't seen each other in a few months. She'd carefully avoided him. And intended to do so tonight if she could.

"If you'll excuse me," she murmured, nodding once again as she brushed past him and headed for safety. He watched her walk away, a smile playing upon his face. Everything about Luce was always neat. Put together. Her fair skin and green eyes were almost startling against her short and sleek dark hair. She was slender and graceful and yet there was a fire inside of her that he knew only a few lucky souls had ever seen. And he was one of them. Luce Porter was all that and more, he thought. A firecracker waiting to be lit.

His eyes followed her as she made her way around the room. Politely stopping to greet everyone. It wasn't a large group. There was Jen and Bill, friends of the Porter sisters and masterminds of Annie's reunion with Chris. Mark, Chris's editor and his wife Julie, who lived nearby as well as a few of Luce's friends from work.

Andy watched curiously as Luce headed out the French doors to the patio, with Annie following close behind. When he saw Annie place an arm around Luce's shoulder, he frowned. Was she upset? Something wrong? He shook it off. Not his business, he thought. Not going there. Not again.

"Come on, Luce, cheer up. What's got you so down?" Annie's voice was soothing, but there was concern in it. Luce was always in control, but right now, she didn't appear to be.

"Other than the fact that I'm thirty-seven, my eggs are drying up, and Matthew87 isn't actually six foot two with an eight figure bank account?"

"OK, I'll bite. Who's Matthew87?"

"Last night's date." Luce unlocked her phone and scrolled down, then handed it to Annie.

"Wow, he's smokin' hot, Luce..."

"No, he's not. This photo is. Only that's not him. Do you have any idea how mortifying it is to go to Alvino's on 64th, and spot this absolutely amazing guy waiting for you, waving and smiling, and when you approach his table, you discover it's all for the woman behind you? And you realize *your* date is the guy with the hoodie and the man-bun drinking Pabst Blue Ribbon?"

Annie pursed her lips, but it was no use. The laughter just burst right out of her, so hard she started coughing, and now it was Luce patting her on the back and offering comfort.

"Look, Luce, come inside. We've got a huge surprise, and you are gonna love it, and it will make everything better, I promise! And if it doesn't, we'll have Chris invite some of his friends to the wedding, and you can have your pick."

"Promise?" Luce grinned as she turned to head back inside. "Just not you know who, Annie. What's he doing here, anyway?" Luce lowered her voice, not sure where Andy was at but somehow knowing he'd eavesdrop if he could.

"Come on, Luce, the guy practically saved my life. And he and Chris are inseparable now. Plus, you and he have some pretty hot sparks flying, you know." Annie chuckled and elbowed her sister. "Come on, I mean he's seriously hot and you know if he were anyone else…" her voice trailed off as the very subject of their conversation approached.

Luce eyed him suspiciously. The smile on his face wasn't a friendly one at all. She knew that look. She just didn't know what it meant. He was up to something, though. He always was. And while it's true, she did owe him for saving Annie from a psychopathic stalker, she hadn't yet forgiven him for busting her at a crime scene during her days as a cub reporter for the New York News. It wasn't her fault she accidentally stepped around the crime scene tape and tripped on a wire and contaminated the evidence. Not totally, anyway.

But after that? The only assignments she was given were local social events and celebrity funerals. Though truth be told, it did lead her into TV news production and her current career. It wasn't all bad. She refused to let him in on that revelation. No way she was going to give him the satisfaction.

"Hey, everyone, can I have your attention!" Chris stood in the center of the room with an envelope in his hand. "What I have here, ladies and gents, is going to make Luce the happiest birthday girl in the world!"

Luce eyed him suspiciously, especially with Annie, standing next to him, looking up at her fiancé as if he hung the moon. For her, he did. Perhaps for any woman. Chris Gregory was good looking, a bestselling author, and a genuinely nice guy. And he was devoted to Annie. She sighed. Unless Chris was going to magically produce the perfect guy for her from that envelope, he might be disappointed in her reaction to whatever he had in his hands. She glanced over at Andy, standing off to the side, still wearing that silly smirk. He knew what was in the envelope. She narrowed her eyes at him, but he wasn't having any of it. Just shook his head slightly.

"What I have here, in my hot little hands, is the one thing Luce Porter will not be able to turn down."

Now Luce was really curious. She started ticking off ideas in her head. Maybe tickets to Hamilton? John Legend? Celine Dion? She searched Annie's face for clues, as she was just beaming. As if she'd waited her whole life for this. Wait. No. It couldn't be. Could it?

## CHAPTER TWO

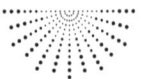

"*S*hhh... ready? Here we go!" Chris smiled as he handed Luce the envelope. Still wary, she took the envelope and shook it. Nothing. Carefully running her finger along the inner seam, she popped the flap open and reached in to pull out a single embossed card.

*Mrs. Adeline Bowers cordially requests*
*the pleasure of your company*
*At the Annual Ghost Ship Mystery Dinner*
*Friday, June 10<sup>th</sup>*
*Please RSVP 516-555-1212*

"No way. It's the Ghost Ship dinner? The mystery dinner? I get to be there?"

"You, Luce, are the investigative reporter this year!" Annie practically shouted with glee. "Is that not awesome?"

Luce was for once, speechless. This was indeed the ultimate birthday gift. One she never even thought possible. It was on her bucket list. Like everyone else, she had one, a short one, but a list nevertheless.

1. *Take a tour of the castles of Scotland*

2. *See Celine Dion live*
3. *Solve the mystery of The Cow Neck Ghost Ship*

The last one really should have been number one, but Luce really had no hope of ever accomplishing it. When she and Annie were small, their dad had loved to tell them the story of the ghost ship that disappeared off the coast of Long Island. Fifty two lost their lives, but one survived. And was haunted for the rest of her days. But for Luce, it was more than just an old tale. Much more.

She'd heard rumors that Old Lady Bowers had started inviting a group to dinner every year and handed out clues, allowing guests to mill about and try to solve the mystery. Figure out where and how the ship went down. And now Luce was actually going to get to participate.

She threw her arms around her sister, then around Chris, and before she could stop herself, almost around Andy. Realizing her error, she stepped back, stumbling, eyes wide.

Andy just smiled, shaking his head. Seeing Luce this happy for some inexplicable reason made him happy too. Though it shouldn't. She truly could shoot him down with her sharp tongue and buttoned-up demeanor. But then again, sweet and demure wasn't his style anyway. He knew there was more coming and couldn't wait to see the expression on her face.

"How did you get this? Who else is invited? Are you all going?" Luce was almost breathless as the questions poured out.

"We're all going, you, me, Chris, Mark and Julie, Jen and Bill, and of course..." Annie laughed and looked over at Andy.

Luce frowned.

"Sorry, Sis, but Andy's the one that scored the invite."

Luce looked over at him in surprise, a blush creeping up her face. "You did? How did you know? Annie, did you tell him?" Nobody but Annie knew about her obsession.

Andy smirked. "I'm not sure what it is I know or don't know, Luce, but I happened to notice your bookshelf had a number of books on ghost ships. I heard about this dinner and thought of you."

Luce was literally speechless. Embarrassed too. She tried to recall when or how he was in her apartment. Must have been during that terrifying episode when Annie's apartment was broken into. Lucky for Luce, Andy was the detective who handled it. Lucky for them all actually, he was good at his job. Too bad, his personal skills were sorely lacking most of the time.

She sighed. This was quite possibly the best gift ever, and the one guy she couldn't seem to handle or control was the one guy who'd thought of it.

Andy watched her expression and laughed. "Do I get a hug now too?"

Luce found herself stammering. "Um, no, well, I mean, thank you?"

He laughed again, a deep, genuine laugh. "It's OK Luce, you can thank me later," he winked as he turned and headed over to the bar. Leaving Luce stunned. And everyone else wondering just what lay ahead.

"Annie, why didn't you warn me?" Luce grumbled.

"Because Luce, you need to loosen up. Go with the flow. We're all going to have a fabulous time. You know it."

"Fine. But don't think you're getting off that easy." Luce really wanted a refill, but since Andy was still pouring a drink, she'd have to wait. Nervously tapping her empty glass, she looked around. Wondered where Jen had gone off to, seeing Bill talking with Mark. You couldn't miss Bill. He was like a huge red-headed lumberjack. Southern style. He and Jen had a fairytale romance. Mark and Julie? High School sweethearts who reconnected after college. Annie and Chris? Star-crossed lovers. And then there was Luce. She sighed and shook her head.

Glancing over at the bar, seeing nobody there, she headed that way, almost walking straight into Andy.

"Looking for this?" He grinned and held out a glass to her.

Luce took the glass, holding it up, sniffed, took a sip. "Pinot Noir. How'd you know?"

Andy just raised one eyebrow. "A gentleman never tells," he said.

"Well, thank you. Again." Luce shook her head softly and smiled as she laid her empty glass on a nearby tray. "I seem to be saying that a lot lately."

"Well, I don't mind." Andy smiled back. "But, I do need to warn you, Luce."

Luce rolled her eyes. "Here it comes, I knew this was too good to be true."

"Mrs. Bowers' invite cost me dearly. So I might have to call in a favor."

"Favor? You need a favor from me?"

"I do." Andy swirled his drink, pursed his lips. He almost looked nervous, Luce thought.

"OK, spill it. What's the favor?" Luce couldn't even imagine. Whatever it was, though, it was awfully hard for him to ask. "I won't bite, you know unless, of course, that's the favor?" She laughed at her own joke, but it didn't seem to relax him.

Her mind once again started ticking off possibilities.

*He wants tickets to a studio recording.*

*Daytime talk shows aren't his thing.*

*His cousin needs a place to stay in the city.*

*Does he have any cousins?*

*He needs a ride back to the city.*

*No, his car's out front.*

Clearly, she had no idea. She held her breath and waited, watching his expression.

"It's not for me, you know. I mean, I would never ever..." Andy hesitated. Hopefully, she really was who he thought she was. Guess no better time than the present to find out.

"My niece. Her internship fell through for the fall semester. She's a comm major at NYU. I was wondering if maybe you might check and see if you had any openings at the station. If you know, you don't mind? If not, I totally get it." He paused, trying to gauge her reaction.

Luce felt herself relax. This was a favor she could deal with. And truthfully, she did need an intern. And having Andy in her debt could be quite useful. She might also get to learn a little bit more about him.

"This niece of yours. Tell me about her." She was fishing, of course.

"Oh, well, she's a senior. Just turned 21."

"I see. Does this 21-year-old have a name?"

"Yeah, sorry, Kat. My sister's kid. Sweet but a bit nerdy."

Luce reached into the outside pocket of her purse and grabbed her business card.

"Here, have her send me her resume. I'll see what I can do."

She was startled to see Andy's face light up. His smile just beamed. And she was struck once again with how aristocratic he could appear at times. Chiseled features, flashing dark eyes and a full thick head of sandy blonde hair. The kind she wanted to run her fingers through. *Perish the thought.*

"Thanks, Luce, really, you don't know what this means. There is one thing, though." This was it. He hesitated, not sure how she'd react, just hoping.

"She's in a wheelchair." He waited.

"And?" Luce looked at Andy curiously.

"And she's in a wheelchair."

"Do you want to elaborate? Is she independent, or does she have a caregiver? Is she smart and capable?" Luce didn't mean to sound inconsiderate, but she really didn't care whether Kat was in a wheelchair. As long as she could learn and do what's asked of her.

"Not at all, I just thought to warn you," Andy responded a bit brusquely. "Look I'll understand if you don't want to hire her, I just wanted you to know."

"Andy," She sighed. "If I hire her, It's because I think she can do the job. Do you think she can do the job?" Luce hoped that sounded more professional than snarky.

"I do. Absolutely."

"Then just have her send me her resume. If she's got some merit, I'll interview her. I don't hand out job favors."

"Okay, I'll have her get in touch, and thanks." Andy slipped the card in his pocket. Looked around for someone to save him. He didn't like asking favors from anyone, Luce, in particular. He was also quite fond of Kat and wanted to help her out. Whether putting her in the same space as Luce was wise… that was yet to be seen.

"It's all good, Andy, really. This business is all about who you know, nothing else. If your niece wants in, we'll give her a shot. If she's not compatible, I'll send her to someone who is. Deal?" Luce hoped it eased his mind. She didn't have any nieces or nephews yet, hopefully soon, but she did know what it was to have family. Seeing the crack in his armor when it came to family was more than interesting—just one more piece of the puzzle she needed to work out.

By the time Luce arrived home, she was exhausted and exhilarated all at once. The whole idea of the Mystery Dinner was truly more than she could grasp. Her investigative inner nerd was screaming with excitement. Having all her friends along for the ride? Even better. Though Andy she wasn't so sure about. He was that temptation sitting in the bakery window, screaming at her to indulge, while her better self reminded her to stay in control. She wondered about his niece. And his motivation. She didn't have to wonder long.

## CHAPTER THREE

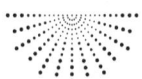

*L*ike any true type A, Luce found that organization and routine were essential. And bedtime rituals were sacred. A cup of Lemon Balm tea, one last check of her email, a chapter or two of a good romance, and then sleep. Every night was the same. The routine was something she hated but somehow craved. Maybe she needed to add one more thing to her bucket list. Something to change her life from ordinary to extraordinary. Whatever that might mean.

As she sat at her café table by the window, she gazed out at the softly lit up street lined with brownstones and carefully placed trees. Her uptown Manhattan townhome was her one indulgence in life. Her comfort zone. After her parents' tragic and sudden death, Luce purchased it with her share of the life insurance money. Annie lived with her for a short time, then found her own place. It was better that way, grown sisters shouldn't live together. She and Annie were different as night and day. But Luce, being older, felt a responsibility to make sure Annie had what she wanted and needed in life. Up until now, it had been all about Annie. But Annie's life was on track now. And it was Luce's turn. At least that was what everyone kept telling her.

Opening her email, she was surprised to see that Andy's niece had already submitted a resume. Opening it, she scanned it briefly. And was immediately impressed. 4.0 GPA. The attached recommendations were stellar. But it was her cover letter that sealed it.

*Dear Ms. Porter:*
*Thank you so very much for allowing me the chance to apply for an internship. As you know, I'm sure, the only way to really experience what media production is like is to hit the pavement running per se. Which, as I'm sure my uncle mentioned, is not something I can physically do. Which makes me no different from half the women in New York trying to race to the subway in stilettos.*

Luce chuckled. Good. A sense of humor goes a long way. Kat seemed direct, as well. She continued reading.

*What I can do is provide you with a keen and creative eye, as well as a damn good cup of coffee when needed. Or tea if that's your thing. I'm driven, and I'm hard working. And most of all, I need to step into the real world and get off my figurative ass and do something! I've spent my life being coddled. Being the exception. Not having to live up to any great expectations (no pun intended.) I've heard rumors that you are tough but fair and an excellent mentor. Which is why I begged Uncle Andrew to talk to you. I heard all about your adventures last year, so I can't wait to hear your version.*

What? Luce had no idea why Kat thought her version would be different, but there'd be time enough to find out. And Uncle Andrew? She'd never heard anyone use his full name.

*I look forward to hearing back from you soon, and hopefully scheduling an interview... please, please, please! Sorry about the begging, but let's be honest. I need this!*
*Respectfully yours,*
*Kat Downing*

Luce smiled and immediately hit reply. Her schedule was wide open, but no need to let Kat know. Better to see how eager she is.

*Dear Ms. Downing:*
*After carefully reviewing your resume and credentials, I feel an interview is warranted. I have an opening Monday morning at 7am. Our offices are at 401 7th Avenue, in the Hotel Pennsylvania. Use the main entrance and take the elevators to the 18th Floor.*
*If you are unable to make it, we can reschedule.*
*Regards,*
*Luce Porter*
*Executive Producer*
*New York Today*
*KNNY*

Luce sat back in the chair, sipping her tea, and waited. If Kat were eager, she'd be waiting at the ready to respond. Ding. Luce smiled and glanced at the time. Two minutes, not bad.

*Dear Ms. Porter:*
*7am Monday works perfectly. Thank you so, so much! I will see you then.*
*Regards,*
*Kat Downing*

Luce shut her laptop with a smile, grabbed her book from the end table by the sofa and headed to her bedroom. She found herself smiling all the way. And looking forward to meeting Kat. She had a feeling she was going to like her. A lot. Spunky, self-deprecating, clearly a fabulous sense of humor.

Her phone buzzed just as she was setting it down on her nightstand. Incoming text. Odd. Not typical for midnight on a Saturday. She glanced over and saw the familiar nickname. *Satan's Spawn.* She could have labeled him anything, but when he put his number in her phone, uninvited, she was in a huff. She wondered if he knew she'd done it.

**Did you hear from Kat?**

Clearly he knew she had. But she'd play along.

*Yes*

*Well?*

*I believe that's confidential*

*Come on, Luce, please?*

That made her grin. The detective is begging…

*Is that you begging?*

*Not nearly. But if you'd like…*

No. I am not going there, she thought. But that was the problem. Now she had a hot detective on her brain, begging… and that would never ever do. As much as she complained about being single and never finding quite the right guy, deep down, she knew it wasn't the men she was meeting, it was her. She had perfected the art of repelling men.

Except for Detective Andy Holman. She didn't seem to quite put him off. She could be the ice queen, and he saw right through it. Which means he could probably break her heart. Which was the one thing that was never going to happen to her again.

## CHAPTER FOUR

    *L*uce looked up as she heard the elevator ding. Poking her head out into the hallway, she saw the young woman carefully wheeling her way down toward her. Making sure to check each door to avoid getting lost.

"You must be Kat," she called out as the girl wheeled toward her. As she approached, Luce realized the chair was never going to squeeze through her doorway. "Looks like you need a smaller chair, do they have different sizes?" She smiled as she said it, and then outright laughed as she saw Kat's eyes widen in disbelief.

"Sorry, was that out of line?" Luce asked her, still smiling.

"Um, no, it's just well, people usually don't joke about it." Kat was clearly mystified. "I can walk a bit, so if you need me to leave the chair out in the hall, I can do that."

"Not a chance, Kat, sit tight, I'll come out there, but first, a phone call."

Luce pushed the intercom button on her desk phone and chewed on her lower lip as she picked up the cordless receiver. Diplomacy was required. And she didn't have enough coffee yet.

"Dan, yes, it's Luce Porter… yes, I'm fine, just need a favor." She took a breath. "Seems my office door is a few inches short of ADA regulations, can you fix that?" She waited, nodding. Listening to his excuses about how it takes time and work orders, etc. "OK, I'll handle the work order red tape, but I'll need this done by tomorrow." She hung up and leaned back with a satisfied look on her face. She was totally pissed off that the door wasn't regulation size—another bit of skimping to save a buck. The previous station owners weren't exactly on the up and up, one of the reasons they'd been bought out.

She looked up at Kat, who still sat outside the doorway in her chair, her facial expression a bundle of nerves. She was pretty, Luce noted. Her golden-brown hair, thick and wavy but neatly framing her heart-shaped face. She dressed simply, but Luce realized her clothes were intended to be functional and simple. A loose cotton skirt and blouse, nothing flashy. Andy had said she was independent, meaning she probably lived alone and cared for herself. Not sure of her physical limitations yet, Luce understood the need to ease into it. She certainly didn't want Kat to be uncomfortable. But she also knew she had to be able to cope with a fast-paced work environment and the lack of decorum at times.

"Let's head over to the conference room, we'll talk there." Kat was still staring at her. Hesitantly.

"Something wrong?" Luce asked, concerned.

"Did you really just ask them to fix the door instead of having me walk into the office? I mean, I could have. I just want you to know that."

Luce sighed and nodded. "I get that, I do. But it's on us to accommodate when necessary, please don't think that means I won't have you making coffee runs. I will. Frequently!" She smiled, happy to see Kat relax.

"So. Obviously, I'm Luce Porter. I'm assuming you're Kat Downing. And now that the introductions are out of the way, let's go hit the coffee bar."

"Not the conference room?" Kat looked confused again.

"Sorry," Luce laughed. "Same thing, actually."

Luce kept pace with Kat as they headed down the hall to the meeting room. It truly was an all-purpose room with snacks and beverages and a great big table for everyone to sit and brainstorm. Rarely used by anyone for more than a few minutes otherwise.

"What can I fix for you?" Luce waved her arm towards the beverage center in the corner, complete with everything from a complicated cappuccino and espresso maker to an Iced Tea brewer.

"Wow! Um, can I? I mean, can I make something? What do you like? I've used these before at my grandparent's so I know how…"

Luce grinned; she saw how excited Kat was. Who was she to deny her?

"Absolutely. I like a good strong brew, 14 oz, cream, and a shot of that monk fruit extract over there for sweetness."

"Got it," Kat grinned as she wheeled over. At least the coffee machines were at waist height, not the executive height counters that made it difficult.

Luce took a seat and rifled through the folder she'd brought with her with Kat's information as well as some notes she'd put down regarding the job responsibilities. She had a really good feeling about Kat and wanted this to work out. Her budget was tight, but judging from Kat's clothing, mannerisms, and extremely tasteful jewelry, Luce could smell the money. Somehow she had a hunch this wasn't about money. She just needed to make sure. New York isn't cheap, and internships don't pay the rent.

Kat returned to the table and placed the cup in front of Luce. Taking a careful sip, she sighed.

"Perfect! You're hired!"

Kat laughed. "Really?"

"Not yet, but let's talk and see," Luce smiled. This was working out well.

She waited for Kat to fix her own and watched as she carefully made a cappuccino. Yep, working out well. They chatted about nothing for a bit. The weather, the humidity, the cherry blossoms coming into bloom. Then it was time for the nitty-gritty. This was always the part that made the interviewee uncomfortable, but Luce knew how necessary the pressure was.

"Your grades obviously are impeccable. Your recommendations, as well. What I want to know is why? Why media? Why this internship? Where do you see yourself going with it?"

Kat relaxed, took a sip of her coffee, and looked at Luce directly.

"People always tell me not to let my disability define me. To limit me. But clearly, it does. Clearly, at times," she paused and grinned, "it makes getting your foot in the door impossible."

Luce chuckled. "Touché."

"But nobody seems to mind me and my chair with a camera. They let me wander around, taking photos and video, they smile and react well. I realized I could do something with this. And of course, there are no limits to what I can do with digital media. There's nothing in my way."

"I don't want to burst your bubble or step on your reality, Kat, but I know some incredible CEO's in a variety of industries who have one or more physical limitations. Though I'm guessing they had to work three times as hard and fight a lot more battles to get there. Society is a cruel mistress at times. And changing perceptions? Too slow. I just want to know you aren't settling for something when there's a dream around the corner waiting for you."

"Not at all. I love it. It's just that loving it is almost the icing on the cake. I just want to be honest. I think that's important."

"It is. How's your arm strength? Some of our equipment can get heavy."

"Well, I'm the Tri-State Women's Wheelchair Tennis Singles Champion 3 years running... so I'd say my upper body strength is pretty damn good." Kat grinned.

"I'd say that's as good as it gets. How about salary? Internships aren't known to pay well, I'm sure you realize that."

"Not a concern for me, though I know that sounds privileged and all, but the truth is, whatever you pay is fine. My family supports me, as much as I usually resent it, right now I'll take the humble route and appreciate it." Kat shrugged. "I can afford to be a lowly intern. I know some can't, and it's unfair."

"You're right, Kat, and I'm glad you realize that. It is difficult for most students to give up higher-paying part-time jobs for the time-consuming grunt work of an internship. It's a sacrifice for most. Which begs the question, what do you feel you'll sacrifice for this? What are you willing to put into it?"

"As it will be full time, independent study credits, I won't have any classes to interfere. I spent the first two summers taking the additional credits I needed, so I guess you could say I already did make the sacrifice, in a way…"

"All right, then moving on, what questions do you have for me?"

They went on like that for another half hour or so, chatting and getting to know each other and about each other. Luce was not only satisfied that Kat was perfect for the job, but she also looked forward to having her around. While Luce's façade for the world was the cool, collected, untouchable one… that's all it was. A façade. Having some refreshing honesty around her was just what she needed.

"Well, Kat, I think we're done here. I'll let you know what we decide within the next few days if that works?"

"Oh, absolutely. And Ms. Porter?"

"Luce, please."

"Luce. I just want to say thank you again. I know my Uncle called in a favor for this, and I sure hope whatever he gave you in return is worth it."

"I'll tell you what I told him. This isn't a favor. I wouldn't meet with you nor hire you if you weren't qualified. Rest assured on that."

"Well, thank you again for the opportunity." Luce watched Kat as she wheeled herself to the elevator and smiled. She'd make her wait, of course, but this was a no-brainer.

Her phone buzzed, not 10 minutes later.

*Well? Did it go well? She's great, isn't she? You'll hire her, right?*

Luce decided to mess with him.

*You'll be the last to know, I promise*

*But you liked her, right?*

Luce shook her head grinning.

*What do you think?*

*Come on, Luce…*

Time to turn the tables, she thought.

*Impatient much?*

*When it comes to you?*

Luce had no idea how to respond to that, so she left it alone. Instead, she put her proposal together for HR and emailed it. She hadn't been kidding about the salary. But she could sweeten the deal by allowing her to start in June rather than September. As long as HR approved it. But Luce was sure they would. She wasn't normally one to push for someone based on their disability, but the HR director was big on diversity and actively seeking to hire a broader spectrum of employees. All she could do was cross her fingers and wait.

CHAPTER FIVE

*L*uce's phone rang precisely 24 hours later. On the dot. Already at work at her desk, she expected it.

"Luce Porter," she answered promptly.

"Ms. Porter, it's Kat Downing? We met yesterday?"

"Of course, Kat, and again, it's Luce, please," she chuckled.

"I just wanted to thank you again and tell you that I am most definitely interested in anything you have available. Not to sound desperate, but I kind of am!"

"Well, naturally, or maybe it's just you know your uncle has been texting me incessantly and I desperately want him to stop!"

"Oh my god, I am so sorry! He's very overprotective. I'm not sure I mentioned it, but he's kind of more of a parent than an uncle. We're really close."

"No worries, Kat, I get it. I'm like that with my sister, and she's only a few years younger than I am. The good news is, you can tell him to put his phone away. If you could possibly come in this afternoon, we can talk about details, OK? The internship is yours if you want it."

"I want it. Oh my god, really? I so want it. Anytime? Or I can come now or whatever?"

"Relax, Kat, anytime today is fine, how about lunch. My treat. I can meet you in the lobby, say at 1 O'clock. Any earlier, we'll spend 2 hours just waiting to order something."

"Perfect, and thank you, Luce."

"I'll thank you to stop thanking me. You earned this. Got it?"

They said their goodbyes, and Luce smiled as she relaxed in her chair. Kat was going to be an awesome member of her crew. She wondered what it was that kept her using a wheelchair. She seemed robust and healthy otherwise. And she did say she could walk a bit. She could ask Andy, of course, but that would be wrong. No, she'd wait, and when the time was right, Kat would tell her.

The lunch idea turned out to be a perfect one, as maintenance had arrived to fix the doorway anyway. She was also expecting them to bring up a desk for Kat. The job wouldn't officially start for another week, but at least things could be ready for her.

She headed down to the lobby and found a lone bench to sit on. The lobby, which had once been the epitome of New York elegance, had been 'renovated' and was now empty of cozy seating and lush carpet. The crystal chandeliers had been replaced with contemporary lighting, and the elegant mahogany phone desks replaced with touchscreen kiosks. It had been modernized, which in Luce's mind simply meant sterilized. No character or personality. Much like her townhome. She'd always thought to redecorate it after moving in. Make it her own. Put her stamp on it. Instead, she'd left it as is. Elegant, cold, and sterile. Giving everyone who entered the impression that's who she was. She wondered if that's how Andy saw her. Aloof and unapproachable. The ice queen.

She glanced over as she saw Kat come in and stood up to meet her. They headed outside, and Luce suggested they head to a café around the corner. It was a good spot, quiet, away from the hub of $7^{th}$ avenue. They placed their orders, and Luce wasted no time.

"Kat, I need to go over some job details. First and foremost, it's full time. And we're not talking 8 hours a day, we're talking salaried, beck and call... I know you live downtown near campus, so be assured we'll cover the ride share costs if you have to head home after hours—no late-night subway rides. But there will be late nights. Can you do that?"

"Absolutely."

"The job pays $3000 a month. Which is more than some, less than others. No benefits. But your daily expenses, for the most part, we'll cover."

"It's fine, really. My rent is already covered, so I'm good."

"The office hours are 8 to 5, but if you need extra time in the morning, you tell me."

"I don't want any special treatment, Luce. I need to live in the real world, if I need to get up an hour earlier, I'll make it happen. Promise."

Luce grinned at Kat. "Well, if you have a hot date and are out really late, just text me."

Kat laughed. "It's about as likely as being asked to headline a runway show at the fashion institute."

"Don't sell yourself short. You've got a good sense of humor Kat; can I ask about it?" She motioned towards the chair.

"Not much to tell really, I was born with a rare deformity in my knees. They can't hold my weight, so I can only take a few steps without them giving way."

"Nothing can be done?" Luce asked openly.

"Knee replacements, but not until I reach full growth, which could be a year or two away, or another five. Until then, there's no point. I'll outgrow the replacement."

Nodding towards her legs, Luce continued. "Your legs appear well-toned, not that I'm interested in them, but how do you manage that?"

"It's important that I keep the muscles strengthened and toned. I have a strict exercise regimen. It's just my knees that don't work, so I have a personal trainer a few times a week but I can reschedule around work. He usually comes at 7, but I'll just have him come at 6."

"You're quite remarkable, Kat, and determined, I believe. You'll be a great asset to our team. You're probably wondering exactly what you'll be doing?"

"I am!"

"Well, mostly, as we discussed, you'll be my shadow. I juggle quite a bit, from production schedules to programming changes to new programming concepts. In fact, I know you don't officially start until next

Monday, but I've got a file full of concepts for new programming I need to be screened. Meaning you sift through and tell me what's worth looking at and what's not..."

"Wow, that sounds fun, actually! I'd love to. I'm done with finals so plenty of time on my hands."

"Good," Luce chuckled. "We get at least 25 or more log-lines a day. Are you familiar with those?"

"OMG, I must have done 50 of those last semester! I actually enjoyed it, though. It's like creating the perfect tweet, isn't it? Telling an entire story in one sentence!"

"Exactly, so I'll forward what we have, just mark the ones you think have merit. Leave the others. We don't delete anything, and we always respond. You'll be doing that as well. Don't worry, we've got a template to use."

"So now it's like I'm the cruel professor, eh?" Kat laughed. "I had so much rejection in the class I'd have stuck pins in a voodoo doll if I'd had one."

"Sounds like this is the perfect way to start off. I'll send the file over later. I've got you set up with an email account as well as a secure laptop, by the way. We'll stop by IT for those. And look, if you need to start an hour later on your training days, you let me know. That's certainly something we can work with."

"Yeah, but you shouldn't have to. I really need to be just like everyone else, Luce, it's important." Kat sighed and leaned forward. "Listen, I love Uncle Andrew, he's the best there is, but he's worse than a helicopter parent. I guess I should tell you that upfront. Knowing him, he'll be interfering. Checking up on me. Checking up on you. He can't seem to help himself. He's always been that way."

"Why? I'm just curious? I mean, I'm sure he loves you. You're his niece, but why so involved?"

"My parents weren't." She shrugged. "They had this vision of having the perfect child. And I wasn't. My uncle took over their role. He was always there, they weren't." Kat looked down for a moment, then looked up directly at Luce.

"I'm not telling you this so you'll pity me. Please don't."

"I wouldn't, Kat. But it helps to understand your situation. I can handle your uncle. I have before." Luce winked and smiled.

"I know," Kat replied with a grin.

"I don't want to know, do I?" Luce replied.

"Nope," Kat took a bite of her salad. "You definitely don't."

Luce pondered that but decided to tuck it away for later.

They finished up their lunch and started to head back towards the office when Kat's phone rang. It was actually quite loud, startling Luce. Especially the ringtone. Sounded suspiciously like the theme from Miami Vice. Luce thought that was odd for someone so young.

Kat grabbed her phone from her purse and barked into it.

"I'm kind of busy," she said abruptly. Clearly annoyed, though there was a smirk on her face. Must be her uncle, Luce realized and looked at Kat for confirmation. Yep.

Nodding to her phone, she whispered "Give it to me," and reached for it.

"Andy?"

"Oh crap, did I interrupt?"

"Yes, you did. We are having a final interview. And if you don't want to blow this for her, I suggest you wait until she's ready to bring you up to date. And let us finish our conversation."

"Just tell me, are you hiring her?"

"Confidential, Detective. I'm hanging up now." And she did.

Kat was doubled-over laughing. "I cannot believe you did that. That was awesome."

"Yeah, but I'll probably end up paying for it somehow, though it was worth it."

"Thank you, Luce, really. I wish I could do that. I always come off sounding ungrateful and bitchy. I don't mean to."

"No, you don't, you're just a young woman trying to live her life, and he's stepping in all the time, right?"

"How'd you know?"

"Ha! I did it to Annie. Only it was worse. I'm sure when you meet her, she'll tell you."

"I look forward to it. I can't believe I'm finally going to have a life! Yes!" Kat did a little bouncy thing in her chair, raising her hands in the air, making Luce laugh. It would be fun having her around. Someone to mentor, someone to take care of again. Someone to fill that hole.

## CHAPTER SIX

*L*uce hadn't been this excited in a very long time. The Ghost Ship event was coming up in a matter of days. Maybe she'd finally discover the secrets behind it. Would she be the one to solve the legendary mystery? It was going to be amazing, that much she knew. She finally had a little downtime, thanks to Kat. What a godsend she'd been. For the first time in months she felt like she had all her ducks in a row. Kat had turned out to be the perfect intern. Smart, enthusiastic, and always up to take on more and more. Which left Luce with a little free time in the evenings, and what better way to spend it than selecting an outfit for the Mystery Dinner.

Normally, she'd have just chosen a simple pencil skirt and blouse, neat, tidy, nothing flashy. But for some reason she wanted to make a splash. Oh, who was she kidding, she thought with a smirk eyeing her closet. Somewhere, deep down, or maybe right there obvious to all, she wanted Andy to notice. She suspected he did notice her already, but the friction that seemed to always be there, right at the surface, twisted her stomach in knots. She was Luce Porter. Cool, calm, collected and never flustered by a man. But Andy Holman? He wasn't your typical man. Her efforts to maintain control seemed to slip away in his presence.

She hadn't always been that way. She sighed as the negative thoughts creeped in. The ones she held at bay. The ones she refused to allow access to. Shaking it off, she grabbed her phone.

"Pick up, Annie, hurry up." Luce muttered, pacing her room. She needed Annie to distract her.

"Um, hey Luce, not a good time" Annie spoke quickly, a laugh in her voice.

"OMG you two are sickening. Listen. The teal cocktail dress or the black capris?"

"What's the occasion?"

"My gift? Mrs. Bowers? Ghost Ship?"

"Hmmm. Who are we out to impress? Wouldn't be a certain detective now would it?"

"Hell no. I mean, no. Not at all. I just want to look good, is that a problem?"

Annie laughed. "The cocktail dress, Luce. Definitely. And that's not why you called. Spill. What's up?"

"Nerves. I don't know why that man makes me nervous. I don't do nervous anymore. Not since Jack. You know that."

"Jack was a class A bastard, Luce, and doesn't represent the male species. He was a one of a kind jerk."

"You say that now, but back then…" her voice trailed off with a shake. Jack had been, at one time, that guy. The one she imagined spending her life with. Ticked off all those boxes. Until things got messy.

"He played you Luce; made you think he was a stand-up guy but when push came to shove his true colors oozed out of him. Now. Enough of Jack. Let's go back to Andy and the dinner shall we? Are you coming out with Jen or taking the train?"

"Hadn't decided yet. I'll let you know after I talk to Jen."

"Cool. We'll all meet here, at our house and drive over. You realize it's only a half-mile or so from us."

"I didn't realize that, no. But that's good. If it's boring we can always just sneak off."

"Luce, you are going to have an amazing time. Now, tell me about Kat? You like her?"

"I hate to admit it, but Andy's the one who did me a favor with her. She's perfect. Just don't tell him that."

"Oooh… so you owe him big time. The dinner invite *and* Kat. Hmmm. I'm sure he'll find a way to have you pay it all back!"

"Don't go there, sis, leave it alone."

"No can do Luce, he's seriously hot!"

Luce could hear Chris whispering in the background and Annie giggling.

"Save it Annie, I'll see you Friday night."

Luce hit a button and tossed her phone on her bed, deciding to try on every dress hanging in her closet. She needed to be prepared. Make sure she had the right accessories. Stripping out of her work clothes, she reached into her closet when her phone rang again. Probably Annie with one of her *one more thing* calls.

Glancing at the screen her eyes widened.

*No. Not a good time.*

"Hello?"

"Hey Luce, it's Andy."

Luce started to shift uncomfortably. Standing in her bra and panties was definitely not the way to have this conversation. Her whole body buzzed.

"Andy? Um, what can I do for you?"

*Oh my god did I just say that standing here half naked?*

"Want to carpool Friday night? I'll pick you up around 4. Or is that too early?"

"Aren't you supposed to wait for me to say yes?"

"Seems you just did. See you then!"

"But," Luce let out a sigh. He'd hung up. Should she call back? Text him? Say no thanks?

She glanced in the mirror. Still half-naked. With a body blush to boot. Nope, not calling him back. Tossing the phone onto her dresser, she flopped down on her bed and stretched out, staring at the ceiling, wondering how she'd get out of this one. An hour or more in the car with him could be the end of her sanity. But the little devil on her shoulder was saying it could be the beginning of something too.

He was annoyingly prompt. Precisely at 4pm her buzzer rang. Luce was ready, naturally, she'd been ready for a half hour. She'd chosen the dress Annie had suggested, and she had to admit it was a good choice. She stopped nervously pacing back and forth and buzzed him in, gnawing on her lip nervously. Something she rarely did. Annie was the lip gnawer, never Luce. Except around this one singular detective. *Nothing to be nervous about, she thought. She should be excited. It was going to be amazing. This was all just nervous energy. Breathe.*

She had the door open the minute he knocked. Slipping by him into the hall, she quickly locked the door and headed out.

"I'm not double-parked you know, and hello to you too," Andy called after her. He smiled though, admiring the way she swayed as she walked. Shaking his head, he followed after her, picking up the pace to catch up as they exited her building. And chuckling as she nearly jumped when he took her elbow to steer her towards his car. When he stopped, she glanced up at him, a look of confusion on her face.

"I thought you drove a Subaru?" she questioned him suspiciously. "That's what you were driving last time."

"I like to mix things up," he laughed as he opened the passenger door.

"This is a Lexus. How is it you drive a Lexus?" Luce was now confused. As confused as last summer, when he'd arranged for her to fly out to see Annie after she was run off the road in Ohio during a crazy and dangerous adventure. She knew then he'd sprung for the airline ticket, the hotel and anything else she needed. Which would be nearly impossible on his NYPD salary.

She slipped into the passenger seat and waited until he'd settled in and started to pull out. She'd had a chance to give him a good once-over now. Designer slacks, expensive cotton tailored shirt, no tie, a few undone buttons at the collar. Even more expensive cuff-links. She'd never seen him dressed in anything other than a pair of jeans or khakis and a polo or t-shirt. Well, that along with his leather bomber jacket that seriously made him eye-candy. Attire that fit a guy like him. This was suspicious.

"You're not on the take, are you?" Luce asked suddenly. It occurred to her, and she was known to be fairly unfiltered at times.

He let out a laugh. That wonderful deep throaty laugh that made her sigh. Only this time it was in frustration.

"Don't laugh, you're dressed like a GQ model and drive a Lexus. Unless you've been promoted or changed jobs… seems awfully suspicious. Wouldn't you agree?"

"And you're a TV program producer who's got a fabulous 2-bedroom on the upper west side. But does that make you a high priced escort?"

Luce blushed furiously and sputtered. "An escort? Seriously?"

"On the take? Seriously?"

She bit her lip and clamped down to stop from responding.

"OK, fair enough Luce. I know that reporter in you is just going to stew on it. Ask me anything and I'll try to answer it truthfully. Just not about work. That's off limits. And since turnabout is fair play, I get to ask you anything too."

They had an hour or so to go, and she didn't want to ride in silence, so she simply nodded her agreement.

"But I go first," she tossed out, and without waiting for an answer, because again, no filter, she dove in.

## CHAPTER SEVEN

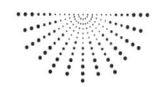

"Middle name?" Luce tossed it out.

"Seriously?"

"Yep." She had her reasons. Middle names often told a story. She'd learned that from one of her journalism professors. And Chris as well. He said authors spent more time on middle names than given ones.

"Delano." He said it quietly, awaiting a reaction.

"Hmm," Luce remarked. Her brain completely engaged now. Delano was a prominent name for anyone who studied American History.

"Age?" Luce knew he was somewhere around 40, but just wanted to confirm.

"Nuh uh, my turn." Andy grinned. "And I already know your middle name. Skye. Suits you."

"Suits me how? And how do you know that?" Luce didn't know whether to be angry or flattered.

"Police reports Luce, we're pretty thorough you know. Moving on... single? As in not dating anyone, or single as in serial dating?"

"That's a ridiculous question. Next?"

"Come on, play along."

"Single. At the moment."

"At the moment, technically, you're on a date."

"Says who?" Luce crossed her arms in front of her. This was not a date. No way. "We're carpooling, that's all."

"Yeah, about that. The dinner is a couples only kind of thing, everybody invited gets a plus one."

Luce glanced over and sure enough, he was smirking.

"My invite did not say plus one, I read it carefully."

"I know, but that's because you're my plus one."

Now he was outright grinning. Luce had no idea what to say to that. She'd never quite been trapped into a date unknowingly. And having Andy trick her into it was unsettling to say the least.

"This is a friend date, though, right?"

"Guess we'll see," Andy glanced over at her a bit nervously. His eyes flashed with something. She needed to change the direction of this conversation fast.

"My turn. How'd you score the invites?" She'd googled Mrs. Bowers quite infamous mystery dinners and discovered how exclusive they were. Previous attendees were all socially prominent and wealthy. No exceptions.

"I have a connection or two. I called in a favor." Andy smirked, glancing over at Luce. "It's quite a long story. Perhaps next time I'll tell you the whole thing."

"Next time? We have not agreed there's going to be a next time. You assume a lot don't you?"

"Guilty as charged. Moving on, my turn. Annie tells me you grew up in Pelham."

"Annie talks too much."

"Leave your sister alone, she's adorable."

"I know, I know. Annie's always been the adorable one. Sweet, innocent Annie. Yeah, we grew up in Pelham. You?"

"On the Island."

"Which is why you are so familiar with it. I always thought you were too comfortable driving out this way." She shook her head as he smoothly exited out onto the Long Island Expressway. "You don't even need the directions do you?"

"No, but I do spend a bit of time out there with Chris, which you know since you spend a lot of time with Annie."

"Which begs another question, Detective."

"Nuh uh, my turn again." He laughed.

"Why are you so fascinated with the Ghost Ship?" His tone was light but curious.

"Our dad used to tell us stories about it."

"Truth, Luce, you have to be truthful." He snickered and shook his head.

"How do you know that's not the reason?"

Andy raised a brow and remained silent.

Huffing with annoyance, she started to tap nervously on her thigh.

"You can tell me anything Luce, really. Out with it. It might help us solve the mystery if I know what you know."

She silently admitted he had a point. But she also knew he might just burst out laughing.

"I have your word you won't laugh?" Luce asked him, her tone indicating if he did, she might injure him.

"My word," he laughed and held out his hand. "Pinky swear," he said.

She really didn't want to link fingers with him. She already knew what it would do to her resolve.

"Well?" he asked.

"I've seen it. OK?" She quickly looked away, out the window... waiting for the laughter. The *are you kidding* remarks. But they never came.

"Tell me," was his only response. His words left hanging in the air. Quietly spoken. Serious. He believed her? She looked over to make sure. Not even the hint of a smirk.

Taking a deep breath, she recounted her tale.

"My dad used to take us out sailing. We had a sunfish. Just a small boat but we learned to sail and we'd go out into the sound and picnic on the islands. One day we sailed out to Execution Rocks. You know it?"

Andy chuckled. "I happen to be one of those idiots who tried to swim out there, when the sandbars were high."

Luce smiled and rolled her eyes. "Why does that not surprise me? In any case, we sailed out and pulled up, tying up the boat so we could sit on the rocks and have lunch. I got up to walk around the rocks, go check out the lighthouse and I saw this ship coming toward the island. I was nervous about even being there, since the whole place is quite creepy. You know they killed slaves there. Who would do that? I mean having slaves is evil enough, but they say they were chained to the rocks and left to drown."

Luce paused, the whole story made her incredibly sad and angry all at once.

"You're right. The ship, tell me."

"So yeah, I saw it. It looked like an Armada ship. You know about boats?"

"A bit, yeah."

"Well it was large, with maybe 6 sails billowing, and cannon heads coming out below deck from the sides. It sailed right past me, and there wasn't a soul on it. I went stumbling back over and pointed it out to Dad and Annie. Only they didn't see a thing. They thought I was nuts."

"I don't."

Luce smiled at him. "Thanks. In any case, to humor me I suppose, my dad researched it, he was a history teacher, and he learned about the legend of the ghost ship. Every so often, someone would report seeing a ship pass through the same area of the Long Island Sound. The more he learned the more he shared with us as kind of a bedtime tale. I think it mostly amused him, but I knew it was real."

"Well, no time like the present to find out," Andy chuckled.

They chatted on for a while, until Luce realized they were already exiting off the expressway, not too much further. Would tonight be the night she finally confirmed her long ago vision? Or would she be disappointed once again by people mocking the true mystery. At least Andy wasn't mocking her. That was a start. She glanced over at him and wondered though. Why all the sudden interest? He usually liked to taunt her a bit, rile her up. He was acting more and more like a guy interested in starting something up and it perplexed her. Another mystery to solve.

The chiming of a cell phone through his Bluetooth startled her.

"Talk to me."

Luce grinned, such a typical NY greeting.

"Hey, you guys getting close?" Chris's voice boomed through the speakers, causing Andy to quickly turn the volume down.

"Yeah, a few miles away, sat in traffic for a damn hour, be there by 6."

"Great, everyone's here, Annie's worried Luce might have chopped and diced you into pieces by now and left you buried in the marshes."

"No such luck!" Luce said with a laugh.

"All right, we'll see you soon, and by the way, we've got news." With that, Chris hung up.

"News?" Luce looked at Andy who appeared just as baffled.

"What do you think it is?" Andy asked curiously.

"No clue." Luce shook her head. "But it better be good…"

## CHAPTER EIGHT

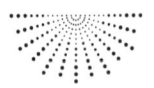

"OMG Luce finally! What took you so long?" Annie didn't wait for Luce to even get her cardigan off before practically crashing into her as she was shrugging out of the sleeves.

Laughing, Luce hugged her and let her have her moment. "OK, spill. What's the big news!"

"Lucey goose, you're gonna love this. Seriously."

"I'm afraid to ask now, but what has your news got to do with me?" Luce looked at her sister's face closely for hints.

"Hang on, no, come on hurry in… to the living room, everyone's here and they all need to hear this too. We were just waiting for you guys to get here."

Andy grabbed Luce's sweater, and handed it to Chris to hang up, and placed his hand lightly on her back, steering her. And making her jump.

"Luce, relax." Andy smirked, and Luce just shook it off. She really was out of her element in all this. As if Andy had some scheme up his sleeve and everyone was aware of it except her.

She took a few steps ahead to put some distance between them, and headed over to the couch, then quickly changing her mind, grabbed a chair instead and settled in to await the big news. Her eyes tracked Andy as he made his way across to the bar, and she couldn't hide the smile as she watched him pour not one but two glasses of wine. She'd had her fill of dating hipster dudes, self-proclaimed feminists and gamers. The worst of them though was a furry. Literally a man dressed as a stuffed animal. Though she knew there was more to it, she had no desire to learn. It had been so long since she'd had a date with someone, well, like Andy, that she'd forgotten the basics, it seemed. Not that it really was a date. Was it?

"Here, this ought to help. Are you nervous about the dinner? Or me?" Andy took a seat on the sofa and stared frankly at her. Luce stared back, trying to contrive an answer.

"Attention Ladies and Gentlemen! We've got an announcement!"

Chris's voice rang out, though not as deep and husky as Andy's, it had a warmth to it that always made Luce smile. She truly did like Annie's one and only.

"Well, out with it!" Bill called out, his boisterous voice causing laughter.

Chris turned and gave Annie a soft kiss and a smile. Luce smiled too, and noticed Andy did as well. It couldn't be helped. Chris and Annie were the epitome of happily ever after. They'd had their share of difficulties, but in the end, they were meant for each other. And Luce knew she could trust him to be there for Annie, through anything.

"We've got one more guest coming to the wedding."

Everyone waited, clearly that wasn't big news.

"And?" Luce prompted him. "Celebrity? Single billionaire? Out with it!"

Annie waited a heartbeat, then handed her glass to Chris for a refill. And Luce noticed for the first time what her sister was drinking, immediately tearing up. Annie smiled at Luce and nodded. Luce jumped out of her chair, grabbed Annie and hugged her, not saying anything at all. She couldn't. She was too choked up. Extricating herself from Luce, Annie looked out at her friends.

"Let's just say I'm going to need an expandable wedding dress!" Annie smiled, placed her hand gently on her belly and looked up at her friends, then looked at Chris. Cheers went up all around. Luce was smiling so hard her cheeks hurt. And when she suddenly caught Andy's eye, she realized he was too. This is what happiness feels like she thought. Good friends and family to celebrate the small things and the big things. She wanted that more than anything. And somehow she had to learn to open up and allow herself that. She knew she was going to go into emotional overload at some point. But this wasn't the time or place for it.

She thankfully didn't have much time to really contemplate all the momentous events in their lives as they were interrupted by the arrival of a limo and driver, sent by their hostess. It was a stretch limo with plenty of room, but somehow Luce found herself tucked neatly between her sister and Andy, not quite scrunched in, but close enough to keep her on edge. Luckily it was a short ride, and with all the chatter and excitement, she was able to relax by the time they arrived.

It was still light out, the late spring skies offering a dramatic view as they pulled up to the gates of the estate. It was one of those fabulous old manor houses tucked away on the North Shore. Stone and ivy and images of bygone days. Pulling into the circular drive in front, Luce gazed at the impressive home. While Annie had always dreamed of a cottage by the sea, Luce always dreamed of the castle. The Bowers Estate may not qualify as an authentic castle, but it gave off that same vibe.

Reaching in, Andy took her hand as she stepped out the rear of the limo and smiled to himself. She was staring so intently at the manor she didn't seem to notice he hadn't let go. Progress, he thought, as he studied her expression with interest. He knew she wasn't impressed by wealth. He'd already found that out about her. It was more a fairy tale syndrome he thought to himself. There were so many layers to Luce, and he wanted to peel them off slowly. Tonight should reveal quite a bit he figured. Maybe he'd solve two mysteries, Luce and the ship.

Though he'd never attended anything like a mystery dinner, he'd heard about them. In fact, most of the other detectives he works with love to joke about the amateur detective business of murder mystery dinners. This was just an offshoot of that. Having some inside knowledge of what it means to actually solve a mystery should give him an edge.

Luce suddenly seemed to realize Andy was still holding her hand and she felt the flush creep over her as she quickly tugged it away. She would have made some sort of remark, warned him off, but the massive oak door suddenly opened, and there stood an actual uniformed butler. Luce couldn't recall ever having encountered one before. It was like something out of a movie. A tuxedoed butler. She jolted when Andy nudged her.

"Come on... it's time. You look star struck," he said with a laugh.

"Not star struck, just a little startled is all," she replied with a huff. She needed to get her act together. It wasn't like her to lose her cool. And even if she wouldn't admit it to Andy, she was indeed star struck in a way. The whole throwback to the glamour days where people rode in Rolls-Royce limos and had live-in servants. She knew without even stepping foot inside there'd be a marble foyer with a chandelier. Part of her felt the romance of it all the way to her toes, while the other part of her felt it was over the top and ridiculous nowadays to live such a wasteful life.

She'd reserve judgement though, until meeting their hostess. She had a feeling she knew exactly what to expect.

## CHAPTER NINE

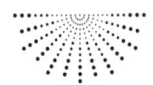

They were all led into the dining room by the butler, whose name they learned was *Mr. Peabody*. Luce had smiled when she heard it, then realized quickly he was serious. Playing a role? Or for real? This was a Mystery Dinner after all. Perhaps they were all supposed to role play. Nobody seemed to know the rules.

They were seated at a massive twelve foot mahogany table, perfectly set with Waterford crystal, bone china and Sterling silver. Everything meticulously laid out for them. Flowers lined the runner in the middle, kept low enough to make conversation across the table possible.

Luce, Andy, Mark and Julie were seated on one side, with Annie, Chris. Jen and Bill on the other. There were settings at both ends as well, but their hostess had yet to appear.

The dining room itself resembled something out of a classic movie. A massive stone fireplace to the side, crystal chandeliers and a mix of seascapes and portraits lining the shiplap walls. A man dressed as what Luce guessed was a footman of some sort entered carrying a tray with an assortment of beverages. Everything from wine to diet coke.

"Do you feel like we're in a time warp?" Andy whispered. She could feel his breath against her ear. Too close.

"Affirmative," she whispered back. It was almost a bit creepy; something was off. And she had to admit, having Andy next to her settled her nerves a bit.

The butler stepped back into the room, clearing his throat. "Ladies and gentlemen, may I present Mrs. Adeline Bowers," he said with a light bow. Stepping aside, he made room for the hostess to make her entrance.

*Wow.* That was the only thing that went through Luce's mind. The woman was decked out. A sparkling sequined sapphire gown. Diamond drop earrings and a sparkling necklace that could have been worn by a princess. Her snow-white hair swept up into a soft knot. She looked timeless yet Luce guessed she must be pushing 80. Though she was smiling, there was a chill to it. Luce felt as if a rush of cold air was blowing in with her, and she nervously reached out to Andy, not quite grabbing his hand, but tapping it lightly. She pulled back quickly but didn't resist when he reached out and covered her hand with his own, squeezing gently. He must have felt it too.

She stood next to her chair, waiting for Peabody to seat her.

"Good evening. Welcome to the annual Ghost Ship dinner, I'm so glad you all could join me. It is my sincere hope that tonight will be the night we finally solve this ancient mystery. It is important that you all do as you are asked, and please follow all the guidelines." Her tone was somewhat brusque and arrogant. Condescending even. Luce was definitely not feeling it. What nerve, inviting people and treating them like children.

Mrs. Bowers went on. "In front of each of you is an envelope. You will find your instructions inside." With that she sat down and nodded to Peabody, a signal of some sort as he immediately left the room.

It was then that Luce realized the name cards were actually envelopes. Reaching for hers, she recognized the stationery. It was the same as the invitation. Pulling the card out, she read it to herself, as everyone else was doing the same.

*Welcome to The Ghost Ship Annual Dinner Ms. Porter.*
*Your partner for this evening is: Mr. Holman*
*Your goal is to collect at least seven clues to the Ghost Ship Mystery.*
*Your investigation will take place in the Ballroom.*

Luce held back a snicker. The ballroom? Really?

The chatter began immediately, each of them looking about wondering if they were all to do the same thing.

"If I may have your silence please," Mrs. Bowers called out suddenly, and all conversation ceased.

"You are not to reveal to the other couples what your mission is. After supper, Mr. Peabody will lead each of you to your destination. When you have completed your task, you will be escorted back to the library where we will try to solve the puzzle."

Luce spoke without thinking, as was her habit.

"So this is like a game of Clue then?" She cringed as their host glared at her.

"Not at all, my dear. This is no game at all." With that, she rang a little bell in front of her and the footman entered with a silver domed platter.

Andy gave Luce's hand one more squeeze and she glanced over at him. Was it just her or was this over-the-top crazy? By the look on his face, raised brow, slight smirk, he agreed with the latter.

"Is there a list of clues? This just says collect seven clues?" Annie asked, a bit confused. "Usually a scavenger hunt lists the items you must find."

"You must decide whether an item is a bona-fide clue or not," she replied succinctly.

"Now. Tell me a bit about each of you." Suddenly Mrs. Bowers was friendly? Luce was skeptical. But she'd play along.

"Mr. Gregory, please, if you would begin?" Mrs. Bowers looked pointedly at Chris.

"Well, I'm a writer. You may already be aware, I write mysteries. I have several series out now, and just launched a new one last year."

"Ah yes. Max Colby, the hopelessly romantic sheriff. I believe the lovely young woman next to you was your muse, no?"

"Guilty as charged," Chris laughed, and placed his arm around Annie, who was beaming. Her long lost love had become a bestselling author and Annie was his inspiration.

"You are quite lucky, young man, not everyone gets second chances, and you, Ms. Porter, I take it, realize that, don't you?" She looked directly at Annie, who nodded.

"I do Mrs. Bowers, believe me. I do."

"Ms. Stolz, you are in publishing as well, no?" Mrs. Bowers turned her attention to Jen and Bill. "Do you work for Mr. Simeon then? His assistant perhaps?" Uh oh, Luce thought, that was a bit insulting.

"Actually, no, I'm an editor as well." Jen wasn't volunteering any more than that. She and Mark were actually competitors. Always seeking out up and coming authors. She was probably ticked off at the assumption, but Jen was too nice to let it show.

"And Mr. Stolz, what is it you do?"

"A bit of this and that I suppose. I freelance." Bill grinned, an infectious smile that usually keeps anyone from prying further. Luce had been down this road before. None of them knew what Bill actually did. They assumed he was a handyman of some sort, as he had a full workshop in his garage. But whenever anyone asked, Jen always laughed and said he did odd jobs. But the money was good. Clearly tonight would reveal no more than usual.

Mark and Julie were next.

"Mr. Simeon, you work with Mr. Gregory, do I have that right? You're his editor?"

"Yes, I've been working with him since his debut novel. Though really at this point our friendship is really more important than our working relationship."

"And Mrs. Simeon, what is it you do?" Her tone was slightly condescending again, and Luce had a feeling that Mrs. Bowers had no appreciation for working women.

"I have a little girl, and she takes up a lot of my time." Julie smiled sweetly. She also was quite a popular blogger but they all knew she was just playing the part. And it was quite effective. For the first time since she'd stepped into the room, Mrs. Bowers actually smiled.

"Well isn't that lovely, dear, a good old-fashioned girl. Nobody appreciates that anymore."

Luce knew what was coming next. She was probably going to get the death stare.

"And you, Ms. Porter? You are a career woman, are you not? TV is it?" Her tone rang with disdain. Luce cringed knowing that was just the beginning. "You must be what, 40 or so? In my day you'd be a thornback twice over."

Luce felt her face flush with anger. And all decorum was lost.

Back straight, head high, she got ready to give as good as she got. But Andy beat her to it. Resting an arm on the back of her shoulders, Andy smiled.

"Never fret, Mrs. Bowers, Luce won't end up alone. Will you sweetheart? No, of course not. But you know she's just been waiting for her sister to get settled down. She's always been devoted, you know."

Luce pasted a smile on her face as she kicked him in the shin under the table. She wasn't sure who she was angrier with. The primped up hostess or Andy. She did realize it was probably all an act for him, and he was just trying to help. Though the smirk on his face was not helping his cause.

As the footman began serving, conversation had ceased once again, and Luce looked across the table and studied her sister. She looked happy. Not just happy. Ecstatic. Which is all Luce ever wanted for her sister. The last few years had not been kind to them. Especially for Annie. The dreamer in the family. The only thing she'd ever really wanted was what she had right now. It just took a whole lot of heartache to get it. And now maybe, just maybe it was Luce's turn. She stole another glance at Andy and mentally kicked herself. She'd learned the hard way not to base her own happiness on anyone else. Maybe though, there was room for a little flexibility?

Her eyes next flicked over to Jen and Bill. Jen and Annie had one of those friendships that Luce envied. They'd met in a thrift store and just clicked. It must have been serendipity, for without Jen, Annie might never have found Chris again. Annie was always harping about fate. If Annie hadn't met Jen, she wouldn't have found Chris. Luce sighed. And if Annie hadn't found Chris, she wouldn't have been terrorized by a stalker, and they'd never have met Andy. Maybe, just maybe, there was something to all this. No time for it now, she thought, as she leaned back to allow the food to be served. Eat, relax, find clues, solve the mystery. *Focus*, Luce, *focus*, she told herself.

## CHAPTER TEN

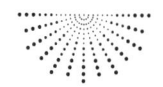

Dinner was relatively quiet; it seemed conversation took a back seat to proper etiquette. Luce took the opportunity to study Mrs. Bowers. Noticing her hands were smooth and pampered. Her makeup was flawless. If she were to guess, she'd say born into money and lots of it. She'd googled the estate. It had been built by her late husband's great grandfather, sometime in the nineteenth Century. She'd yet to research the woman herself, but she would over the weekend. Now that she'd met her, she had every intention of digging deeper. If only to learn whatever deep dark secret she held. Luce was certain there was one.

At precisely seven pm, the towering grandfather clock at the end of the room began to sound. Mr. Peabody appeared, seemingly out of nowhere.

"Shall we begin? Mr. Holman, if you and Ms. Porter would follow me."

Luce scowled. His tone was haughty and rather abrupt. But she allowed Andy to pull out her chair and followed him as they headed out of the dining room. Looking back, she locked eyes with her sister, who seemed perfectly content. Excited even. But Luce couldn't shake the feeling that something was off with this whole evening's events. Whether it was the hostess with the mostest attitude or the generally creepy ambiance, she wasn't sure. But it clearly wasn't what she'd been expecting. And by the looks of it, Andy wasn't feeling it either. She noticed he'd stiffened up a bit as if he was on alert. He again placed his hand on the small of her back, to usher her out of the room, and as he did so, leaned down to whisper in her ear.

"Stick with me. Just follow my lead."

Luce darted a glance up at his face. He was dead serious. Something was off, and he felt it too.

They were led into the main foyer, then up the circular staircase to some sort of mezzanine level, then down a hall through a set of French doors.

Luce gasped softly; the room was stunning. Jane Austen would have a field day with this. The room was large, with a domed ceiling painted with a magnificent seascape. Antique wall sconce lighting gave it atmosphere, reflecting their glow on the glistening marble floors. The pièce de résistance, though, was an entire wall featuring small personal balconies—the kind used by illicit lovers in all those historical novels she loved to read.

Andy nodded towards them and smiled, raising a brow, causing Luce to give him a warning glance. They'd been around each other enough, and this was not his usual MO. Oh, he liked to tease her, but it had always been more of a snide teasing. At least she'd thought so. This wasn't. Clearly, he had ideas about them. Or maybe not. Maybe her imagination was running wild.

"I'll leave you here, you have one hour to find the clues, then I will return and take you back to the library." Mr. Peabody gave a short bow and departed, leaving Luce and Andy still gazing about and shaking their heads.

Still whispering, Andy leaned down once more. "There are cameras in here, so don't say or do anything you don't want them to see or hear. Clear?"

Luce glanced up in the corner, saw the red dot on the camera. She hadn't expected that. Maybe it was just security. Maybe. But she nodded at him and smiled, as if they were sharing a secret. She could play along.

"Well, *sweetheart,* where shall we start?" Luce used the same phony endearment he had.

Andy looked about, then pointed to a window overlooking the water.

"There, I think, by the window, *honeybunch*." He smirked, and Luce actually let out a laugh.

"There's a window seat, usually a good hiding spot, no?" Luce looked at Andy for confirmation. He nodded, and they headed over in that direction.

The east wall of the Ballroom was an alternating pattern of balconies and majestic tall narrow windows in between. And each of the windows had a window seat. Luce held her finger out and counted seven.

"I know where you're going with that, and it's too easy. It's never the obvious." Andy smirked and gave a small shake of his head. "Nice try, though."

"Au contraire, detective, it's always the obvious." Luce laughed and crouched down to lift up the padded bench on the first one to see what was hidden inside, if anything.

"Aha! Told you." Luce cried triumphantly as she reached in and pulled out a large folder with a string closure. Setting the lid down, she sat and began to open it. The seat was built for two, and Andy took a seat next to her and began looking over her shoulder as she slid the contents out.

It was a single piece of paper with what appeared to be a watercolor print of a ship. A ship that looked exactly like the one she'd seen as a kid. She was stunned. Not by the picture, though, rather by her reaction. She wasn't surprised. She should have been, but she wasn't.

"That's it," Andy said softly. "That's the ghost ship."

Luce turned to look at him, narrowing her eyes.

"How do you know that?"

"Isn't it? Isn't that the ship you saw?"

"Maybe, but maybe it's any old ship. Maybe they're trying to fool us. You said it like you knew, Andy. Like you were sure."

Andy looked away for a moment, then looked back at Luce, as if trying to decide something.

"Out with it, detective."

He glanced up at the corner where the camera was. Luce followed his gaze.

"Later," he said softly. Luce nodded as she looked back down at the drawing.

"Here, give that to me, I'll hang on to it. Let's go to the next one," Andy said quietly.

As they walked the few steps over to the next seat, Luce paused suddenly.

"I feel like they made this deliberately easy, Andy. Why would they do that?"

"Don't jump to conclusions yet, Luce, let's see what's in box number two first, shall we?"

Luce lifted the next seat lid, and once again, the clue was right there. This time, a small plastic bag containing the remnants of a seaman's patch. Frayed and faded, they could still make out the design—an anchor with a chain. Luce looked at Andy, who nodded, holding out his hand. He slipped the bag into the folder he was carrying, and they headed silently over to the next one.

"This is way too easy, Andy," Luce muttered.

"Seems so, Luce, but let's wait and see how it all plays out."

Luce detected a note of seriousness in his voice. She sensed they were on the same page.

The next window seat contained a flask, tarnished and old. No markings, though.

Three down four to go, Luce thought. She felt a sudden chill as they approached the next one and shivered.

"Cold?" Andy asked.

"Actually no, just a sudden chill. Maybe there's an open window somewhere."

Andy looked around, and just as he suspected, all the windows were closed. He'd felt a chill at the same moment. He also had a sense that not only were there cameras in the room, someone was watching them. His instincts told him this wasn't all fun and games. Something was going on here, behind the scenes.

"Remember what I said, Luce. Stay close, OK?" Andy's voice was barely audible, but Luce heard him. And right now, she was really not feeling all that comfortable anyway, so she didn't argue.

She lifted the next seat and reached in to grab another plastic bag. Lifting it out, she took one look, gasped, and dropped it.

"What the hell? What's wrong, Luce?" Andy looked at her with concern.

She nodded at the bag inside the compartment.

Reaching in, he realized as soon as the light hit it what it was. A knife. Not just any knife. A knife coated with what appeared to be bloodstains.

"Relax, it's paint, Luce. Just paint." Though he had to admit, it looked incredibly authentic—a bloody knife. "Damn, what the hell is that about?" he muttered to himself.

"I know it's paint, it just startled me," Luce huffed out. She was embarrassed to have reacted like such an amateur.

"You OK?" Andy asked, knowing she wasn't really.

"Of course, let's move on," Luce said briskly and headed to window seat number five. "But maybe you should see what's in this one," Luce offered. "You know, to be fair."

Andy smiled to himself and took the hint. Let her put on a brave face.

He reached in and grabbed a small envelope lying at the bottom.

It was old, clearly. In fact, so old, Andy paused and took out a pair of thin plastic gloves from an inside pocket in his blazer. Luce rolled her eyes. *Figures,* she thought. Of course, he carries gloves.

She waited patiently while he oh so carefully opened the envelope and slid out an even older looking scrap of paper. Thin, like parchment.

"Well, what is it?" Luce whispered with a bit of impatience. Andy's expression was curious, she thought. Eyes narrowed; lips pursed.

"A bill of sale."

"What kind of sale."

Andy looked at Luce with an odd expression.

"It appears to be a bill of sale for a slave."

Luce's eyes widened as she held out her hand. "Let me see."

"Be careful, I'll hold it, as it's fragile and I've got the gloves on." Luce shook her head and tried to read it as he held it flat on his palm.

"Damn," Luce whispered. "It is. One female. 70 Pounds. Is that her weight or the cost?" Luce didn't wait for an answer. "To be delivered on the morrow to... crap, that's where it ends. But at least there's a date at the top. 10 June, oh my god, that's today. June 10th." The year is smudged but looks like 1790. She looked back up at Andy, and their gazes locked. They knew as silly as this whole mystery dinner was, this wasn't. This felt all too real.

They retrieved the last two clues. One was a wax insignia sealer, the other a broken seashell.

Having found all seven clues, with plenty of time to spare, they slipped out onto one of the balconies and sat down on the stone bench. All the items were now in the folder. Luce clasped her hands together nervously in her lap.

"I don't like this, Andy. It's not fun. I thought this would be fun. It's not. Something terrible happened here. I can feel it. And please don't tell me I'm imagining things, I'm not." She spoke quietly. Nervously.

"I know."

She looked at him in surprise. "You do?"

"Something I probably should have mentioned earlier."

"What's that?"

"I told you we used to try to swim out to the lighthouse?"

"And?"

"I saw it too."

## CHAPTER ELEVEN

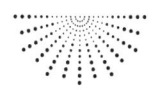

"What?" Luce hissed. "You've seen the Ghost Ship and didn't bother to say a word?" her eyes narrowed. Here she had been revealing her deepest secrets, and he certainly hadn't returned the favor. She stood and paced the balcony. "What kind of partner are you anyway?"

"Pretty hot I'm told," Andy replied, laughing and wiggling his eyebrows. Luce pursed her lips, trying not to laugh.

"OK, points for that. So, you saw the same ship I did? In the same spot? Execution Rocks?" Luce asked, then went on without waiting for another reply. "How old were you? When was that?"

"Summer of '94. I was 11. You?"

"Me too. Same year. Same age. Huh, I thought you were older than me," Luce chuckled. "Being bossy and all," she added.

"I remember the date too. The day I saw it. Maybe you should sit back down." Andy reached up and grabbed her hand to tug her back to the bench.

She sat down, and looked at him, curious.

"It was my friend Gordy's birthday. June 10th." Andy waited for Luce to react.

"I wish I could remember the date I saw it, but it was so long ago. I just know it was summer."

"OK, listen, Luce, think. Try to remember anything else about that day. Maybe why you went sailing, was it something you did every weekend? Was there something else?"

"I don't know. I mean, school was over, so we were kind of celebrating. I know that."

"Good, that's good. Now you were celebrating school being out, we can look up the school calendar and approximate."

"I guess it had to be June, we always started after Labor Day and finished in June."

"That narrows it down. Saturday or Sunday?"

"It was a Friday, actually, now that I think about it. School was out so dad wasn't working…" Luce's voice trailed off.

Andy pulled out his phone and started tapping on the screen rapidly.

"June 10th was a Friday that year." He said it quietly as he looked up from his phone.

"Today's the 10th," Luce said just as quietly. "Creepy or coincidence, detective?" She meant to ask it lightly, but they both knew it wasn't a light question.

Andy stood and reached to pull Luce up. "Let's go in. It's almost time for us to be *escorted* back." Luce nodded, but quickly tugged her hand away. The whole evening was becoming a bit surreal. She felt things were closing in a bit and needed some space.

As they stepped back into the ballroom, Mr. Peabody seemed to simply appear out of nowhere.

"If you'll follow me," he said, brusquely, holding open the door.

Andy leaned down toward Luce, their height difference becoming increasingly difficult for her to ignore. "After you, Luce," he whispered, and they followed the butler back through the hallway and down the stairs.

"The library is this way," Mr. Peabody nodded toward a small door to the side of the stairs, and they followed him cautiously. Entering the room, Mr. Peabody suddenly turned.

"May I?" he asked, holding out his hand towards Andy, who was holding the folder.

"Time to turn in our treasure, eh?" Andy asked with a smirk. The butler maintained his stoic demeanor, stiffly took the folder from Andy, then placed it carefully on the mantle of the fireplace.

Briskly walking toward the doorway, he nodded at the pair, and strode out.

"Oh my god, Andy I could live in this room," Luce exclaimed as soon as the butler left them alone. The Bowers library was a dream, Luce thought. Every wall was a built-in-bookcase. There were hundreds and hundreds of books. Old, new, big, small. And the furniture rather than being stuffy and formal, was sumptuous. Soft, broken-in leather sofas and overstuffed recliners. This was a literal book lover's idea of heaven. There was an entire coffee and tea service area next to the large framed bay window overlooking the gardens. Though it was after sundown, the garden lighting was soft and glowing, creating a warm and cozy atmosphere.

"Don't get too comfortable, something tells me she doesn't want us staying too long." Andy muttered with a frown.

"What is it? Something's gnawing at you. I can tell."

"Too many things seem to be falling into place too easily. Remember what I said? It's never the obvious. And this is all just too obvious for my taste."

"It is odd, isn't it? But there's no way she knew about us seeing the ship, on the same day? That's too weird anyway. How could she know that? That's what I find creepy."

"You don't find it creepy that it actually happened?" Andy chuckled. "There's only one possibility Luce, and that is that what we saw was real. Not a ghost ship at all."

"Maybe. Or maybe we both happened to be at the same place, same time?" Luce began peering over at one of the shelves and started to head over to it. Reaching up and stretching she tried to grab for a book she spotted, but it was just out of reach. Shrugging, she turned around, almost bumping straight into Andy.

"Jesus Andy, give a girl some space would you?"

"I was *going* to give you a hand there Luce. Ungrateful much?"

"Oh, well, in that case, do you see that blue faded edition, the one that says, *Cow Neck Historical Society?*"

"Got it," Andy replied, smirking as he reached directly over her head, instead of going around her. He knew he was being slightly irritating, but that was his mission. He needed to keep her off guard. A little off-balance.

"You're really pushing it detective," Luce shook her head laughing. There was something incredibly irresistible about the man and as hard as she fought herself over it, she was in a losing battle.

"Let's sit while we wait. Tell me why this book is so interesting."

They got comfortable on one of the sofas, and Luce began flipping through the book. Her father had many books like this one; as a historian as well as a history teacher, he had worked closely with local groups on historical preservation, genealogy and local folklore, a particular interest of his. He and her mother had been headed home from one of the local society annual dinners the night of the storm that took their lives in a flash.

She turned the pages slowly, rather reverently, looking for something in particular, Andy thought. He was patient though. She looked pensive. Finally, she stopped on a page with several photos.

"This one. See that? This is what it looks like from the shore." Luce pointed to a photo of a lighthouse. "According to the caption, that's our lighthouse. On the island known as Execution Rocks, it says."

Luce began reading some of the text below the picture when the door suddenly opened, and Mark and Julie entered with Mr. Peabody.

Repeating the same request he made to Luce and Andy, he took a large envelope from Mark and placed it next to theirs on the mantel, then left the room.

"Well, I don't know about you two, but that felt like the twilight zone." Julie laughed and took a seat opposite Luce and Andy while Mark just stood in awe at the incredible book collection.

"Fucking amazing," Mark breathed out slowly. "I have never seen the likes of a room like this except in a wet dream."

Julie looked at Luce, and they both burst out laughing. Andy leaned back and swung one leg over the other. He needed to relax. Shake off the nagging feeling that something was terribly wrong with this whole scenario. Including the fact that he was the one that got them into it in the first place.

"Hey Luce, what did you guys find? Anything good?" Julie asked grinning. Clearly having fun, and not, apparently, spooked by any of it, Andy noted. Interesting.

The door opened once more and Jen practically bounced into the room. Like a bottle of bubbly with Bill right behind her, just grinning. Again, the butler took a small box from Bill and set it on the mantle next to the other clues.

"You guys will not believe what we found! But we're not allowed to tell, now are we," Jen gushed. "Wait." She stopped suddenly in the middle of the room and twirled around. "This is oh my god amazing. Bill, I want this. Build me a room just like it. This weekend. Lowe's here we come…" Jen's mouth was left hanging open and she let her eyes roam every shelf.

"Sorry, Jen, I saw it first. I'm redoing my office tomorrow. Just wait." Mark laughed. He did like to one-up his competitor.

Andy watched his friends carefully. None seemed to be bothered at all by any of what they found, nor did they seem at all nervous. So why would he and Luce have a totally different experience. When the door opened next, and Chris and Annie entered, he had his answer.

## CHAPTER TWELVE

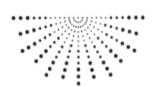

They all watched curiously as Mrs. Bowers made what by all appearances was a grand entrance. Sweeping into the room and heading straight over to the fireplace. Turning to her guests, she cleared her throat.

"Now that we are all gathered once again, shall we begin?" A soft murmur floated around the room.

"Very well. We shall open each set of clues, and after each is opened, we shall all propose a theory. Now, I will give you a backstory."

"The clues you have retrieved are to help solve the mystery of the ghost ship, said to roam the Long Island Sound. There are many theories, but none have solved the actual mystery of the ship to my satisfaction. The ghost ship is said to make its appearance every year on the same date. At the same time. Those who have seen it, describe it identically. Some call it The Phantom. An old ship with billowing sails. And nobody aboard. It's spotted in the same location each time. Reportedly around the lighthouse that you can see from any vantage point along the coast.

The clues that you have all retrieved are items I've gathered over the years in my quest for answers. Some may not have any relevance. Others may be significant. That is for you all to decide. After each set of clues is presented, each of you may select one item of importance for your team.

The remaining items will be dismissed. Ultimately each team will have 4 items in their possession and must provide a theory. Are there any questions before we begin?"

Luce wanted to jump in, but Andy quickly placed his hand on her arm, stopping her with a small shake of his head. She frowned; he was always doing that. Interfering. But for now, she'd let it slide. He must have a reason, she thought, and it better be good,

"Very well, Mr. Peabody, please open the first set."

The butler retrieved the folder containing Andy and Luce's clues and laid all of them out on the table in the center. Mrs. Bowers nodded at him to step back, and went over and picked each one up carefully, announcing the finds.

"Mr. Holman and Ms. Porter, please make your first selection. In this case, you may keep only one of the clues you've found. You may have one minute to decide."

Luce frowned, knowing Andy, he'd pick for them. She turned to face him giving him her best no-nonsense glare.

"The bill of sale." She said softly, but firmly.

"Done." Andy nodded in approval. That was definitely his first choice.

"We'll take the slip of paper in the plastic bag please." If this were a competition, they didn't want anyone else knowing what it was. Not that any of them had a chance of solving this. He knew that now. Only he and Luce were destined to figure it out. Which was the biggest mystery of all.

They went around the room then, the others all selecting as well.

Jen and Bill chose the patch. Mark and Julie chose the knife, while Annie and Chris went for the drawing of the ship.

Next, Julie and Mark were able to choose first. Their set of clues was a strange combination of children's toys and they selected a handful of what appeared to be matchsticks. Old ones at that. It seems their destination had been the nursery. Luce and Andy studied the remaining six clues for a moment and made their decision.

"The doll, please," Luce said, pointing to a cornhusk doll that had clearly seen better days.

Again, they completed the circle, with Jen and Bill choosing a cup and ball set, while Annie and Chris went for what appeared to be dull marbles, made of clay.

Next up were Jen and Bill's clues, clearly straight from the kitchen. They elected to keep a large cast iron skillet. Annie and Chris chose a pewter mug. Luce and Andy selected a hanging salt box, followed by Mark and Julie's choice of a crystal decanter.

One more set of clues remained. Chris and Annie's. Mr. Peabody laid them out on the table, and they all studied them.

"Where do you think all this came from?" Luce asked Andy in a hushed voice, glancing up at him. Her face pale and drawn.

"My guess? A dungeon or a basement full of horrors," he replied quietly. Judging by Chris and Annie's expression when they returned to the Library, it appeared they weren't taking any of this seriously. They assumed everything was simply for entertainment, Andy thought. They were having an adventure. At this point, that was for the best. Nobody else needed to know there was something else going on. Although Annie did appear to be overdoing it a bit. Andy wondered if she weren't masking a bit of underlying tension.

The items were grotesque. And yet everyone else in the room was laughing and smiling as they decided which horrific clue would be theirs.

"Go on Annie, you pick," Chris gave Annie a quick kiss and smiled. "Last one!" Annie studied them all, and smiling hesitantly back at Chris, chose a pair of shackles. Old, dented, rusted shackles. With pieces of chain hanging off.

Luce glanced at Andy nervously. She felt it too. They were real. Not for show. He reached over and squeezed her hand and smiled reassuringly, giving a small nod at the other guests, silently telling her to play along.

Julie and Mark chose an old branding iron.

Jen and Bill selected a frayed noose.

"I can't, you do it," Luce murmured softly.

Andy selected the one remaining item that was clearly the outlier. It wasn't some sort of instrument of torture.

"The signet ring please."

## CHAPTER THIRTEEN

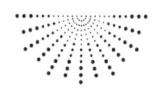

"You have 30 minutes to discuss your clues, Mr. Peabody will be happy to provide refreshments. Then, each team can announce their findings. There is no right or wrong of course, just theories. The theory that I believe has the most merit, I will choose as the winner."

"Oh, is there a prize?" Annie asked, quite enthusiastically, though with humor.

Mrs. Bowers shook her head, and Luce thought she almost saw a smile. Maybe the old biddy had some cracks after all.

As their hostess left the room they all began to chatter.

"Who wants to share clues?" Annie asked.

"I'm afraid that's not allowed, Ms. Porter. You must only confer and share among yourselves." Mr. Peabody interrupted with a sniff, causing Luce to roll her eyes. She didn't know where they'd found this guy, but she sure wished he'd crawl back in his hole.

The chatter returned, and Luce turned to Andy. "Well, detective, where do we start?" She asked quietly. If nothing else, Luce never lost her competitive nature. No use letting others hear.

"I think with the bill of sale." Andy replied.

"Slave ship?" Luce murmured. "Did you see the shackles Annie picked?"

"I did. That's why I chose the ring," he said, reaching to pick it up and take a closer look.

It was old, a deep gold, and actually misshapen. The center stone appeared to be some sort of bluish gray stone, with a faint carving in it.

"Luce, google eighteenth century signet rings, would you?" he suggested.

Luce raised her eyebrows and narrowed her gaze.

"Please," he offered, with a smirk.

"That's better." Luce chuckled. Bantering with him helped her relax.

Grabbing her phone, she tapped in the description and waited. Using data instead of WIFI always slowed things down.

"According to google, often made of 18k gold, they usually featured an intaglio carving in a gemstone. Used to seal things with a coat of arms or initials."

"Well, this certainly could be 18k gold. And definitely there's something carved in this stone. Turn your camera on, maybe we can zoom in?"

Luce shook her head, and chuckled.

"Would you be so kind as to please turn your camera on?" Andy laughed.

"But of course, Mr. Holman, I would be ever so happy to oblige," Luce murmured, smiling.

She switched her phone's camera on and zoomed into the face of the ring stone. Andy leaned over to look as well. Too close, she thought.

They both remained quiet as they studied it.

"Take a picture or two," Andy whispered, then added "Please."

"Definitely a coat of arms. Maybe google image search?" Luce suggested, and Andy nodded. They waited for the images to load, then looked at each other in stunned silence.

Luce spoke first. "There's no way to solve this tonight, you know that."

"I do." Andy agreed.

"So why are we here do you think?"

"I have my ideas on that Luce. For now, let's just decide on a theory, and present it. Then we can follow up on all this later."

"This isn't very fun, is it?" Luce murmured.

"I'm sorry, Luce, I thought this would be something you'd enjoy, I had no idea."

Luce smiled at Andy and shook her head. "It's probably the most thoughtful gift ever, Andy, really. Not your fault at all. I just wish it had met our expectations."

"I like how you said that," Andy remarked. "*Our* expectations." He smiled as a blush crept over her face, causing her to look away for a moment. He gave her a minute to regroup.

She turned back, composed again. "So, what's our theory?" she asked. "Slave ship?"

"No, I mean it is, but let's not even bring it up. How about a British Ship with colonial prisoners?"

Luce nodded. She could go along with that. It was one of the many stories of Execution Rocks after all.

Everyone paused their conversation as Mrs. Bowers reentered the room. Each couple looked around at the others, all smiling, as if they each had the secret to the ghost ship and were eager to reveal it.

"Well now, if we're all ready, who would like to begin?"

"We'll start," Annie called out with a smile. She was certainly loving all of this, thought Luce, and she would be the last person to dampen her spirits. Or scare her. She had watched her sister go through something far scarier, and knew it was best to keep her thoughts about this to herself.

Annie tugged on Chris's hand as she jumped up. Not as tall as Luce, Annie was rather petite and far more relaxed about everything from her clothing to her makeup. She had the natural girl-next-door kind of look. And pregnancy seemed to make her glow.

"The Ghost Ship was clearly a colonial merchant ship. Judging by the items everything screams revolutionary war period. Our guess is it ran aground on the shores of the island, and somehow, they managed to get back in the water and perhaps they sank right there from the damage." Annie finished and looked at Chris who just nodded and smiled indulgently. Clearly Chris had allowed Annie to come up with her own idea, Luce thought. Because Chris would have basically written an entire short story if given the chance.

"Very well, thank you, next?" Mrs. Bowers seemed completely uninterested in that theory. Bored even. Luce frowned. The least she could do is fake it. Or maybe, that was the intent. Maybe Chris really did have a story up his sleeve and was saving it for his next book.

"We'll give it a go," Bill jumped up and pulled Jen up along with him. He towered next to her, but Jen never seemed to mind. Luce envied them. They had a whirlwind romance and managed to keep it thriving for over a decade.

"Well, we also believe it's from colonial times. But judging by the little shop of horrors that Annie and Chris visited? It had to have a mutinous crew!" Bill's voice boomed, echoing throughout the cozy room.

"Yes, so we don't think it was an accident at all. We believe the crew rebelled and hung the captain. But karma probably stepped in, and they got lost in a storm on their return, and with no captain to guide them, they sank."

"Mutiny? Interesting theory," Mrs. Bowers commented. A bit more interested.

"Oh, we'll go next," Julie said. She and Mark remained seated though, as Julie wasn't really the center-of-attention type. "It was a British Ship, overtaken by pirates. The captain was murdered with the knife. His crew was captured, and they were all branded with the mark of the pirate, whose initials were TB. We believe that the pirate wasn't even a real pirate. He was a privateer. But committing such atrocious acts, he had to pretend to be a pirate so nobody could identify him."

"And once they'd taken over the ship, they realized their own ship had been hit with cannon fire. So they allowed it to sink. And sailed off in the British ship, lowered the flag and raised their own. The ghost ship was the pirate ship."

"Privateering, eh?" Mrs. Bowers smiled. "Interesting theory." She turned to Luce and Andy.

"And what have you two come up with? The detective and the reporter, I have high expectations, you know." She seemed quite intent now. As if she really did expect something new, perhaps more noteworthy. Luce glanced at Andy, knowing their theory would disappoint. But they stuck to their plan anyway.

Andy spoke first. "Definitely a British ship. But not taken over by pirates, sorry guys… clearly they ran aground. Carrying colonial prisoners, which I deduced based on those shackles Annie and Chris have. Anyway, they crashed into the rocks, and everyone perished."

"There's more," Luce added. "That's not the phantom ship though. You see on board that crashed ship were the wives and children of several noble British families. The British sent another ship to search for it, but they never returned. To this day it can be seen traveling the waters of the Long Island Sound in search of the missing vessel."

Everyone in the room sat in rapt attention. Including their hostess.

"Oh, that is truly wonderful. Nobody has suggested that before. You know, I have a feeling you are on to something. Yes, quite." She was speaking almost to herself now and smiling.

Luce looked quizzically at Andy. The little story they'd made up didn't fit their true theory at all. Yet Mrs. Bowers seemed all in on it.

Andy shrugged, turned and smiled at Mrs. Bowers.

"Thank you. We think it fits nicely as well. I take it we're tonight's winners, then?"

"Arrogant much?" Luce whispered, laughing.

"So I've been told," he answered with a grin. At least they were both feeling more comfortable, he thought to himself. But he still couldn't wait to leave.

The pop of a champagne cork startled everyone, as Peabody began pouring everyone a glass. Except Annie who waved him off.

After cheers all around, and much discussion, they prepared to leave.

"You have to be anywhere tomorrow morning or should we crash at your sister's?" Andy asked.

"I'm in the mood to discuss all this with some rational objective observers, so let's stay out here tonight." Luce wasn't sure if it was the bubbly talking or the fact that an hour's drive alone with Andy might be a terrible idea. Relaxing with her sister would be the perfect distraction. At least she thought so, until Annie dropped the next bombshell.

## CHAPTER FOURTEEN

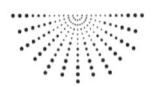

"We lied." Annie said the minute she opened the door. "Quick, come in." She tugged on Luce's arm practically dragging her over the threshold, causing a Rube Goldberg effect where Andy quickly threw an arm about her waist, steadying her. Luce stiffened up like an ironing board.

"What do you mean, you lied?" Luce managed to huff out while trying to compose herself. She felt like a rag doll being pushed and pulled by Andy and Annie.

"Just go sit." Annie pointed to the sofa in the sunken living room. "Both of you."

Luce and Andy shared a look, half disbelief, half guilt at not admitting to their own lies. Sharing the silent message, *what do we do now?*

Raising a brow, Andy nodded towards the sofa, and waved his arm indicating Luce should go first.

"Always the gentleman," she muttered under her breath.

Leaving the recliner for Annie, Luce sat on the couch, only flinching slightly when Andy sat down next to her. And again when his arm rested on the back of the couch behind her head. He really was assuming too much, she thought. On the other hand, maybe she was too. She'd ponder it later.

"Did you guys find anything a little creepy about that whole thing?" Chris jumped in immediately. He had taken a seat on the floor next to Annie, one hand resting on his raised knee, the other on Annie's belly.

"Try a lot creepy," Luce replied, frowning. "But you guys seemed to be enjoying it. What was up with that?"

"Oh, we didn't want to ruin anything!" Annie exclaimed. "When that creepy butler took us down to the basement, which by the way was terrifying, and then left us there with only a flashlight? The minute we saw the shackles I was sure we were all going to end up chained to those damp stone walls." Annie was practically shivering. Chris appeared pensive. Normally he tended to smile and shake his head when Annie's imagination took hold. But Luce noticed he didn't this time.

"I convinced her it was all stage props," Chris commented, "but clearly they weren't."

"The knife was coated in red paint, yes," Andy jumped in. "But I could see the old grayish stains on it. And those were probably real."

Luce glanced at him, nervously. "What do you mean?"

"Blood stains on metal will end up leaving a discoloration," Andy explained. "The older the stain, the greater the discoloration. But I can't know for sure without testing."

"You said it was paint. You thought I was overreacting." Luce poked his chest with her finger for emphasis. "You made fun of me"

"Sorry, but I didn't want you all freaked out. I was calming you down. It worked, didn't it?" Andy looked so apologetic that Luce nodded reluctantly.

"Just don't lie to me anymore," she crossed her arms in front of her chest, mostly to keep from poking him again. She'd noticed he was solid as a rock, and that was just too tempting.

"Too bad we couldn't keep the clues," Chris muttered. "There was one in particular…"

"Which one?" Andy probed.

"The branding iron."

"Well, there's something you all should know," Luce said matter-of-factly. Perhaps a bit smugly.

"What's that *Ace*?" Andy asked with a grin, using the nickname he'd given her the first time they'd met during her crime scene faux pas.

Luce pulled out her phone and held it up. "I took photos." She smiled as she knew that would get them.

"Yeah, she photographed that signet ring." Andy said, nodding.

"I photographed all of it," Luce said, smiling proudly. "All 28 clues."

She stole a glance at Andy who was staring at her with an odd look. Either he was angry or there was some other emotion swirling around his eyes. Always dark, they were practically blazing black.

"What? Nobody saw me do it, it's not a crime, right? I mean you told me to…" Luce was just confused. Andy should be happy she did it. Overjoyed. He should be grabbing her and hugging her and — nope, *not going there*, she thought.

"Anyway, so maybe we can use your printer, Chris, and print out all the clues, and then we can use google image search as well." Luce turned away from Andy's glare. He still hadn't responded.

Annie yawned, involuntarily, covering her mouth to hide it.

"Yeah, let's do that tomorrow. Right now, I think my girls need some sleep." Chris said, standing and holding his hand out to Annie.

"Girls?" Luce asked with a grin. "You're thinking I'm going to have a niece?"

"I know it," Chris said proudly, causing Annie to giggle.

Luce just shook her head. She had to admit she was tired as well. Lucky for both Luce and Andy, they stayed over often enough they each had their own designated guest rooms and had left enough clothing and toiletries behind from their visits to make it easy to stay over when necessary.

∾

THE NEXT MORNING, Luce entered the kitchen bleary-eyed and in desperate need of coffee. Annie was already up, looking like she was ready to take on the day.

"Since when are you a morning person?" Luce mumbled as she sat at the quartz peninsula.

"I don't know, I think it's hormones, sis," Annie laughed. "I can't sleep in, and I can't stay awake at night. Everything is topsy turvy!"

"Coffee?" Luce asked hopefully.

"Sure, dark roast? Or Hazelnut?"

"Hazelnut. And you do have cream, right?" Luce's tone was almost pleading.

"Of course, silly." Annie busied herself making a single serve mug for Luce.

"Where are the boys?" Luce asked looking around.

"Out for a run," Annie replied, handing her the freshly brewed nectar she was craving.

"Ugh, well, how much time do we have?" Luce asked curiously.

"Why? Do we have sizzling detective stories? Some dirt to dish?" Annie's face lit up.

"Nah, sorry sis. I know you're disappointed, but maybe next time," Luce chuckled. Annie had been trying to fix her up with Andy for months. And truth be told, Luce was kind of warming up to the idea. It was only fear that kept it from happening. Nothing more than fear.

"I thought we could start going through those photos. I really think we have a shot at figuring out the ghost ship. And why that whole dinner was such a surreal experience."

"That's the word Chris used as well. Surreal." Annie murmured. "I suppose we should wait for them though. It's only fair."

"Fair to who?" Luce grumbled and held her mug out to Annie. "More please."

"I think you're awake now, make your own!" Annie laughed.

"I liked you better as a night owl," Luce shook her head and got up for a refill.

"I wish I had this kitchen. I love this kitchen."

"You don't even cook, Luce."

"I could learn, Annie. Seriously. It's perfect." Luce sighed, gazing longingly at the white country cupboards with their antique bronze pulls. The sleek quartz countertops and the cleverly hidden appliances. Especially those. Microwave, dishwasher, trash compactor all faced with white cabinetry. It was straight out of HGTV and it had been Chris's gift to Annie.

He'd bought it for her. He really was that guy. The one who'd do anything for his one true love. Annie had to wait a long time for him, but looking at her now, Luce knew it was worth it for her. She radiated happiness. Luce couldn't remember the last time she'd felt pure joy about anything.

The sound of the screen door slamming off the kitchen jolted her back to the present. She grabbed her mug and quickly escaped back up the stairs. A quick shower, some make-up and a fresh change of clothes and she would be ready to face the day. There was one quick thing she wanted to do first though. Grabbing her phone, she pulled up the site she'd bookmarked the night before, ran a quick name search, waited a moment, and seeing the results, froze. No time for a shower. No time to change.

Luce ran back down the stairs shouting. "I knew it. I knew it. Oh my God! You guys won't believe this."

She was so focused on her discovery she ran smack into a hard wall of muscle and sweat at the bottom of the stairs.

"Umph!" Luce's reaction was muffled as an arm went flying around her waist holding her up. And holding her too close. Bringing her palms up to push away, she already knew who she'd run into. A half-naked Andy. Yikes.

"So um, you can let go. I'm good." Luce looked up at his face, noticing the broad grin. Of course, he'd find this amusing. She would have too, if he wasn't sending electrical impulses from her head straight down to her toes. And everywhere in between.

Releasing her, Andy stepped back and let her pass, then turned to follow. He'd been heading up to grab a shower, but whatever this was that had Luce up-in-arms, he'd need to find out first.

## CHAPTER FIFTEEN

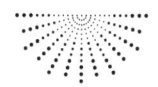

"Mrs. Adeline Bowers inherited that property." Luce stood in the kitchen holding her phone up, pointing to the screen, even though nobody could actually see what was there.

"Well, yeah, her husband left it to her," Andy said. Somewhat disappointed in the news.

"No, silly boy, not her husband. Her father, Arnold Bowers." Luce smirked.

"Wait, what?" Andy was all ears now.

"Arnold Bowers was not her husband; he was her father."

"Holy shit." Chris looked at Andy.

"On it." Andy pulled out his phone and began furiously tapping away.

"She's right," Andy said, sounding a bit surprised.

"Gee, thanks for the vote of confidence," Luce muttered.

"Adeline Bowers, born in 1940. Arnold Bowers died, 1944, during the war." Andy scrolled down his screen. "Get this, Adeline's mother died several years later. Under a shroud of secrecy, it seems… this will take a bit of research. Who raised her, was she married, any children…" Andy was hunting for something. "She inherited from her father… interesting. As her mother was alive when he died."

"So which is the bigger mystery?" Annie asked. "The lady or the ship?"

"I think I'll call the others; we need to all put our heads together." Chris grabbed his phone and immediately began dialing Mark. "I feel a new book coming on!"

"Who's got the Born This Way ringtone?" Andy looked around.

"Oh... hell, that's Kat" Luce murmured, reaching for her phone.

"What?" Andy gave Luce a glare.

"Oh, don't be an idiot. She put it there, not me." The idea that Andy thought she was mocking his niece? Seriously?

"Yeah, Kat, what's up? Everything good?" Luce's tone was rushed, rather than professional, but hey, it was Saturday.

"Yeah I was checking messages, got one from a Mr. Peabody," Kat replied.

"Hang, on, Kat, I'm going on speaker." Luce laid the phone down and pushed the speakerphone.

"OK, he says Mrs. Bowers would like to meet with you regarding an opportunity and can you come by and see her on Monday at 10am and if it's a problem you can cancel."

"Wait, they just assumed I'd be there? How did she get the number?"

"Probably just used the station directory."

Luce frowned. "Huh. OK Kat, thanks. I guess I'll be out of the office Monday morning. Hopefully I'll get back by early afternoon. Give me the number just in case there's a change in plans."

Disconnecting, they all remained silent. This was a seriously shocking turn of events. Why was Luce being invited back? Alone? She wondered if she should go alone or bring someone along. Opportunity meant business. If it was business, she had to go alone.

"You're not going alone." Andy's voice was firm.

"Excuuuse me?" Even though she didn't want to go alone, now that he'd put it out there...

"Clearly she's got a few marbles loose, and there's some crazy-ass stuff going on. Look, I'm your ride, right? It makes sense that I come along with you."

He had a point. But her stubborn nature insisted she get the last word. She just couldn't think of one at that very moment.

"But it's not until Monday," she protested, somewhat weakly.

"Call her, tell her you're headed back to the city tomorrow but you can swing by on the way." Andy then turned and headed up the stairs skipping steps as he went, calling out. "Jumping in the shower, back in a flash."

"Um we're having a discussion here," Luce mumbled in return, shaking her head. "That man is going to drive me to drink."

"Too late for that Luce," Annie laughed. "Now quick, call Mr. Peabody."

Luce held up her hand to silence everyone as she pulled up the contact she'd entered and hit send. She put the phone on speaker and laid it down on the counter.

"Bowers residence," the stiff awkward voice echoed.

"Mr. Peabody? Luce Porter."

"Ah yes, Ms. Porter, I take it you received my message. We'll expect you Monday at 10 then?"

"I'm afraid that won't work. However, I'm happy to stop by on our way out of town tomorrow, say about 11am?" Luce replied.

"Very well, I will confirm with Mrs. Bowers and let you know if there is an issue. Otherwise, we will expect you then." Without waiting for a reply, he disconnected.

Luce frowned and shook her head, muttering a few choice words under her breath.

"Well, since we're waiting on *Mr. I'm In Charge of Everything*, might as well have Julie and Mark pop over here, since they live so close. Then we'll call Jen." Luce grabbed her coffee and headed down into the living room and through the massive French doors to the patio. Collapsing into one of the fabulous comfy chaise lounges, she stared out at the deep blue waters of the Long Island Sound. She could see why Annie loved living on the beach like this. It really was quite the dream home.

She thought about the turn of events. What could Mrs. Bowers, if that's even her real name, possibly want to offer her and why is Andy so gung-ho on her not going alone? The invitation was definitely creepy, but Luce wasn't afraid. Should she be?

It wasn't long before she was joined outside by the others, with Mark and Julie in tow. They lived only about a 2 minute drive away, 5 minutes walking along the beach. Clearly they'd driven this time. Luce smiled, knowing Annie must have made it seem urgent.

As they all took a seat, Andy reappeared as well, now dressed in jeans and a snug-fitting t-shirt. His wet hair slicked back. She noticed he hadn't bothered to shave though. Which was fine by her. He looked pretty damn good that way. Luce was still in the shorts and tee she'd slept in. Her hair loosely tied atop her head. Perfectly presentable but suddenly she felt exposed. And her reaction to him made her nervous.

"You know what, you all get this discussion going, I'm just going to run and freshen up!" Luce announced as she quickly headed back inside and up the stairs. Mostly she just needed to regroup. She was feeling overwhelmed. Too much chaos, not enough Zen.

After a quick shower and change of clothes, and maybe a few minutes getting her look together, Luce headed back down to the patio. Hearing the chatter from outside, she quickly grabbed a bottle of water and joined the others only to be met with total silence and a lot of guilty expressions.

Not good. So not good, she thought.

"What? Come on, cough it up. You're all sitting here like you were caught red-handed. Doing what I have no idea." Luce went over to her seat and plopped down, took a swig of water and looked around again. "Annie?" She used her guilt-the-sister voice.

"What?" Annie looked nervously at Luce.

"What were you all gabbing about before I came out here?" Luce demanded, watching how they all looked at each other.

"So yeah, hey, we need to get Jen and Bill on the phone, right?" Chris said, pulling out his phone and laying it on the small patio table next to him, clearly changing the subject. Tapping the screen, he placed it on speaker, putting an end to Luce's interrogation.

Luce stewed silently, still irritated. They were being very secretive and she had no clue why. Though she had a suspicion it involved one particular hot detective who now seemed to be sitting next to her on her lounge chair. The excuse being he needed to be closer to the phone to hear. She didn't think so. Nervously tapping her foot, she waited for Jen to answer as it would at least break the awkward silence.

"Hello?"

Whew, finally. Luce put her hand on her knee to stop the tapping.

"Hey Jen, it's Chris, listen everyone's here at the house. We're doing a bit of a rehash on last night's adventure. Is Bill around?"

"Yeah, hang on," Jen turned and called for Bill. "We're both here. That was sure something. Weird though, we were a little creeped out you know."

"Yeah, we all were," Annie jumped in. "You guys had the kitchen, right? Was that really weird?"

"Yeah, because it wasn't the actual kitchen that they prepared our dinner in. We didn't get a chance to talk about it last night but it was like a back door off the real kitchen and it was a really old kitchen. As in colonial era I bet." Jen replied.

"Indeed it was," Bill chimed in. "It was like walking into the twilight zone. More like a movie set, not actually real but it felt real. Ya know?"

"Yeah, the nursery was the same way. Felt like I'd walked onto the set of a history channel documentary," Julie remarked.

"Well, I think we can all agree, the whole thing was odd. Jen and Bill, was your theory about mutiny, was that for real?" Chris asked, keeping his voice neutral, not to give anything away.

"Not likely," Bill laughed. "Mutiny? Nah. Something pretty dark and sinister happened. Truthfully? We think it might have been a slave ship."

Andy nodded silently and looked at Luce. "Yeah," he spoke up. "Mark? You and Julie want to change your story?" Andy smiled. Knowing by their expressions and wide eyes, they did.

"Yes, please," Julie nodded vigorously and shared a look with Mark. "Whatever it was, it didn't involve privateering. It involved children. Slave children, actually, based on some things we saw in the nursery."

"It's hard to explain, but some of the toys weren't toys that colonial children would play with." Mark sighed and shook his head "Some were more primitive. We were almost afraid to touch them."

"Primitive how?" Andy asked, his attention focused now.

"There were traditional dolls, set upon a shelf. Beautifully carved and the clothes were silk. But on the floor, in an old pail, there were rag-dolls, made with twigs and things. Clearly not meant for the same children as the ones on the shelf." Julie shuddered. "As if there were two different sets of children."

"We think it was a slave ship as well." Mark added.

"Well, Chris and I also vote for slave ship. That house of horrors basement made my skin crawl." Annie shivered.

"So Luce, maybe you can share those photos with everyone. Then how about we stick with our original teams, only this time, we all study every clue."

"I think we all agree," Luce said. "My next question is why on earth does that prickly old woman, who isn't who she says she is, want to see me?"

## CHAPTER SIXTEEN

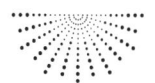

It was quiet. Too quiet. Andy looked about for Luce, but the patio had cleared out after lunch, and Luce had said she'd be back shortly. But it had been a few hours, and she hadn't returned. He'd been sifting through the clues on his own and was feeling a bit annoyed and impatient. He had ideas and needed a partner to bounce them off of. Chris and Annie were in the living room, Mark and Julie had gone back to their place, leaving him alone with his thoughts. Not something he was really keen on. The Ghost Ship was a welcome distraction for him. Something to take his mind off things. He'd needed that. Yet he had a sudden need for Luce. She was more than a distraction. Now that after 10 years he'd finally stopped resisting the pull.

He'd been a rookie cop; she'd been a rookie reporter. Their first meeting didn't go well, but if nothing else, it was memorable. He'd been assigned to a pair of detectives that day, his job was to help protect a crime scene. Somehow, Luce Porter managed to get in his way. He smiled as he remembered cuffing her, torn between attraction and frustration. They'd run into each other again, a few times a year, but it seemed they were fated to simply go their own ways. Until the night he was called to Annie Porter's apartment. A simple break-in turned his life upside down and brought Luce right back into it.

Hearing the door open, he turned to see Luce, stepping out on the patio, tray in hand. Craning his neck to see what she'd brought, he grinned.

"How'd you know?" He asked.

"Know what?" Luce quipped, setting the tray down.

"That soft pretzels and beer would make me do just about anything you asked?"

"Anything, eh?" Luce smirked.

"I'm all yours, Luce." Andy grinned as the flush crept up her neck into her face. He couldn't help noticing that stripped of the professional attire and demeanor she had on in the city, she was, underneath it all, as wholesome as they come. Not unusual for so many women in New York. The struggle to get ahead in their careers was twice as hard as for men. It was the same regardless of what path they chose. But this Luce, the weekend Luce? He wanted more of. He'd been contemplating a lot of changes lately, he realized, and she was top of the list.

"Well, then my first request is about Mrs. Bowers. Can you run a background search on her? I mean, if that's legal?" Luce wasn't sure it was, and knew Andy was a stickler for rules.

"Perfectly legal using public records," he replied with a grin. "I'm on it. How about in exchange you tell me about how Kat's doing in the internship?"

"Hmm. OK, she's wonderful. Best I've had." Luce smiled.

"Truth? Or you're just appeasing me?" Andy raised a brow. Hoping it was true. Kat was so smart and capable; it just took the right person to allow her to flourish.

"Appeasing you? Moi? I think not, Detective, not my style." Luce laughed and relaxed in the lounge chair opposite his, opening her laptop and getting comfortable. "In fact, Kat is really phenomenal. I had my doubts, you know," she continued.

"Doubts?" Andy frowned. "How so?"

"Relax, *Uncle Andrew*, it's not because she's weak in the knees."

Andy glared at the comment.

"Everyone is weak-kneed in my presence," Luce laughed out loud. "I had my doubts because you know, she's related to you. I thought she might have an attitude problem."

Andy's frown turned into a sheepish smile. "I suppose I deserved that. I'm glad you see her potential, Luce, seriously. Not enough people do."

"That bothers you a lot, doesn't it?"

"It does. Until Kat came along, I suppose I didn't pay enough attention to how unfair people could be treated. Or how little the law protects those who are disadvantaged. For example, did you know that if businesses aren't open to the public, they don't always have to make accommodations or be accessible?"

"Do they teach that at the police academy?" Luce smiled, but she was curious. He seemed to know quite a bit on the subject.

"No, law school." It slipped out before he realized he'd said it.

"Law school?"

"Eh, yeah. I might not have mentioned that to you, huh."

"Eh, no, you didn't," Luce chuckled. "What other surprises do you have hidden away? And if you went to law school, why aren't you practicing law instead of arresting budding journalists?"

"I will someday. I wanted to give myself time on the force to learn how to be a damn good investigator. Because a good lawyer needs to be able to rely on themselves to discern the facts."

"Somehow, I think there's more, isn't there?" Luce asked quietly. This was a new side to Andy she hadn't seen. Usually cocky and arrogant, bossy as hell, suddenly she was seeing a spark of something else. She wanted more.

"Perhaps there is, but let's save that for another day, shall we?" He seemed to want to avoid the subject. Luce was willing to let it drop. For the moment.

Andy grabbed his laptop and, placing it on his lap, typed in a few commands.

"OK, back to our mystery ship. So, while we wait on the Bowers check, tell me something. Which clue, out of all of them, strikes you as the most important one?" Andy asked casually, though the tapping of his fingers on his thigh indicated how critical a question it was.

"The bill of sale," Luce replied without a second thought. She knew in her bones it was a slave trade transaction. She'd seen them before doing other types of research. And every time she came across something like that in her research, it made her ill. Especially when researching in the tri-state area. She was taught in school to believe the North had some sort of monopoly on morals when it came to slavery in America, but one of the lessons her father had instilled in them was that the inescapable evil of slavery had been everywhere. It wasn't just the South. It existed even in the small peaceful inlets of the Long Island Sound.

"Agreed. Whatever that ship was, somehow it involved slavery. Maybe," Andy added for good measure. "We are jumping to conclusions. But all in all, it would appear to be a good theory, no?"

"Yeah, I mean the bill of sale, shackles, a branding iron, all the elements of a truly gruesome tale. If those clues are to be believed. Maybe it's all for her entertainment?" Luce mused, knowing the woman could be just bat-shit crazy eccentric.

"Well, once we find out her background, if we do, it will help. Maybe tomorrow will shed some light on things." Andy set his laptop aside and stood up to stretch. "How about a walk along the beach? I bet it's only a mile or so to Mrs. Bowers property line. I didn't get a chance to look last night, but I bet there's a clear view of the lighthouse from there."

"Good idea," Luce replied, closing her laptop. "I'll see if Annie and Chris want to come."

Andy paused as Luce stood and turned to go inside.

"I was thinking just us."

Luce stopped then and turned to look back. He was serious, she thought. Just them? Alone? On the beach? Probably a terrible idea. Worse than terrible. But what if it were terribly wonderful?

"Oh. Okay," it was out of her mouth before she could stop it. Their eyes locked for a moment, and Andy quickly stepped toward her, and grabbing her hand, led her away from the house and down towards the beach.

"Which way?" Luce asked.

"Left. I think her place is near the second jetty down there. Maybe a little past it."

He kept hold of her hand as they walked, making Luce nervous enough to tug slightly. His only response was to smirk. "Get used to it," he said softly.

"Andy, what is this? I mean, right now... me, you... this?" Luce's voice was quiet, but firm.

"Luce, when was the last time you flirted. I mean, really flirted?"

"I don't remember," Luce shrugged and looked out toward the water. "It's been a while. I mean what's the point?"

"Something tells me there's more to this than you just haven't found the right one. I keep wondering what it is that has you keeping up this wall. Especially between us."

"Well, for starters, you've never done this before with me, so you must have your own wall, no?" Luce was defensive, now, he could see that.

"Tell me. Who was he? The jerk who did this to you."

Luce stopped walking and turned to look at him. Check his sincerity maybe. "How do you know that's what this is about?"

"I'm a detective, Luce." Andy smiled then. And something snapped in her. Suddenly she felt the need to put it all out there.

"His name was Jack."

"Jack. Got it. I'm guessing there's more?" He kept smiling hoping she'd relax.

"Yeah," Luce sighed. "Way more." Looking over at the first Jetty, she nodded. "Can we go sit over there? This might take a while."

"I've got all day, let's go." Andy gave her hand a tug and they headed off for the rocks ahead.

"I used to climb these rocks as a kid, then head to the end of the jetty and pretend I was overlooking the ocean. Waiting for my ship and my mates to come get me," Andy mused aloud.

"I can see you out there, skipping rocks, no doubt. I bet you had one of those metal detectors too. Combing the beach for treasure." Luce smiled, picturing the young Andy Holman.

"That I did," he laughed. "Come on, let's sit up here, fewer barnacles." Just one of the hazards on the rocky coastline, he remembered.

They settled down on top of one of the larger boulders and gazed out at the water.

"So. Jack. Spill it." Andy wasted no time.

"So. Jack." Luce took a breath. "We dated a year. He was smart, good looking, very successful. Quite charming. At least I thought so."

"What, no wait, let me guess. Not quite monogamous?"

"No. He was. At least as far I know. I told you how we lost our parents."

"Car accident, right, during the super storm a few years back. Annie's mentioned it a few times as well."

"Yeah. Well, When I got the call he drove me to the hospital, then dropped me at the entrance. I thought he had gone to park the car. He never returned."

"Oh, for fuck's sake."

"He texted me and left messages for a few days, but I didn't see him. He didn't show up to their funeral either. Said he had a scheduling conflict."

"You handled that entire experience alone?"

"No, never alone. I had Annie."

"Yeah, but she needed you to be the strong one, didn't she, and that fucker couldn't be there for you? You know, Luce," Andy said softly, taking her chin in his hand and turning her to face him. "We're not all like that."

"I'm counting on it, Detective," Luce smiled. And for the first time, Andy felt like he could see hope in her eyes. "Now, how about you. Being so perfect and all, why aren't you settled down with 3.2 kids and a house in the burbs?" Her eyes twinkled with mischief as if she was enjoying putting him on the hot seat.

"Would you believe me if I told you I just hadn't found the one?" Andy grinned, knowing she wouldn't buy it.

"No. Try again." Luce's tone was a little more serious now. She really did want to know the truth, and he knew he'd have to tell her.

"You haven't met my sister yet. Brie. She's a few years older and growing up just the nicest, sweetest person. A little spoiled maybe, but money will do that. She married Steve when they were pretty young. Maybe they should have waited, who knows. When Kat came along, at first, everything was good. But I watched them become that couple. The one that bickers endlessly and never has a nice thing to say about each other. I watched their marriage turn into something they both hated. I was still a kid myself, but I became Kat's surrogate parent. Someone had to. They didn't know how to cope. I never wanted that for me."

"But your parents seem to have a wonderful marriage," Luce chided. "Seems to me there's more stopping you, no?"

Andy sighed, and nodded. "Karen. My first serious relationship. She was smart and funny and always quite agreeable. I brought her to Thanksgiving Dinner and then she ended things. Said she didn't want to end up like my sister with a kid like Kat and a miserable marriage. It made my skin crawl. After that, I dated, but not with any future in mind."

Luce studied his expression for a moment. "And now?" She held her breath then, she hadn't meant to let that out.

"And now I think maybe it's time to explore a different path." He smiled and took her hand. Luce had no idea what was coming next and bit her lip nervously.

"Come on, we've got a lighthouse to find." He stood, tugging on her hand to pull her up with him. She breathed a sigh of relief, though in all honesty maybe it was one of disappointment. There was something there, embers crackling away, and at some point one of them was going to ignite it.

They slid down off the rocks, Andy hopped down first, into the sand, and turned to help Luce when shouts erupted from the house. They could see Annie waving her arms frantically on the patio. Andy immediately grabbed Luce by the hand and took off in a sprint, Luce scampering to keep up.

Reaching the patio, Luce let go of Andy's hand and raced over to Annie.

"What happened, are you OK? The baby? What's wrong?" Luce was breathless and didn't leave time for Annie to answer.

"I'm fine, Chris just said to find you. Actually, he said holy shit, go find Andy!"

Luce looked over at Andy, who looked just as bewildered.

Just then, Chris appeared, rushing out the door, his hair disheveled, as if he'd been combing his fingers through it, perhaps in frustration.

"Andy, by god, I found her."

"Found her?"

"Yeah, I found MorningStar."

## CHAPTER SEVENTEEN

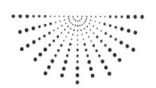

"Who or what is MorningStar?" Luce looked at Chris, then at Andy, who both looked a bit guilty.

"I'd kind of like to know that as well," Annie piped in. "What are you guys hiding from us?"

Chris ruffled his hair again, swiping the falling locks off his face. "Um, yeah, sorry? Forgot to mention that Andy and I discovered an interesting little tidbit on our run this morning."

"Tidbit?" Luce scowled at Andy. "A tidbit you didn't think to mention in the last, oh four hours or so? I'm guessing it has to do with our mystery?"

"No doubt, sis," Annie huffed. "Why are we always the last to know everything?"

"Well?" Luce tapped her foot impatiently, looking from one man to the other. Clearly frustrated.

"We might have passed by the widow's house on our run," Chris began. "Well, if she is a widow. Anyway, we might have noticed something in the yard."

"Might have? You were snooping!" Annie grumbled.

"Please, Annie, of course they were snooping. Look at their faces!"

Luce nodded in their direction, the two now standing side by side, nervously tapping their fingers.

"Say how about dinner, who's up for Lobster? Anyone?" Chris smiled hopefully knowing it was Annie's favorite.

"Are you going to share your little adventure with us or use this as a distraction?" Luce demanded. "Because we're not going anywhere until you explain MorningStar."

Andy and Chris shared another look, then they both sighed simultaneously.

"Yes, we're going to share. And no sense copping an attitude, Luce, I don't even know what Chris knows yet."

"Nice try, detective, but you have some idea and we have none."

Chris held a hand up in the air. "Truce everyone, no bickering. How about Andy and I head to the dock for the lobster, then we'll have a nice meal and everything will be explained."

"Are you going to tell Andy before us? Is this one of those let the women go get things ready for dinner and we'll talk privately schemes of yours?" Annie tried to hide a smile.

"Well joke's on them then, as we'd rather eat at Tristan's Landing." Luce chuckled. "Annie has a craving for their lobster roll, don't you Annie? And we'll all go, together in the same car. Just so there's no conversations without us!"

Luce grabbed Andy's hand, and mimicking his earlier attitude, smiled sweetly. "Shall we go *sweetness?*"

Andy laughed good-naturedly. "But of course, *my dear,*" he replied, returning the smile. And not letting go of her hand when she tried to gently tug it away. Leaning down to whisper in her ear, he warned her. "Be careful, Luce, you know what they say, when you play with fire?"

∽

TRISTAN'S LANDING was a local favorite, located at the end of the pier in the harbor. A floating restaurant, it was charming and inviting. Twinkling lights strung about the outdoor deck reflected off the deep blue waters. The interior featured gleaming wood paneling, antique anchors and wheels, and nautical memorabilia scattered throughout. Always busy, Saturday nights in particular you were guaranteed a wait. After Chris headed in to put their name on the list, they settled on a few benches outside on the pier. It gave them a chance to talk before being surrounded by other diners with large ears. As with all the small harbor inlets, Port Newton was a small town and rumors traveled fast.

The bench was large enough for all to sit on, and Chris and Annie of course snuggled up in the chilly early evening air, while Luce tried to give herself a little distance from Andy. Though he wasn't having any of it and kept sliding towards her.

"So, MorningStar. Who wants to explain?" Luce jumped right in. She had left it alone on the ride over, knowing she needed the element of surprise to launch the discussion.

Andy looked at Chris, who gave a small shake of his head and grinned.

"Last night," Andy began talking quietly, "it was dark and you couldn't tell, but there's a small pond in Mrs. Bowers' garden. We saw it from the street as we ran by her house today."

"We thought we might, you know, take a look," added Chris.

"Please don't tell me you actually *were* snooping around her property," Annie's eyes widened. "That lady has a few screws loose. Remember that movie, oh what was it called, Misery? With Cathy Bates? She kidnaps that author?"

"Well I wasn't alone; Andy was there too." Chris looked at Andy, hoping for backup.

"I told him not to go in there, but he did it anyway, so naturally I followed, you know, just to make sure he was safe and all." Andy grinned and gave Chris a conspiratorial wink.

"So, we crept in along the side hedges, and slipped through the garden gate. It was early enough there was no one about. We could see objects floating around the pond, so we felt we should get a little closer." Chris added.

"I told Chris, we needed to avoid anyone spotting us through that window overlooking the garden. The one in the library. We decided to hunch down, maybe crawl over to it." Andy chuckled. "Might have removed an article of clothing or two, so they wouldn't get muddy."

"Oh, for the love of cake, you two did a commando crawl in Mrs. Bowers yard?" Luce laughed outright. "What I wouldn't give to have pictures of that."

"Chris, really, your firstborn is gonna have a prison daddy!" Annie shook her head and laughed along with Luce.

Chris smiled, and went on. "Want to know what was floating in the pond?"

Annie and Luce nodded eagerly.

"Mini ship replicas. Model ships. Colonial ships." Chris beamed.

"And carved on the outside along the hull of the largest one…." Andy teased. "Drum roll please…"

"MorningStar!" Luce and Annie both said at once.

"Wow. MorningStar is a real ship, I take it? You said you found her?" Luce turned to Chris. "What kind of ship?"

Chris looked around, ensuring no prying ears, "A schooner. Built by a plantation owner on Long Island. A guy named Lionel Bowers."

They sat in stunned silence.

"It disappeared off a small island of rocks in the Long Island Sound in 1790."

"Wait, 1790?" Luce jumped off the bench. "You know what that means?"

"It wasn't a ship hauling colonial prisoners. At least not soldiers." Chris mused.

"It's also the date of that Bill of Sale," Andy remarked, narrowing his eyes a bit as he concentrated.

"Did you get a picture?" Annie asked.

"But of course!" Chris shook his head. "That's how I was able to research it."

"Well, let us see," Annie huffed.

"Hold up," said Luce. "I'm sorry, but if you were crawling around commando style in the garden, how is it you had your phone handy to take a picture?" Luce looked from Chris to Andy, trying not to playback the whole thing in her head.

"You don't want to know," Andy leaned over and whispered. "Trust me."

Chris pulled the photo up on his phone and leaned in so Luce and Annie could take a look.

Luce looked closely at the photo, then at Andy for confirmation. As far she knew, no one else knew he'd also seen the ghost ship. But to her eyes the MorningStar sure looked just like it. Looked just like the drawing they'd found as well. They'd have to compare the two closely when they got home.

"As fascinating as this is, and it is fascinating, I'm kind of starved and the guy over there is waving us in!" Annie tugged on Chris to get up.

Andy stood up quickly, and deliberately took Luce's arm to escort her in, causing her to shake her head and smile. Progress, he thought to himself.

They were seated at a booth with a large window. Luce and Annie slid in to be next to the window, allowing them a breathtaking view of the sunset reflecting in the gently rippling water. Completely relaxed, Luce turned to Andy, a question in her eyes.

"Tell me something, you grew up around here, right?"

"I did." Andy smiled, knowing that Chris was the only one who knew that. And clearly hadn't told her. He didn't share that information with too many people.

"But yet you didn't know Mrs. Bowers before now, right?"

"Right again. Full confession, my mom does. They belong to the historical society and serve on different committees together."

"That's how you got the invite, then." Luce grinned. "Connections. What else are you hiding?"

Andy held both hands out above the table, turning them over and back again. "Not a thing. Unless you'd care to search?" He laughed out loud then, watching her fidget as she picked up her menu and hid behind it.

"Not right now, I've got a lobster to eat. Perhaps though, another time?" Luce smiled and ducked her head, stealing a glance to see if her comments had the desired effect.

Yes indeed, Andy Holman was struck speechless.

## CHAPTER EIGHTEEN

Peabody, as they now referred to him, had opened the door and immediately frowned at seeing Andy. He stepped aside and let them in but had them wait in the foyer.

"I'll need to check with the mistress of the house. She wasn't expecting both of you."

"Is that Miss Porter?" Adeline called out as she entered, and upon seeing Andy, frowned.

Not waiting, Andy jumped right in. "How are you today Mrs. Bowers? My mother does send her regards. Said your Tulips this year were outstanding. I was supposed to mention that on Friday, and I'm afraid I lost track."

"Oh, well," she smiled broadly and straightened up. "Thank you and thank your dear mother. She's always been a helpful woman. You take after your father, though, don't you?"

Luce pursed her lips, trying not to laugh. She could just store all this away for later. After being seated in the living room, Luce took a breath. She was already uncomfortable and she felt as if she were being swallowed whole by the enormous wing back chairs. Andy, meanwhile, appeared perfectly relaxed. Except she could see the twitching of his lips. She knew he was stewing about something.

Mrs. Bowers was dressed once again as if she were hosting Sunday brunch with the ladies. Maybe she'd just come from church. Luce couldn't decide whether all this was simple eccentricity or something far weirder. She had no idea how weird it would get.

∼

"Well, do we have a deal, young lady?" Adeline Bowers didn't take no for an answer and clearly had little patience. Luce had barely digested the last half hour's worth of chatter from the woman, and now she wanted an answer?

"I want to make sure I understand," Luce said slowly. "You would like to sponsor and fund a reality program exploring the history of the ghost ship. On WNNY. With me producing."

"Yes yes, are you daft?" Mrs. Bowers choice of words was odd at best.

"No, no, I admit it's a wonderful idea. But there are logistics to consider, time frame, scheduling."

"But of course there are, and that's your job. I'll expect you the week after the 4th. Give you time to plan. Then maybe you can wrap it all up by the fall. All the new series begin in the fall, don't they?" She went on without giving Luce a chance to answer. "I'll provide full access to the estate. And I will make myself available for interviews, which you may record, to help with the research as needed. Give it that air of authenticity, as they do on PBS you know."

Luce felt oddly as if she were having an out-of-body experience. Her mind was simply floating about trying to reconnect. This was so far from what she'd expected, though in truth, she had no idea what to expect. But a TV show? About a haunted ship? *Her* haunted ship?

She looked at Andy, hoping he'd offer some sort of confidence boost. Anything to snap her out of this strange fog. His gaze wasn't one she could read. It was penetrating, as if sending her a message. And then she saw it. The slight shake of his head. *No?* Why was he telling her no? This was a fabulous opportunity. She frowned and shook her head slightly as well.

"I'll tell you what Mrs. Bowers, I will promise to study the opportunity carefully and get back to you this week. I do have to confer with my production team and do a little of my own homework as well. I'm sure you understand."

"Perhaps we could have a little tour, as we didn't get a chance to fully explore the other night. Might convince her," Andy flashed a grin at Mrs. Bowers, and reached over and grasped Luce's hand, giving it a squeeze. She realized he was up to something, and she had to admit it was a good idea. She could scope it out and decide if it would make an interesting location shoot or not.

"You know that might just help," Luce nodded in agreement. She tried to smile, though she felt it looked more like a nervous tic. Something in this room was really unsettling and she had a sudden desire to get out of there. She could swear the drapes were moving as if a window were open. But it was stuffy and warm, and she was certain no air was blowing.

"Certainly. In fact, if you'll just wait for a few more minutes, my grandson is arriving any moment and he can show you about. I'm afraid my stamina isn't what it used to be."

Luce stifled her gasp and darted a look at Andy who looked just as shell shocked. *Grandson?*

Andy recovered first it seemed. "You know we certainly don't want to intrude on your visit, and we're happy to come another time if that's more convenient."

"Don't be silly, Lionel will be thrilled to have someone other than his crotchety old grandma to entertain him for a bit. He comes every Sunday when he's in town." Luce couldn't help but smile at the sudden change in her. Her grandson must mean the world to her, so somewhere in there is the real Adeline Bowers. It's as if a switch was flipped the minute she mentioned him. Her curiosity couldn't be held at bay.

"Mrs. Bowers, if I may ask, how long have you lived here. The property has been in the family a long time I assume?" Luce had to be careful not to reveal what they knew.

"That it has. Originally built by Lionel's namesake, back in 1750 or so."

"Do go on, please," Luce smiled, hoping it looked sincere.

"Ah well, it remained in the family for generations, until it was lost in a high stakes card game. It was several generations before it was back in the family. Since then it's transferred ownership a few times. But I've made sure that it is in a permanent trust now. It will remain in the family from here on out." Adeline's expression turned wistful. And Luce was chomping at the bit to learn more. The story they'd come upon, about it being built in the eighteen hundreds was clearly incorrect. Or deliberately planted to mislead. But why?

No time to ask more, as a young man practically ran into the room, bustling with excitement.

"Nana! How's my girl," he shouted, laughing as he leaned over where she sat on the couch to hug her affectionately.

"Lionel, we have guests!"

"So I presumed from the car in the driveway. Who do we have here?" He turned to study Andy and Luce, looking from one to the other, raising his brows and grinning. He was about as different from Adeline Bowers as they come, Luce thought. Faded torn jeans, a body hugging t-shirt, canvas sneakers and a mop of blond hair just slightly longer than his shoulders.

"Lionel, sit a moment," she smiled as she patted the seat next to her on the sofa. He dutifully obeyed. "This is Andy Holman and Luce Porter. Luce works for WNNY."

Lionel frowned slightly and narrowed his gaze. "I thought we said no more interviews, Nana," he scolded.

"This is very different. Luce is very interested in the Ghost Ship, and I've asked her to produce one of those TV series to investigate it."

"A reality show? Here? Nana, no. Absolutely not!" Lionel jumped up and strode around the room, pacing.

"Look, I'm sorry my grandmother has wasted your time, but occasionally," he paused and glared at her, "she gets it into her head that there's a ghost ship traveling around in our backyard. Please accept our apologies."

Adeline stood then; her facial expression clear. She was angry. "Lionel. Stop this nonsense. I am not some crazy old fool. This is still my home. If I choose to open it up to explore the world of the supernatural, that is my decision. Now, please, sit back down. I'll order some tea, and then you will show our guests the property."

They stared at each other for what seemed like an eternity to Luce, then finally the young man sat back down, followed by his grandmother. The temperature in the room had dropped about 20 degrees, and Luce shivered. Things were getting stranger by the minute.

## CHAPTER NINETEEN

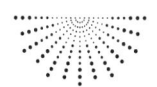

Luce was surprised at how affable Lionel was on their tour. Once he discovered Andy was NYPD, and their families were acquainted he completely switched gears. He'd obviously served as a tour guide before and had a remarkable knowledge of the history of the property.

They started the tour in the library, giving Luce a chance to voice the question topmost on her mind.

"Everything I've read says this house was built in the eighteen hundreds and it has that feel to it, but your grandmother said it was much older. Colonial in fact." It wasn't exactly a question, but a prompt.

"Yes, it's been built and rebuilt, several times over in fact. The original home, the stone structure you see in the front, was in fact built in 1750 according to the cornerstone. But as is wont to happen with these old homes, time and the elements take their toll. War too. Not just the revolution, but 1812 and again during the Civil War. Many changes." Lionel paused, then looked about at the books lining the shelves. "You'll find much of the history of the estate in the books here. I've read a few, not all, obviously," he chuckled.

"You're a man of letters, then," Luce smiled.

"Well, I travel quite a bit and reading helps me unwind."

"It's good to have a hobby that feeds the mind," Andy chimed in. "I'm afraid I don't read enough." Though if trapped in this particular room, he might just read a hell of a lot more, he thought.

"Shall we head up to the ballroom?" Lionel began to usher them out.

"We've actually been there, but I am interested in the basement. I've heard it's quite... let's just say, interesting?" Luce was hopeful. "I'd like to make sure the atmosphere will come across to viewers, before making a decision."

"My grandmother hasn't managed to persuade you yet? I'm surprised," Lionel shook his head. "She must be losing her touch. OK, this way." He pointed towards the bookcases. "We can get there from here."

Pushing a button along one of the shelves, Lionel pushed gently and one entire panel of shelving swung inwards, revealing a broad stone staircase.

"Wow, a secret door, I love it," Andy commented enthusiastically, causing Luce to take notice. Maybe he'd come on board after all.

Andy took a moment to let his eyes adjust and noticed the panel of switches on the wall to the right. Lionel stepped down onto the first step, and flipped several of the switches, bathing the stairwell in the light from the LED panels lining the walls on both sides.

"Watch your step, it's well lit, but there are some cracks in the stones here and there," Lionel called out as they descended into the unknown.

As they reached the bottom, Andy watched as Lionel flipped another set of switches, flooding the basement with more LED lights along the old stone walls.

Luce looked about, confused. The room was cavernous, yes, but quite empty. She noticed openings in several places that appeared to be passages. Perhaps leading to other chambers in the basement? She looked at Andy, who didn't seem at all phased at first glance. Until she saw him tapping his fingers against his thigh.

"My mother would be green with envy at this place, our basement looks like the storeroom for an antique shop!" Andy's tone was relaxed, but Luce could see his mind cranking. *Where was everything?* She'd ask Annie later. They must have gone into a passage or two.

"I'm afraid this won't quite sell the viewers, but I'm sure there's plenty more to see," Luce commented softly as she looked around.

"Oh quite, Ms. Porter. I guarantee it." Lionel smiled and nodded back toward the stairwell. "Shall we go up?"

Andy and Luce followed, disappointed but curious at the same time. Annie and Chris didn't mention it being empty or using secret passageways. But the damp stones with the bit of moss and areas of condensation would definitely give off the atmosphere they'd need. Reality TV was all about the camera, the angles, the edits. Without a script, they had to create the drama, often out of nothing. Far from reality, Luce knew the secret was illusion.

They headed up to the main level, and then to an old elevator, complete with a brass polished scissor gate, taking them up to the residential quarters, as Lionel put it.

As they stepped out, he pointed to the left. "The family suites are that way, and without permission, will be off limits. Down here to the right," he paused and nodded, "are a half dozen guest suites. Back in the day visitors often spent weekends, even full summers here, as guests. I imagine you will stay here when you are filming as well."

They followed him as he practically leapt down the hallway. Luce had to smile as she watched him. He couldn't be more than 25 she thought, and full of that boyish charm too many men lose. Though, looking at Andy, certainly not all.

Lionel stopped in front of one of the suites. Luce looked closely at the brass plate adorning the door. *MorningStar*. She quickly glanced at Andy who gave a slight nod. Indicating he'd seen it too.

"This is the MorningStar suite." Lionel said, opening the door.

"What an interesting name," Luce remarked as casually as possible.

"Yes, it was a ship. All the suites are named after ships. Our family built them way back when." Lionel quickly moved on to the décor, whether purposefully or not, Luce couldn't tell. Pointing to the various antique pieces of furniture, he explained the connection each piece had to the family. But Luce wasn't listening, as her eyes had fixed themselves on the view out the window. It was east facing, over the water, and directly in view was the lighthouse at Execution Rocks.

"Ah, I see you've spotted our gem," Lionel said, jolting Luce back to the present. "No coastal home is complete without its legendary lighthouse."

"I agree," Andy spoke up, noticing Luce's nerves were on edge. "I had a view of this from my attic window as a boy."

"Well, if you like that, you'll love what I have to show you next." Lionel waved them both out of the suite and back to the elevator. Stepping in behind them, Lionel pulled the gate closed and latched it. "Who's up for the Bowers Tower?" he said with as sinister an accent as he could muster, accompanied by a grin. "Ready or not, here we go," he said, and pushed a button labeled WW.

CHAPTER TWENTY

No one was more surprised than Luce when the elevator opened and they were practically on the roof. Well, technically, it was the roof. A widow's walk. She'd never been on one before and was just a bit nervous about stepping out onto it. She'd seen them in photographs of course, but never one with elevator access.

"Shall we?" Lionel was awfully cheerful, and Luce had a sudden premonition of being pushed right off the roof into the sea below. Shaking it off, she gave Andy a nervous look, but he simply nodded softly, and ushered her out on the strange platform. If they'd been anywhere else, she would have simply figured it was a rooftop deck, albeit oddly shaped. It was more of a raised platform with a railing, that extended out over the rear of the home. It appeared sturdy enough, but who knew?

"You go first. You know, just in case?" Luce nudged Andy. "If it holds you, I'll follow."

"Nothing to worry about," Lionel assured them. "I've been coming up here for years. It's my favorite meditation spot." Somehow Luce couldn't picture the animated young man meditating, and the thought made her smile.

"Then it's a widow's walk, where the wives would wait for their seafaring husbands to return?" Andy turned to Lionel; brows raised in question.

"Exactly. It was also a lookout, so they say, during wartime, and even during prohibition."

"Prohibition? You mean they were transporting illegal booze here?"

"Well, there are rumors you know," Lionel laughed. "My favorite legend? Some say that there was a British war ship chasing Washington and his troops that crashed right on those rocks. Penance for chaining our patriots there to die. And that the only one to witness it was my ancestor, Lionel Bowers. I figure if there *is* a ghost ship, that's it."

Luce had begun to regret not bringing a pad and pen, or at least hitting record on her phone. Hopefully Andy was making mental notes as well. She looked out over the water and found herself staring straight at the lighthouse. She imagined the view from there would give anyone a clear sighting of any ship, moving in any direction. She knew then her mind was made up. This project was definitely happening.

"I've got one more surprise, if you're up for it," Lionel's voice held a teasing note.

"Always, my friend," Andy responded with more enthusiasm than usual. Maybe his irritation at her meeting with Mrs. Bowers was just a bit of envy and nothing more.

But when he glanced her way, she saw it was an act. The same concern was in his eyes as earlier.

They headed back down in the elevator to the first floor, and then around the corner and down the hall to a side door. Exiting out, they ended up in the gardens, which Luce knew Andy had seen already.

"Wow this is certainly lovely," Luce mused, looking around. There was a pathway, which it seemed had been carved out of the flower beds, rather than the flowers planted around it. As they meandered around, Luce noticed various little gnomes scattered about, dressed as sailors and captains and even an admiral or two. It really was enchanting. The delicate and assorted pastel blooms of pink and white impatiens lying close to the ground, set against a backdrop of the tall, soft pink and purple hydrangeas was really quite stunning.

"Wait until you see this!" Lionel grinned as he led to the far end of the gated garden area, straight to the pond that Andy and Chris had discovered. Luce snuck a peek up at Andy's face, to see how well he masked his lack of surprise.

Very well it seemed, as he stopped short just as they approached it. "Wow, you have got to be kidding. There's an entire flotilla here." Andy leaned forward and crouched a bit to get a better look. "Are they models of real ships, or just hobby models?"

"They're real alright. See that larger schooner over there? That's the MorningStar. Behind it, to your left? That's her sister ship, the Nightwind. And this one right here," Lionel pointed to a small sloop in front of him, "they say that it was a scouting ship. During the The Battle of Long Island."

"Who built these? They are superbly done," Andy remarked.

"My father. He was quite the model ship builder. He probably would have loved the family business, building real ones, but that died out with my great grandfather, sorry to say." Lionel looked disappointed for a moment, then his face brightened again. "But probably a good thing, I'm not much for business I'm afraid."

Luce was about to ask exactly what Lionel did, if anything, for a living, when Peabody snuck up on them.

"Will you join us for lunch?"

"Thank you Mr. Peabody, but my parents are expecting us. We'd probably better get moving, so we'll just come in and say our goodbyes."

"Very well, follow me please," he responded in his usual haughty tone.

As they did, they dropped back a few steps, and Luce looked at him curiously. "Lunch with your parents?" She whispered. "You neglected to mention that to me." She chewed on her lip for a moment. From the look on his face, she'd been set up. She knew it.

"Relax Luce, you'll love them. I do." He grinned, took her elbow and steered her forward to catch up with the others as they went back through the side door.

"Well, Ms. Porter, do we have an agreement?" Luce was startled, not expecting Mrs. Bowers to meet them at the door.

"I'm not positive, but it does seem like an excellent idea and a good opportunity, but as I mentioned earlier, I do have to clear it with the powers-that-be."

"Very well, I'm disappointed you can't commit, but I suppose that's the way of things now. I'll expect to hear from you this week. Good day." With a nod to Luce, then to Andy, Adeline Bowers turned and simply walked away.

∽

As they settled in the car, Luce fastened her seatbelt, and turned to face Andy.

"Do your parents expect us?" she blurted out.

"Of course!" Andy chuckled.

"And how long have they been expecting us?" Luce asked, watching his expression. Busted.

"Hmm, well, I might have mentioned that we would probably stay out at your sister's this weekend after the dinner. And then she figured of course I'd stop by for lunch on the way back to the city."

"I see. Basically the whole time." She frowned. "You've known the whole time and not mentioned it?"

"Come on Luce, it's just lunch."

"With your parents."

"Yeah but still, just lunch."

"Andy Holman, you better not have any more tricks up your sleeve," Luce could barely suppress her smile. She really needed to put a stop to his shenanigans, but at the same time, she simply couldn't. No need to be nervous. Meeting his parents? When they were just acquaintances? Well maybe a little more, maybe friends who flirt? Still, it was just lunch. Maybe his mother could provide some intel on Adeline Bowers. She focused on that and found herself relaxing enough to think of questions to ask.

Until they pulled into a long tree-lined driveway and pulled up to Andy's childhood home. Then all bets were off.

## CHAPTER TWENTY-ONE

"You have got to be kidding me." Luce simply stared at the massive structure. "This isn't a house, Andy, it's a mansion. A massive Tudor mansion. This house makes old lady Bower's place look like the slums of the neighborhood."

Andy laughed out loud. "Disappointed?"

Luce couldn't help but smile. His laugh was contagious. "Please tell me Peabody's cousin isn't going to answer the door?"

"Nope, that'll be Ms Trunchbull."

Luce's eyes widened. "You're joking," she humphed out, crossing her arms over her chest. Looking down, she was glad she was at least dressed appropriately. Simple summer skirt and blouse rather than her skinny jeans and a t-shirt.

"I am. Her name is Molly."

Luce slumped back in the seat. "What have you gotten me into here, detective? Is this really your home?"

"Nope!"

"No?"

"It's my parents' home. Mine is a 2 bedroom walk-up about 3 blocks from yours." Andy grinned, and patted her knee. Sending electrical currents straight to her core. "Come on, it'll be fun," he said, winking as he opened his door and stepped out, coming around to the passenger side and getting the door for her. She glanced up as he grabbed her hand while she stepped out.

"You live 3 blocks from me?" Luce wondered how she didn't know that though it explained how he was always popping up in her life.

"I do. Convenient, no?"

"No. Now, lead the way, detective. And by the way, you so owe me for this." Luce's nerves were in full force. She could handle it, she silently chided herself. Maybe they were nice? Maybe he wasn't really a spoiled filthy rich kid at one time. Maybe this was a terrible idea...

In those brief moments walking up to the door, she let her imagination run wild. Envisioning a stiff, formal pinch-faced woman with a penetrating glare. Someone who would believe Luce to be completely undeserving of dining in her home. His father would be imposing and gruff. She would sit ramrod straight for a painful amount of time just wishing it would be over.

She was rendered speechless when the door opened and there stood a petite blonde with brilliant blue eyes, a smattering of freckles and a huge grin. One just like Andy's. Dressed in denim capris and a loose fitting button down shirt, she was as far from formal as it gets.

"Come in come in," the whirlwind gushed as she opened the door. "I can't believe he's finally brought you here!"

*Finally?*

"It's certainly great to meet you as well." Luce smiled.

*Yeah cause I've heard nothing about you... OMG I'm going to kill him,* Luce's mind raced.

"Luce, this is my mom, Molly." He grinned and winked.

*Molly? OMG I'm going to kill him twice,* she corrected herself.

"Gil's just finishing up out back, so why don't we head out there as well, enjoy the sunshine."

Luce assumed Gil was Andy's father, since she was completely clueless thanks to the smart-ass leading her along with his hand on her back. They followed his mother through the main hall, through a door leading to a fabulous sunroom, where the sliding doors led to a beautiful redwood deck. Overlooking the water, naturally. Luce looked around in astonishment. It was gorgeous. From the deck, the rolling green lawn seemed to seamlessly flow down into the pebbly beach. The deck itself had a full outdoor kitchen, which is where she instantly spotted Mr. Holman himself. There was no mistaking him. He was tall, and broad shouldered like his son, his hair much darker, though, and speckled with gray. Handsome would be an understatement. He was quite stunning. And if Andy were going to age that well, oh boy. Luce was in trouble.

They all sat outside and enjoyed a luncheon smorgasbord of grilled shrimp and veggies, prepared by Gil, who as it turned out was a remarkable chef. Molly regaled Luce with tales of Andy's childhood while Gil filled in some of the mischievous blanks that mothers seem to be unaware of. Luce knew that part was all a ruse. She could tell by the glint in Molly's eyes, she knew. As time went on, the drinks flowed freely, and the stories even more so. Andy quit at a beer or two, but Luce was finding it difficult to refuse the daiquiris Molly kept pouring.

"You know Andy, you really must show her the clubhouse that you built." Molly grinned at Luce. "It's quite the thing."

"Hmm, a clubhouse? Let me guess. So you and your buddies could hide from your sister?" Luce looked over at Andy, noticing the blush creeping over his face.

"Not exactly." He murmured.

"Well, we didn't have any boys in the house," Luce remarked, dryly, "but our neighbors had three of them. And they had a *clubhouse* with a big sign that read 'no girls allowed.'"

"Oh, my no, Luce, Andy certainly did not have a sign like that. He built it *for* the girls." With that Molly burst into laughter. "He didn't feel like the house had enough privacy." Molly was gasping and practically doubled over. Andy was shaking his head trying not to laugh, and Gil was just leaning back, smirking and twirling an unlit cigar in his hand.

Luce was suddenly reminded of those times before the accident. Times with her parents, the laughter. The memories. The time spent she couldn't get back. Though for the first time she wasn't overcome with sadness. She felt her eyes tear up, but it wasn't overwhelming. She wiped them gently and tucked her head for a moment. A gentle tug of her hand from Andy had her looking back up at him curiously.

"Wanna see it?" Andy grinned. "I promise you'll love it."

"Wonderful idea. We'll get things tidied up and meet you back here in a little while." Molly nodded toward a gate on the side of the home. "It's just over there, and it really is adorable."

"Come on," Andy stood, and pulled Luce up out of her chair. "Your castle awaits."

"I bet you said that to all the girls," Luce couldn't help but grin. She felt so at home, so welcome. It had been a long time since she'd felt this way.

She followed Andy around to the gate and watched as he unlatched it and slid the door open, like a barn door. Stepping through, she gasped in astonishment.

There in front of her was a full-blown cottage. She hadn't even seen a glimpse of it driving up, it was so carefully and discreetly hidden from view by a line of trees.

"Clubhouse? This is not a clubhouse. This is a cottage. This is a guest-house. This is not a little boy's clubhouse." Luce gave Andy as stern a look as she could. "Now stop grinning and explain." Andy was having trouble keeping a straight face seeing Luce's expression.

"I wasn't exactly a little boy. I was fourteen, and my dad helped. He's an architect. Now come on, come inside. You'll love it."

The first thing Luce noticed was how clean it was. Not an old club-house left neglected, as she imagined. And it oozed charm. Nothing frilly or feminine, but simple, quaint and tasteful décor. It wasn't large, per se, but roomy enough to have a cozy sitting area, a mini kitchen, a bathroom and even a daybed. In the center was a large round game table, the type that could be converted to a half dozen or more games. From checkers and chess to poker. Plantation shutters, and a few area rugs strewn about gave it a homey feel. But it was the window seat over in the sitting area that drew Luce's attention.

Walking over to it, she paused and looked back over at Andy. "May I?" she asked softly, nodding towards the cushioned bench.

"Of course," he said, smiling. "Have at it."

She lifted the bench seat, letting it rest up against the window ledge. Peering inside she whistled softly. Straightening up, she turned and looked at Andy, this time her gaze curious. "You never said a word. This is how you knew?" Luce asked softly. "In the ballroom, you knew just where to find things."

Andy nodded. "It's the first place I would have looked, yes. Want to see it?"

Luce nodded back. "Do chickens squawk?"

Andy strode over and reached in with both hands, carefully retrieving the hidden treasure and setting it over on the table.

"It's our ship," Luce whispered, gazing at the perfect model of the ghost ship. It was exactly as she remembered. "You built this?"

"I did." Andy replied with a shrug. Though he wouldn't admit it, he was basking in Luce's reverence toward his handiwork.

"How did you do this? I mean there wasn't a kit called "ghost ship" was there?" Luce was truly astonished.

"No, but dad helped. I was into that stuff as a kid. Building things. Recreating things."

"You're full of surprises, aren't you, Detective?" Luce shook her head and smiled. "I sense there is way more to you than meets the eye."

"And I could say the same about you." Andy murmured softly. His gaze locking on hers. She was quick to look away though, disappointing him.

"This must have been a fabulous hideaway," Luce sighed. "Exactly how many girls did you bring home to your teenage love nest?"

"A gentleman never tells, Luce." Andy replied, "But you're the first grown woman if that counts." He nudged her, hoping to get a reaction, but Luce was a step ahead spinning quickly and stepping back outside. He knew she was simply prolonging the inevitable. He just had to make her realize it. And suddenly, it struck him. He knew exactly what needed to be done.

## CHAPTER TWENTY-TWO

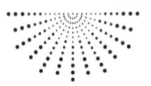

"Ready?" Luce looked over at Kat and grinned.

"Ready as I'll ever be!" Kat replied. It had been a week of chaos; Luce having thrown Kat into the fire feet first. They had a presentation to put on, one that would either have Luce producing her first reality show or slinking off, tail between her legs. With Kat's help, she was confident though that they'd succeed in the former.

With a quick nod at Kat, Luce pushed open the conference room doors and entered with as much of an air of authority as she could muster. Holding the door so Kat could wheel in, Luce made a mental note to find out why it was taking so long to put the automatic doors in she'd requested. The annoyance only served to fuel the fire in her to make this project happen.

∼

"So there's the nuts and bolts. Are there any questions?" Luce looked about the conference table, where the programming board all seemed relaxed and tuned in. She knew this was a good sign. She'd stuck to the basic pitch. Authorities in the area of history and local lore explore a historical property in search of answers. She'd noted how timely the topic was, the local interest and the fact they had a weekend prime slot empty in the fall.

"Just one." Stuart Manning held up a finger and smiled. His signal for everyone to pay attention. She bit back her own smile. He was a teddy bear in a lion's suit most of the time. As the station's general manager, he had the final say in almost everything. And she had a hunch he was on board.

"Who's our host?" he asked. Knowing this was the big question.

"Ah, yes. The kicker. We're hoping our lovely morning anchor will agree to it," Luce replied and looked over at Alicia with a grin. They were friends as well as colleagues, and she had the perfect personality for this gig.

Luce frowned slightly when she saw Alicia's face. She didn't look happy at all. She looked distraught.

"I'm so sorry Luce. I would have loved to jump on this." Alicia paused and looked around the table then sighed. "I suppose the cat will now be out of the bag, but I'm afraid the stork has other plans."

Stunned silence was immediately followed by whoops and whistles and congratulations. Luce quickly ran to her friend and grabbed her in a hug. She didn't want to put a damper on such wonderful news. Alicia and her wife had been going through IVF, and this was huge for them. Though Luce did feel that quick sting, first Annie, now Alicia. Was anyone *not* pregnant? Oh wait, that would be Luce.

"Well, I guess it's plan B then?" Luce tried to play down the sudden obstacle.

"You mentioned Rodney Court, the local historian you'll be using as well as author Christopher Gregory who will also be on site." Stuart went on as if nothing had happened. "How about an investigative authority? Some who can be the debunker should strange things occur. Perhaps our host should be a detective? Some of them have awesome screen appeal." Stuart smirked then. His wife was a retired officer.

"I believe we have just the right one on our list, Ms. Porter," Kat jumped in. "We can certainly screen test him and have that ready by tomorrow afternoon."

Luce squelched her reaction. She knew from Kat's face who she was talking about but Luce hadn't had any discussion at all with him.

"Well then, how about we meet again tomorrow afternoon to confirm a new host." She tried to remain calm and unruffled.

"Perfect, Ms. Porter, and if all goes well, we'll expect a rough cut of the pilot in 2 weeks please. There's no time to waste!" Stuart stood then, indicating the meeting was adjourned. Luce waited for everyone to exit and turned to Kat.

"Please tell me you're not thinking what I think you're thinking?"

"Luce, face it. Stuart wants a hot detective. Now I may not see him that way, but no red-blooded woman would ever turn the channel on him and you know it." Kat smiled and raised her brows. "Admit it!"

"OK, but I will not be the one to ask. And furthermore, maybe he can't get the time off of work. Maybe he wants more than we can afford?"

"Not likely, Luce. Money is not an issue. And he doesn't work weekends anymore."

Luce sighed. She was in a bind now. But this was a monumental knife in her plans. A twisted knife.

"Fine. Just take care of it." Luce knew she sounded a bit snippy, but it was more nerves than annoyance. Two weeks. They were asking the impossible. Sure, it was a rough edit, meaning almost anything with a few good shots to entice would do, but still. She picked up her things and stuffed them back in her tote, and headed out, holding the door for Kat once more.

"Lock up Kat, I'm headed home," Luce called out as she turned down the hall towards the elevator. She needed a time-out.

～

SHE'D BARELY BEEN HOME a half-hour, just enough time to change, relax on the sofa with her favorite facial mask and a glass of wine. Her phone buzzed. She shook her head as Satan's Spawn appeared on her screen.

*Are you sitting down?*

Luce fired back automatically.

*Why?*

He fired right back.
*Did you hear from Kat?*
She frowned as she quickly replied.
***No. Is everything OK? Is Kat OK?***
*Of course she's fine. Looks like I have a new career path. See you bright and early.*
Reading his response, she narrowed her eyes.
Oh no. No no no. Too soon. She wasn't ready for this. Besides, tomorrow was Tuesday. Andy works on Tuesday. Wait. Something's not right.
*You work on Tuesday. Won't they be ticked off if you're late?*
She waited for his explanation, tapping her fingers nervously.
*What time do you head to the office?*
She knew he was up to something.
*Very early.*
*More specific please*
Luce sighed. Whatever she said, she knew he'd show up to meet her.
*I'll be out of here by 6:30am.*
*See you then.*
Crap, she thought. She should have said 5:30.
Luce debated calling Kat but decided it could all wait. She needed downtime. Time to clear her head. Closing her eyes and leaning her head back on the armrest, she swung her legs up on the sofa and tried for a short catnap. But the images in her head were anything but relaxing. Because they were all about Andy. And so were her dreams.

∼

NOTHING COULD PREPARE her for what awaited her in the morning. She cursed herself up and down for telling him she left for the office at 6:30 in the morning. She should have just ignored him. Because the minute she hit the sidewalk, there he was, leaning against his car, thankfully the Subaru, with a shit-eating grin. If it weren't for the fact that he was holding *two* cups of coffee, she might have had a few choice words. But there was no need to rattle him quite yet. Coffee first.

Smiling, she took the one he held out, took a small sip and sighed.

"Light and sweet, right?" Andy seemed to know which buttons to push. Perfect coffee being one.

"Yes, thanks. Why are you here? I thought we'd meet at the office?"

"Well, silly for us not to ride together, especially if we're going to work together," he grinned as he let her settle in the passenger seat before closing the door.

Slipping in the driver's side, he put his own coffee in the holder and checked for traffic before pulling out.

"You know you were illegally parked, right?" Luce looked pointedly at him.

"Was I?" he laughed.

"And you know I haven't actually made a decision on you yet, for the show. What if you suck?"

"What if I do? Come on, this whole thing is perfect for us. You know it. You can't say no to me anyway."

"I can't?"

"Nope." Andy smiled broadly and reached to turn on the radio. Which was fine with Luce, because she had too many thoughts to sort through and not enough time to make sense of all of it.

## CHAPTER TWENTY-THREE

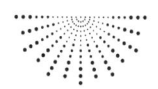

"No."

"Luce, come on be reasonable. If I'm not available to devote myself full time we'll never solve anything."

"Full time? You mean every time I turn around, there you'll be?"

"Well, not every time…" Andy grinned. "Come on, I'm fun to have around."

They were in her office, having just come from the conference room, where it took only two minutes for them to hire Detective Andrew Holman as the host for the upcoming series, Phantom of Execution Rocks And only two minutes more for her to discover Mrs. Bowers had already arranged everything with the station. The crew would be staying out there full time, beginning that weekend.

"My schedule, one I've carefully arranged, has you being available on set twice a week. That's all we'll need. You can do everything else remotely."

"Yeah, but maybe I'd rather stay there too. Maybe I'll spend some time with the fam. Maybe I just want to watch you work."

"You're really enjoying this, aren't you?" Luce shook her head and bit back a grin. Truthfully, the screen test was amazing. The camera loved this man. He oozed intelligence and charm and something else, a mystique, that just didn't let the viewer go. And all he did was say a few lines about his memories of the ship. Luce knew it was good. In fact, she played it back fifteen times to be sure. And saved a copy in the cloud to watch later.

"Well, I guess what's done is done." Luce sighed dramatically but smiled across the desk at him. His boyish enthusiasm for this was infectious. "How did you get all this time off anyway?"

"Accrued PTO. I haven't taken time off in years. Figure now's as good a time as any."

"Somehow I know I'm going to regret this whole thing."

"No way Luce, we're going to go on a great adventure. Maybe solve a great mystery. What do you say we celebrate? Dinner? You must be done for the day, right?"

"Done? I'm just getting started! Filming starts this weekend. Kat and I will be going 24/7 until then getting things ready." Luce shook her head in disbelief. "You realize this is work, right?"

"Say no more. I'll get out of your hair. For now." He stood and turned to go, then stopped suddenly turning back toward her. "You haven't told me yet what I should plan on bringing, you know, to wear? Or do I get a wardrobe?" He wiggled his eyebrows and winked.

Luce closed her eyes briefly. "Sorry, forgot. OK, look. You'll need a bit of prep. I get that. Clearly you have no clue how low-budget TV works." She sighed. "Might as well sit back down. It's going to be a long night."

∽

LUCE BARELY SLEPT ALL WEEK, there was too much to get done. The production schedule. Getting the team settled into a routine. Determining strategy. Deciding who would lead the actual investigation. After all, it was a reality show and there really was a mystery to solve. So many details. Plus she had to make time to help Annie firm up the wedding details. She was maid-of-honor after all. Thankfully Kat was as creative as she was brilliant. Luce couldn't pull this off without her. She'd almost decided, in just a few short weeks, that once Kat graduated, Luce would hire her full-time.

The plan was to have everyone meet up Saturday morning at the Bowers place. Settle in and have an initial production meeting, scout the grounds, then film the intro. When the doorbell rang Friday afternoon, interrupting her last minute, albeit careful, packing, it startled her. Luce, puzzled, headed to the door. She tapped the buzzer, and spoke cautiously. "Yes?"

Nothing.

"Hello?" she spoke again, exasperated. Still nothing. They must have called the wrong apartment, she shrugged, annoyed, then headed back to her bedroom to finish double checking her *don't leave home without it list*. And nearly jumped when the door buzzed again.

"Damnit!" She swore loudly.

Smashing her palm against the intercom button, she wasn't so calm anymore. "What the hell do you want?" Luce practically snarled, then immediately felt bad. What if it were her elderly neighbor, locked out again, or the hearing impaired teenager from upstairs. *Crap.*

"Someone having a bad day?" The deep baritone boomed with familiarity.

"Andy?"

"Candygram."

"Oh for forks sake, come on up," she laughed as she buzzed him in.

She opened her door and waited, poking her head out into the hallway until he appeared. Then sucked in a breath when she saw him. He had this uncanny way of simply looking at her and with one glance, she melted. GQ cover models had nothing on this guy.

As he approached, she noticed the package in his hands. "What's that?"

"No clue, but it was sitting outside with your name on it."

"Huh. Not expecting anything." She wrinkled her nose as she looked at it. When she looked back up at him, his face bore a curious expression.

"Did I interrupt something?" He looked around, almost as if he expected to see someone.

"No, just packing, why?"

"You were a little jumpy when I buzzed." He looked at her expectantly.

"Someone buzzed a few times, nobody there. Maybe that's who left the package. I guess." Luce shrugged. "Sit, I have to finish packing. Why are you here anyway?"

Andy laid the small cardboard package on the coffee table and followed Luce as she headed into her room, then took a seat on her bed.

"You don't really follow instructions very well, Detective."

"You said sit. I'm sitting." He grinned and leaned back on his elbows as he watched her carefully mark off items on her list. Double checking first one suitcase and then a duffel. Each one containing a series of color-coded packing cubes.

"So again, I ask, why are you here?" Luce paused, tapping the tip of her pencil on her bottom lip as she nervously considered the guy with the danger sign flashing above him comfortably seated on her bed.

"Dinner. And a sleepover."

"Not happening." Luce laughed and shook her head. "Early start tomorrow. And even if I had nothing planned, it wouldn't happen."

"Oh, that's where you're wrong, but irrelevant at the moment. We're going out tonight and having dinner at your sister's and staying there so we can get that early start you so desperately want. Clearly you're about done packing, right?"

Turning to face him, she raised her eyebrows and pursed her lips.

"As I thought. Ready?"

"Ready as I'll ever be."

As they headed out towards the front door, Andy stopped short. "The package. Maybe we should see what that's about?" His tone clearly meant it wasn't a question.

She stepped over to the table, picked up the box, shook it lightly and examined it.

"No return address. Just my name, clearly it was just dropped off. Should I be worried?" Luce tipped her head and looked at Andy. Hoping he wasn't concerned.

"Do you mind?" He asked her, glancing at the box and nodding.

Shrugging, she waited while he slipped a pair of gloves on.

"Always prepared, aren't you?" she snipped as she handed him the box.

"Let's sit, take a look," he said quietly, examining the box.

As they sat on the sofa, he placed the box on the table and began to examine it more carefully. Checking the seams, the tape and tapping the sides.

"Well? Aren't you going to open it?" She began tapping her foot nervously.

"Scissors?" he asked, holding out his hand. Luce just stared at it.

"Why did you have me sit down here if you needed me to go get scissors?" She huffed as she stood and headed into the kitchen. Andy bit back a grin. He knew he shouldn't tease her like this, but really, he thought, it was too easy. And the way her eyes blazed when she got fired up was irresistible.

Returning, she handed him the scissors, then stood hovering over his shoulder as he slid the scissors neatly through the top seam and popped the top two flaps open. Luce had to lean all the way over to peer inside, realizing too late her chest was practically in his face. Quickly straightening up, she regrouped and stepped back.

"Maybe you could take whatever's in there out?" She asked quietly. Directing her gaze anywhere but his direction. Knowing he probably had that smirk on his face.

"My pleasure, Luce," he replied chuckling. It was about as awkward a moment as she'd had in a while and was really throwing her off her game. Until he placed the object on the table and removed the bubble wrap.

Without thinking, Luce instinctively placed her hand on Andy's shoulder as she stared at it, stunned into silence.

"Is that for real?" Luce whispered.

"I think so," Andy replied in a hushed tone as well. "The question is, who sent it?"

# CHAPTER TWENTY-FOUR

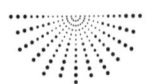

"You didn't tell me everyone else would be here," Luce remarked as they pulled up, spotting the other cars in the driveway. "I recognize Bill's truck, and Julie's bug, who's SUV is that?"

"Kat's. When Chris said we should come tonight, have dinner and stay over, he told me to invite her as well. One last summer barbecue before the chaos begins." Andy shrugged. "You could use some down time. You do realize we'll miss the annual 4$^{th}$ Barbecue, right?"

"Yes, and that's another thing. We weren't supposed to have to start filming until *after* the holiday." She shook her head.

It had been a crazy week. Putting a new series together in two weeks' time from idea to fruition was a monumental task. Impossible some would have said. But as Luce came to learn quickly, when there's money and power behind decisions, they get implemented quickly.

"You know, I couldn't have done this without Kat. Thanks for sharing her with me." Luce said quietly. "She's really quite amazing."

"Got that right," Andy replied as he got out and came around to open Luce's door. "Shall we?" He grinned as he held out his arm, elbow crooked, to help her out. Luce grinned back. If nothing else, Andy Holman was sure nice to have around sometimes. *Sometimes.*

"So, is everyone clear on the schedule for tomorrow?" Luce dove right in once they'd all settled around the large patio dining table.

"No work talk, sis," Annie laughed. "Tonight is just good food, good company and free flowing cocktails. For those who can have them," she added, patting her tummy.

"Are you sure, Annie? Really sure? Because Andy and I have something to show you all. But if you aren't interested of course," Luce let her voice trail off haughtily. Picking up her glass, she took a sip of her wine and placed it back in front of her, twirling it between her fingers. "I suppose it's nothing really."

"If it's nothing, darlin, you wouldn't have mentioned it," Bill called out.

"Very true," Chris remarked. "What do you have?" he demanded, turning to Andy, who held his hands up in mock surrender.

"Not my show," he laughed.

"So today as I was finishing packing, the buzzer rang. When I went to answer it, nobody was there."

Everyone waited silently for her to go on.

"I went back to packing and it buzzed again. Again, nobody was there."

Luce reached down to pick up her purse, which she'd set down by her feet. Placing it on the table, she reached in and gently lifted out the item she'd received earlier, which they'd carefully repackaged in the bubble wrap.

"Then Andy arrived, and found this on my doorstep," Luce continued, raising it in her hands so everyone could see.

"And? What is it?" Annie demanded, earning a quelling look from Luce.

"Patience, sister dear," she replied dryly, turning to Andy. "Maybe you ought to do this, Andy. Do you have those silly gloves?" Luce smiled at him, he was seated next to her, leaning comfortably back in his chair.

"Not silly," he chuckled, "but yeah, hang on." He reached into a side pocket of his cargo shorts and magically produced a pair of blue gloves.

He snapped the gloves in place on his hands, and took the curious item from her, while she slid his plate away to make room, and wiped the tablecloth as well.

"Well then, shall we?" Andy began to carefully peel off the wrapping, occasionally popping a bubble or two for fun, causing Luce to raise her eyebrows and roll her eyes.

Once the wrapping was removed, he laid it out in the center of the table as a protective surface and set the object down so everyone could see.

"What is it?" Mark squinted his eyes, "other than old and tarnished?"

"Looks like one of those snuff boxes, if you ask me!" Bill said gruffly.

"No way, it's a pill box!" Jen said emphatically.

Everyone was standing around the long rectangular table now and leaning into look, nudging each other out of the way.

It was an old flat silver box, only about a half inch in depth.

"Looks like a powder puff or a pocket mirror," Julie remarked.

"It's engraved with something," Mark called out.

"Who's got a magnifying glass? Chris you must have one, right?" Annie pulled at Chris to move him aside, laughing.

"I've got one."

Everyone stopped talking and looked at Kat, who was grinning and reaching into the tote bag hanging on her chair.

"Listen, when you don't have mobility, you learn to cope." Kat chuckled. "You become that game show contestant who packs the kitchen sink in her bag. Now since I've got the eyepiece, I get to look first!"

Luce grinned at her assistant, and nodded to Andy to give it to Kat, who was at the end of the table.

Gently picking up the strange flat metal box, he stood, and carried it carefully over to Kat, and then stood next to her as she began to examine it. He knew it was only fair to let her have first crack at it. They hadn't had time to examine it back at Luce's apartment, but they had opened it. And knew there was more to come.

"Damn," Kat whispered. "Too much tarnish. Can't make it out but I think they are initials."

"May I?" Andy asked, nodding at the eyepiece. Kat handed it to him, pursing her lips, indicating her displeasure. "You won't do any better, but here."

"Damn," he whispered. "She's right."

Kat smiled, shaking her head, sharing a glance with Luce.

"Can I open it now?" Kat looked at her uncle. "Please?" she added for good measure, somewhat sarcastically.

"Oooh, it opens?" Annie cried out, clapping her hands. "What's in it?"

"Maybe if we give her a chance to open it, everyone can find out!" Luce laughed.

Andy reached into his pocket, producing a second pair of gloves, causing everyone to laugh at his preparedness.

"Ok, drum roll please?" Kat spoke quietly as she snapped her gloves in place, mimicking her uncle, then delicately grasped the old hook clasp on the front side of the strange piece. Releasing the hook, she lifted the lid very carefully.

"Well shitfire and sandstone!" Kat exclaimed loudly.

"Language, Kat!" Andy responded instinctively.

"All grown up here, Uncle Andrew," Kat reminded him, laughing.

"Say Kat, are you going to show us?" Annie asked in frustration. "Come on!"

Kat reached in the box and pulled out the tiny key lying inside. It was small but ornate and just as tarnished as the box.

There was silence for just a moment as everyone stared at the key.

Chris spoke first. "Any idea what it's for?"

"I'll tell you what it's not. It's not a door key," Andy stated matter-of-factly.

"No way that could open, or start, anything I own," Bill shook his head, confused. "And I have every kind of toolbox and gadget known to man."

"How about we make a list of things it could open?" Annie suggested.

"Good idea, Annie, could you do that?"

"Of course. As I'm not allowed *on set* at least I can do something!"

"We still need to figure out who sent it, don't we?" Chris asked as he sat back down. "That might help."

"So. Do we include this in the show? Or use it behind the scenes?" Luce mused out loud.

"Judging from the shows I've seen, the host always discusses the clues they have," Jen tossed in.

"True, but Andy didn't receive it, I did." Luce replied.

"But he found the package, therefore, it's part of his reality," Mark mused.

"But what if the sender doesn't want it to be revealed?" Kat piped up. "We don't know who sent it, we don't know why, and we don't know the state of their mental health. Just putting it out there."

They all pondered that for a moment.

"I don't think there is anything sinister about the key or the box." Andy remarked. *Only about the delivery of it from an unknown sender*, he thought. "What say we pack it up and put it away for now. I heard a rumor there's cheesecake?" Andy grinned and looked over at Chris.

"Three kinds!" Annie jumped up. "And I get first dibs on the toffee caramel."

Everyone began to chatter once more, as Luce put the box and key away, while Jen and Bill began clearing the dinner dishes to make way for dessert. Andy once more relaxed in his chair, this time resting one arm along the back of Luce's chair. It was turning out to be a perfect night, he thought. Good friends, fabulous food, intrigue and mystery. And Luce. Most would say at their age, this whole mating dance was unnecessary. Why flirt? Why waste time? Because Luce needed time. He sensed her skittishness right alongside her attraction. She needed time to see that they were just as meant to be together as Chris and Annie. Time to recognize that he wasn't Jack. And that this wasn't fleeting. He turned toward her and smiled, gauging her reaction. His gaze remained steady as she returned it, flicked a glance towards his arm and back to his eyes. Soon, he thought. Soon.

∼

LUCE WAS USED to episodes of insomnia. Staring up at the dark ceiling. Thoughts racing through her head. Especially the night before a new production shoot. But that's not where her mind was going. It was Andy. She fought the images. The striking good looks. The charm. The attraction. She'd been battling with herself for a decade over the same man. Maybe it was time to give in and see where it went. Maybe that would be the only way to end her misery. Sighing, she sat up, swung her legs over the side of the bed, stood, and walked over to the window and sat on the small bench beside it. The view was spectacular and calming. The soft glow of moonlight reflected on the water. The occasional flickering light from a passing boat, not yet ready to dock. Leaning her head against the windowpane, she imagined how this might have looked exactly the same several hundred years earlier. Closing her eyes, she slowly dozed into a light sleep.

Only to be woken suddenly by a boom and flash. So sudden she didn't know if it was part of her dream or if she'd been awake the whole time. What she did know, was that she was awake now and the fiery orange glow of the blaze in the water was no dream.

## CHAPTER TWENTY-FIVE

Andy awoke with a start, immediately succumbing to an urge to spit and heave. As he became more aware he realized his mouth had a gritty, sandy, salty taste. Lifting his head, he took note of his surroundings. He was lying on his side, at the water's edge. The water gently lapped at his feet. Rolling his shoulders and flexing his feet, he felt no sharp pains. Nothing to indicate any injury. Slowly sitting up, he rubbed the wet sand off his face and ran his fingers over his scalp to massage it out as well. Dressed in a pair of fleece sweatpants, no shirt, he was soaked. The tide was going out but it didn't explain how the hell he'd ended up there. Last thing he remembered, he'd awoken in the guest room to the sound of an explosion and looking out had seen a fireball over the water.

Standing up, he looked about. It was quiet. Nothing to indicate anything had happened at all. Turning to go toward the house, he spotted a shadow in the distance by the rocks. As he headed over to investigate he realized what it was and quickly ran over.

"Luce, wake up. Hey, Luce" Andy spoke softly, gently shaking her shoulder. "Come on babe, let's open those eyes." He exhaled a long breath, and reached down, picked her up out of the sand, and, cradling her in his arms, strode quickly back over to the patio, setting her down in the chaise lounge. She hadn't woken, but she was wet and chilled. Wearing only a pair of shorts and a skimpy tank, hypothermia could easily set in.

Not wanting to wake anyone in the house, he tried to stay quiet. He looked around and noticed the wooden chest by the door. Figuring it must contain the beach supplies, he gently lifted the lid and blew out a sigh of thanks. Towels. Grabbing a few, he noticed a plaid blanket as well. Perfect. He quickly went back to where he'd left Luce and laid the blanket over her. Andy took one towel and began drying her off. Her unresponsive state had him worried, he was willing to do anything to wake her. He picked her up once again, and headed inside and up to his room. Laying her down in his bed, he crawled in next to her, and wrapped his arms around her to keep them both warm until she woke up. Whatever had caused them both to doze off on the beach like that wasn't anything normal. He knew that. He felt her move and whispered softly.

"Luce, hey, wake up honey. Open your eyes."

"Ouch!" He let out a muffled cry as Luce's head came straight back smashing into his face.

"What the hell?" Luce practically shouted as she tried to move away.

"Shh… it's just me, and it isn't what you think, just relax for a sec. I'll explain," Andy kept his voice low and calm.

Luce turned toward him, then gasped realizing how close they were.

"This better be good, detective," she warned him, keeping her voice down. She wasn't sure why, but she knew she wasn't going to like whatever he had to say. Whatever landed her in bed with Andy Holman had to be a doozy.

"There was an explosion, out on the water," he began quietly.

"Yeah, I saw it," Luce murmured. "What was it?"

"I have no idea, but somehow we both must have gone to check it out. Whether together or alone, I couldn't say."

"I don't know, I don't remember anything after that. Just a big ball of fire low in the sky over the water." Luce shook her head softly.

"Same here. I woke up and found myself lying in the wet sand, at the edge of the water. When I got up, I found you lying quite a distance away. I tried to wake you, but you were out like a light."

"Well, that's one way to cure my insomnia," Luce muttered. "How'd we get here?"

"Um, hmm… maybe I'll save that part for later?" Andy joked, then let out an "oomph" as Luce's elbow backed into his rib cage.

"How long were we out? What time is it?" Luce lifted her head to look at the clock on the nightstand. "That can't be right, Andy. It says 12:32 am. It was almost 12:30 when I saw the explosion!"

"I know. I'm not sure. Maybe there was a power outage. Hang on, I'll check my phone." He scooted away from Luce, regretting the action the minute he felt the cool air between them. Knowing once he got out of the bed, he wouldn't be able to crawl back in.

He stood and walked over to the dresser where he'd left his phone.

"Well, it's not 12:32."

"Whew," Luce sighed.

"It's now 12:33" Andy murmured.

"What? That can't be," Luce grumped. "Impossible."

He turned toward the bed and watched with amusement as Luce gathered up the blanket and snuggled deep under the covers. Sprawling out, she left no doubt that she was claiming her space.

"Impossible or not, we're not going to solve this tonight. We saw something. We investigated. And we've no recollection of what happened. We'll determine what everyone else saw or heard in the morning before we head over to Mrs. Bowers."

"Oh my god I almost forgot we start production tomorrow. Holy…" Luce's voice faded out.

"Holy what?" Andy prodded.

But Luce was already asleep again. This was definitely a conversation for another day.

## CHAPTER TWENTY-SIX

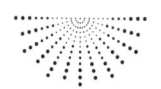

"So, we're agreed? We tell no one, not even Annie," Andy said quietly, gripping the wheel so tightly his knuckles were visibly white.

"Or Chris," Luce replied, hands clasped in her lap, fingers intertwined tightly. "No one will believe us anyway." She sighed. Just like her sighting of the ship all those years ago. Nobody called her a liar, but they had all been more amused than concerned.

"I know. Believe me. They'll humor us, but that's all." Andy shook his head. "I'm not sure what I believe when it comes to this stuff Luce, I like to deal in facts. But at the same time, I can't discount what happened." Pulling out of the driveway, he turned onto the winding tree-lined street and headed towards the Bowers estate, just a few minutes' drive away. They'd practically snuck out of the house to avoid conversation with anyone. They'd all be there to help set up production later in the day. No need to stir the pot just yet.

"Maybe it was one of those shared dreams you see on unsolved mysteries," Luce mused. "Maybe we're psychically connected."

Andy glanced over at Luce and smirked. "We're connected all right."

Returning his gaze, with a half-smile of her own, she chuckled. "Focus here Andy, we've got a show to do. You know, priorities?"

"Oh, I have priorities too Luce, keep that in mind." He chuckled and turned his attention back to the roadway. Too many little creatures like to scamper across, and he knew Luce wouldn't appreciate participating in any roadkill adventures.

"Looks like the crew's arrived early," Luce murmured as they pulled through the gates to Adeline Bowers' estate. "I see Jamie's van, and Kat's here as well. I feel like I'm late to the party!" Luce chuckled.

"This historian, when does he show up?" Andy was curious.

"Rodney, yes, he won't be here until tonight for the opening dinner segment. Then after that, he'll come by once or twice a week to help explain whatever findings we have. You and Chris will be the investigators, so most of the time the cameras will be on you."

"How many camera guys do you have?"

Luce smiled. "Just one and his assistant. Mostly we're going to have cameras mounted throughout the house so we can capture all movement and then one handheld to follow you for close-ups and things."

It was actually far more complicated, but Luce figured it was best to keep it simple. He didn't need to know all the technical details, or bits of trickery involved in filming.

"Will they run all the time?" Andy wondered aloud.

"That's the plan." Luce chuckled. "Why, were you planning a midnight rendezvous?"

When he didn't respond, she looked over and saw the cheeky grin and flare in his eyes.

Shaking her head and laughing, she knew he'd be a handful. And the butterflies in her stomach told her he might just be a bit more.

∼

"LADIES, gentlemen, if I may have your attention." Mr. Peabody was in full-on butler mode. Standing at attention in the foyer, trying to make himself heard over the din of noisy voices echoing throughout.

When he got nowhere, he began clapping his hands. "May I *please* have your attention!" This time his voice was louder and quite a bit more stern. The noise level quieted down, and he cleared his throat.

"Mr. Holman and Ms. Porter, you will be staying upstairs here in the main house. Your crew, with the cameras and things, will be in the guesthouse. Ms. Downing, if you'll follow me, please, you will be in the lower level guest suite. I'll get you settled first. The rest of you, please wait here until I return."

Kat smiled at the stern looking man as he did exactly what she'd hoped. Instead of taking the handles and pushing her chair, he simply nodded at her to follow along. Too many people simply assumed she needed help. She decided as grumpy as he seemed, somewhere inside he had some redeeming qualities. She followed him down the hall past the stairwell, and down toward the library.

"Oh my, can we just poke our head in here?" Kat was surprised when he stopped and set her bags down.

"But of course, Miss." He said. Kat grinned as she suspected he'd almost cracked a smile.

He opened and held the door while she wheeled herself in and simply paused. Looking about, her eyes widened.

"This is amazing. I mean look at this!" She quickly wheeled over to get a closer look at the bookcases. Gazing up at one of the shelves, she pointed. "That's not what I think it is, is it?"

Mr. Peabody headed over to the shelf to get a closer look at the target of her curiosity.

Pulling it down, he read the title. "The Hitchhiker's Guide to The Galaxy," and this time Kat knew he was smiling.

"May I?" She held out a hand.

"Wow," she sighed, flipping the cover open. "It's a first edition! Holy prefect!"

"It is, I've had the pleasure of reading it myself. Good choice. You may take it to your suite if you like."

"Awesome," Kat breathed out slowly as she placed the old paperback carefully in her lap.

"Ok, I know they are all waiting for you back there so I suppose we better get me settled, eh Peabody?" Kat grinned and he returned one of his own. He rarely softened his stance for anyone, but this young woman had something special about her. Peabody was only human after all.

As she followed him out of the library she heard him call out a greeting.

"Good morning sir, we didn't expect you until lunch."

Coming toward them was a vision, Kat thought. Couldn't be. She recognized him immediately but decided to keep her mouth shut for now.

"Good morning Peabody, and who's this?" His voice held a touch of humor, as his eyes raked over her.

"Lionel Bowers, may I introduce Kat Downing? She's interning for the station this summer and will be working here on the project."

Lionel grinned. "Really? I see you've already hijacked my book collection," he commented, nodding at the book in her lap.

"Oh! I'm so sorry, I didn't know," Kat gasped, lifting it up to give it back and biting her tongue before saying anything to get her into more trouble. She was already in too deep. Lionel Bowers, aka Sticks, was the drummer for her favorite band. The one she went to see play every chance she got. The poster on her wall. Her major crush. And now she'd stolen his book? How did no one tell her? She realized her mouth was still open and she was staring.

He laughed outright then. "No please, I haven't read it in years, enjoy it. It's rare anyone pulls it off the shelf and gives it a proper reading. You know books are like instruments. They need TLC and attention. They need to be read."

He caught her eye then and flashed a look she couldn't quite read as he turned to go. Then turned back suddenly.

"I'll see you at lunch, Kat. Pleasure meeting you," he said with a wink.

Kat simply stared as he turned back around and continued on his way down the hall, then she looked at Peabody. She knew she must be ten shades of crimson by the expression on his face.

"What? I've made a fool of myself, haven't I?" She put her hands over her face and shook her head.

"Don't be silly. I'd say you made quite an impression. Come, we'll get you settled before they all send a search party after us."

## CHAPTER TWENTY-SEVEN

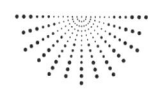

*G*azing out on the water from her guest suite balcony, Luce had to admit the accommodations were first class. She'd already received a text from Jamie that the *crew quarters* consisted of a 3 bedroom guest house rivaling a 5-star villa. She smiled as she recalled his exact words; *My ship has landed.*

She'd been given, of all things, the MorningStar Suite. It was truly unbelievable she thought as she gazed around the room. It was designed to replicate a first-class stateroom, albeit from days gone by. Gleaming wood-paneled walls with brushed bronze lighting fixtures. A palm frond ceiling fan was the only off-kilter element, being more tropical than stately. Though more effective too. The canopy bed was invitingly warm with an abundance of soft cream throw pillows and sheer flowing drapery tied back to the mahogany posts.

The full sitting area by the French doors leading to the balcony featured not only a sofa and recliner but a chaise as well, perfect for reading. The ensuite was large, offering a claw foot tub, walk in shower and a vanity complete with stool, mirror and all the amenities one could need for an extended stay. She barely needed to unpack her own things. Not even the Ritz could compete with her current situation, Luce thought. The walk-in closet was large enough for her entire wardrobe, and even had a small bench in the center. Her favorite piece though was the armoire.

She'd expected it to hold a TV and was only slightly disappointed when upon locating the old brass key and pulling the carved mahogany doors open she discovered it was a pull-out desk. Designed to replicate an antique Secretary Desk, but with the hidden modern accessories essential for the 21$^{st}$ century. It even had a full panel of plug-in outlets to accommodate any of her electronics. Opening the bottom cupboard doors, she found a small stool tucked neatly away as well. She knew she'd explore more later, but no time for that as she'd asked everyone to meet up out back for their initial production meeting before lunch.

She took one last look outside and her eyes landed on the focus of all her attention now; Execution Rocks. The lighthouse was clearly visible at this angle, with its wide red band around the stark white tower. It was innocuous during the day, she thought. Nothing unusual about it at all. But if last night were any indication of how things can change rapidly, she had to prepare herself. She knew she saw something explode. Andy saw it too. She knew he found her asleep in the sand and his story about waking up there as well rang true. She should be terrified by it. She should be in high-anxiety mode. Or at least nervous. But when she awoke this morning, wrapped in Andy's arms, she was as calm as she'd ever been. She'd slipped out of bed and back to her room, feeling perfectly at ease. Maybe that should be her biggest worry. Turning towards the door, she took a deep breath.

"Show time," she said quietly to herself as she headed down to meet the crew.

EVERYTHING WAS IN PLACE. Filming would begin as soon as the first car pulled up, with Chris being filmed as the first to arrive at the opening night dinner. The guest list was complete, the cameras in place. Jamie would capture the primary footage while remote cameras captured the rest of the activity throughout the property. Luce stepped back and surveyed the scene. The shadows cast by the stone façade added the perfect aura. As host, Chris would stand at the entrance; Annie on one side and Mrs. Bowers on the other, to greet the guests as they arrived. A narrator would record the voice-over to be added later, introducing the participants and offering additional explanations to any scene as needed.

She sensed Kat coming up next to her and turned, offering a smile and a shaky laugh. "OK Kat, this is it! Do or die!"

"It's gonna be awesome. Are you kidding? Just wish we could be there at dinner."

"We, my friend, are not invited to this party. We have to remain in the background. Our fun is later on when we view the footage. Our job is to make sure it all plays out and nothing is overlooked. You have your cue cards, just in case they forget something?"

"Got it all boss lady. We are good as gold." Kat gave a mock salute.

"And it looks like Chris and Annie are right on time. Cue Jamie they're headed this way, then let's slip back a bit and make ourselves invisible. I want to see each entrance, make sure we won't need a retake."

～

"Who's that?" Kat whispered as the last car rolled up.

Luce looked down to check her list. "Friends of Lionel's."

Watching them step out of the car, Kat gasped softly.

"What?" Luce murmured. "What did I miss?"

"That's Jackson Tulley!" Kat whispered excitedly.

"You know him?"

"Geesh Luce, don't you listen to the radio? Like ever?"

Luce grinned. "On occasion, but humor me."

"I told you Lionel plays drums for Pluto's Plan, remember?"

"Yes, you mentioned it about a hundred times at last count, Kat."

"Jackson is the bass player for Pluto's Plan. Damn, is that his girlfriend?" Kat practically whined seeing him turn and help a young woman from the car. "Well that's two down. There's still two more though."

"Two more what? Come on, you're not one of their groupies are you?"

"I am, and damn proud of it." Kat laughed softly. "Hey, a girl can dream, right?"

"Well, don't give up on Lionel quite yet. I saw the way he eyed you at lunch. Like you were his next meal." Luce smiled as she saw Kat blush. She wasn't even stretching the truth on this. Lionel Bowers had been watching Kat most of the day. It would be fun for Kat to have a summer fling. As long as it didn't get out of hand. As long as she didn't get hurt. And as long as Andy stayed out of the way.

As Jackson escorted the woman inside, Luce and Kat followed the camera crew, at a safe distance. Once inside, they quickly blended into the background to watch as the guests were seated in the dining hall. Mrs. Bowers stood at her seat at the end of the long table and looked at her guests, nodding to each one by one. Luce took a deep breath and nodded at her to begin. And with that, Adeline Bowers picked up the dinner bell in front of her, rang it twice, and launched an adventure that Luce hoped would solve a mystery that had long plagued her.

What she didn't realize was that there were others in the room that desperately wanted the same answers, but for very different reasons.

## CHAPTER TWENTY-EIGHT

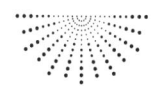

"I'm afraid your historian is a snooze fest, Luce," Kat shook her head and leaned back. "And the camera does not like him. He comes across pasty. Is that a word?"

"That's the least of our worries! That little floozy that Jackson brought had her hands in *all* the wrong places." Luce let out a breath and started pacing. "She better not come back sniffing around again."

"I've never seen my uncle quite so embarrassed, I have to say," Kat mused. "She was practically crawling all over him."

"I want her cut out of every shot. Every damn one." Luce barked.

"We can do our best, Luce, but really, I mean it will get the audience's attention." Kat's eyes widened when she realized Luce was not laughing.

"Come on Luce, he wasn't interested. He made that abundantly clear when he literally picked her hand up off his thigh and moved it." Kat grinned. "I wish I were that bold."

"No, you don't. That was really quite slutty of her." Luce snapped back.

"She just wanted to attract the camera's attention, of that I'm quite sure, Luce."

"Well, you may not see it the same way, but I know what I saw. And your uncle, FYI? He's hot. You've said so yourself."

"Yeah but I like hearing you admit it," Kat laughed outright.

"Yeah yeah, listen, let's just get a rough cut on the dinner and a few of the scenes in the library afterward. Then we can call it a night."

"You know what? I got this, Luce. You go ahead and get some rest and I'll go ahead and finish playing back and marking up the footage. Let me show you how good I am!" Kat knew this was her one shot to show Luce how good her skills were.

Luce stretched her arms above her head and swiveled her neck. Rest sounded heavenly. Especially after all she'd been through in the last 24 hours. She looked around the room they'd been given to set up their editing bay. Luce and Kat would select the bulk of the raw footage for each episode, and hand it off to their studio production team.

It was an office near the Library on the main floor. It was spacious, and comfortable, but had none of the character of the other rooms. Almost as if it had been neglected. She guessed it was one of those rooms only used by staff. Knowing they'd spend a lot of time in it, she quickly decided to have some décor brought in. Some plants or flowers, a print or two for the walls. She'd have to check with Peabody, but she was fairly certain he wouldn't mind. Turning back to Kat, she made up her mind.

"Deal. Kat, I know you have a tremendous eye." She paused. "Just remember to stay tuned in. Listen for snippets of conversation that may be off camera. Let your intuition guide you."

"Aye Aye Captain." Kat grinned.

"Oh and Kat?"

"Yes?"

"Make sure to edit out the slut." Luce turned and headed out into the hall making her way towards the stairs. She paused then, and smiled. Kat was a wonder, and with her help, this show was going to be a hit. As long as the cameras love Andy as much as they seemed to hate Rodney. It was a shame really, but they could interview him in dark shadows and create an atmosphere. They had a few other changes they'd need to make as well, she thought, as she headed into her suite.

∽

"Nice night."

Luce jumped. She'd been so relaxed, sitting on her balcony, enjoying the soft glow of the moonlight reflecting on the dark rippling waters of the sound. A glass of wine in one hand and her other tucked behind her head. Of course, now the wine was all over the sheer tank and shorts she'd chosen to relax in. Luckily it was white wine not red, but the minute the liquid sloshed on her chest it made no difference. Thank god it was dark. Though from the look in Andy's eyes, standing not 3 feet away it didn't help matters.

"Do you always sneak up on people in the middle of the night?" She tried to keep her voice calm and relaxed. But she was most definitely annoyed.

"Free country, Luce, and it's only 9:30. Plus, my balcony my choice, right" He chuckled.

She could see he was still standing there staring at her, and it wasn't her face he was looking at. Looking down, she realized how transparent her tank top had become. Two choices, she thought. Go in and hide or flaunt it.

"Our balcony it would seem."

"It would," he grinned then. "Mind if I sit with you?"

"Would you care if I did?"

Andy laughed then and sat down in the lounge chair next to her, imitating her pose.

"What have I done this time? I can tell I've annoyed you."

Truthfully, Luce knew he'd done nothing at all. It was that girl, Cherise, who rather than some escort floozy turned out to be Jackson's sister.

"Nothing, OK? It's not you. Though if you don't quit staring at my boobs it will be."

"Can't help it. It's a guy thing. You've got good ones."

"You'd think you'd have gotten your fill at dinner," Luce grumbled softly, causing Andy to burst out laughing.

"Oh shit I said that out loud, didn't I?" Luce grinned. She couldn't help it. It was a relief almost to say it. Put it out there and relieve some tension.

"Don't tell me you were jealous, Luce," Andy's voice was deeper, raspier, teasing.

"Moi? Certainly not," Luce whispered softly, her attention solely focused on his face now, as she noticed him drawing nearer.

"Maybe just a little?" He breathed out slowly, lifting a hand and reaching toward her, causing her to lean back away from him.

"What are you doing?" Luce could hear her own voice tremble.

"Eyelash," he said softly as he slid one finger gently over her cheek. Luce shivered.

"Cold?" he asked, answering her question.

"No," she whispered. He wasn't looking at her chest anymore. His face was now only inches away. He's eyes locked on hers.

Luce was as sure as ever what she wanted now, though terrified all at the same time. Licking her lips, she took a breath and braced herself. She knew kissing Andy would be a mistake of gargantuan proportions. She also knew she might regret it if she didn't.

His palm on her cheek, his thumb sliding across her bottom lip, he leaned in.

The instant his lips met hers, their world seemed to explode. She felt lightning bolts run through her veins as he explored her, first with his tongue, then with his hands. They were everywhere as Luce reached over and placed both of hers behind his head to draw him closer. It had been building for so long it was as if this were the grand finale.

A sudden noise caused Andy's eyes to glance just over the rails. "Holy fuck," Andy's words breathed into her mouth, just before he pulled back. "Look over there, by the jetty, Luce."

"That can't be," Luce whispered, staring at the spot he was pointing to.

"Let's go. Come on," Andy said as he took her hand and pulled her up. "Throw on some real clothes and let's go have a look."

"Maybe I should get Jamie, film this?"

"No, just us." Andy's voice was strange. Detached, Luce thought. But it didn't matter. She somehow knew he was right, somehow. Whatever was happening down there wasn't to be shared. At least not yet.

## CHAPTER TWENTY-NINE

"Where do you think he went?" Luce whispered, one hand on Andy's back as she stood crouched behind him. The massive rocks in the stone jetty appeared untouched. But they both agreed they'd witnessed someone walk right into an opening that seemed to have vanished.

Andy felt around carefully with his fingertips, looking for holes, holding his head sideways, listening for air pockets, anything to hint that it was a façade. But it was dark, nothing but moonlight to guide them. He hesitated to shine a light; he didn't want to be seen. He was sure someone else had been out here. He crouched down, and, reluctantly, turned on the bright light from his phone and scanned the sandy area for footprints.

"Andy look," Luce tapped on his back to get his attention. "Above you, something shiny, glinting."

He aimed the light towards the top of the jetty and swayed it back and forth until he spotted it. A lever of some sort.

"What is that?" Luce tapped his back again, leaving her hand there.

"Only one way to find out," Andy replied and chuckled. He thought about offering up a snarky remark about her being handsy, but was enjoying it too much. He reached up and pushed down on the rusty metal lever as he leaned in, then felt the rock grudgingly give way as it swung inward, slowly, about a foot, then stopped.

"A trap door? Made of stone?" Luce murmured, following him in.

He stopped and turned. "Luce, stay here. I mean it. Just stay here. If I'm not out in 15 minutes, go for help." Andy's voice brooked no argument. Though Luce did give him her best scowl.

"Fine but be careful. Okay?" she grumbled as she exited the cramped dark space. Truthfully she didn't want to be in there, so outside was better. But patience wasn't her friend at that moment. She stood at the entrance as he disappeared inside, and listened as his footsteps echoed softly, the sound fading away.

Andy estimated he was about 100 feet in, when the damp hallway seemed to veer off to the left. Following the wall with his hands, keeping the light off so as not to alert whoever had entered the passageway before him. He paused every few yards, listening. He heard nothing but the slow steady sounds of condensation dripping. The wall abruptly came to an end, his hands touching air. Hearing nothing still, assured nobody was there, he switched on the light and realized he had stepped into a large chamber.

"Son of a bitch," he said softly, shining his light around the room, taking it all in. Heading over to the far wall, he crouched down, examining what looked like fossils at first. But on closer examination, they were bone fragments. Human or animal, he couldn't tell. He needed better light. More tools. He knew he'd have to come back. In fact, Luce may have been right all along. They should have brought Jamie. This was going to be a fabulous scene for the show. More importantly, he felt the first twinge of real excitement, outside of the fun he was having with Luce. He'd only agreed to play TV adventurer to be near her anyway. Part of his overall plan.

He heard a scream and quickly stood up, tuned in. It wasn't a yelp or a mild, help me I've fallen scream. It was blood curdling. And he'd know that voice anywhere.

"Luce! Luce where are you?" He yelled impatiently. Her shouts had come from somewhere she shouldn't be. Too close. He'd left her with strict instructions to stay put. How hard is that? He shook his head in frustration.

"Luce!" He was getting worried now.

"Rats, Andy, there are rats." Luce came stumbling into the chamber, eyes wide.

He wanted to wring her neck, but the look on her face told him she'd learned a lesson. Instead, he shook his head softly and stepped over to her, wrapping his arms around her.

"You still don't follow orders very well, do you?" He whispered. Still unsure of their surroundings. "It's OK, Luce. They're just mice."

"Tell them that," she replied, still shaken by the little rodents that had scampered by her feet. Leaning her head against his chest, she closed her eyes and took a deep breath, then pulled back.

"OK, I'm fine. Just startled. What did you find?" Her voice still shook, indicating she wasn't *fine* at all, causing him to bite back a smile. Luce was always the one to put on a brave face. It's one of the things he admired about her. But no time for that now.

"I was just beginning to look around when you gave me a heart attack," he said quietly. "It's a treasure trove in here. Look over there, by that puddle, there's a set of boxes. And over there? Some very old books. I was just digging into this little pile over here," he aimed the light. "I think they might be old bones. I thought they were fossils at first." He stepped back over, paused to slip on some gloves, then crouched down again. Lifting a small object, he weighed it in his palm, then plucked it up with his other hand to study it.

"I have to get this on film, Andy." Luce took out her phone and began fiddling. "Just keep doing what you're doing…" her voice trailed off as she began recording with the nighttime setting on her video. Luckily, her phone was pretty new and the camera was amazing. She tried to keep steady as she recorded though she really wanted to crouch down next to him. She also wanted to go through the books and boxes though she knew she had to remain in the background. This was Andy's investigation. She thought about calling Chris though. He should be here too.

"We should come back tomorrow night with Chris, and film this properly, right?" Luce was torn between being the consummate professional and giving in to her curiosity.

"I suppose you're right Luce, though I would like to look around a bit more. Do you mind?"

"Not at all, I'm just going to peek at one thing myself," she replied. "Just one." She smirked knowing she'd have a hard time sticking to that. Heading over to the books first, she spotted exactly what she wanted right off the bat.

It lay flat, off to the side. She crouched down and blew off the dust and sand that had settled on it. Using the light of her phone, she could tell it was unusual. The cover appeared to be a light colored embossed leather, but the spine had what looked like a cloth binding. She peered closer to read the inscription.

*MorningStar*
*Bowers Shipping LTD*

"Andy! Look!" Luce stared at the book in awe.

"Well I'll be damned." He whistled softly, crouching next to her.

"Do you think it's the ship's log? Journal? Whatever they called it?"

"More than likely. Can you open it? Here put these on," he said, quickly peeling off his gloves and handing them to her.

Luce didn't bother to put them on, instead using them as she would a cloth, to gently pull on the cover to lift it. "Nope. Wait. There's a lock."

Looking at each other the realization was immediate.

"The key," they both said in unison. He grinned and leaned in to give her a quick kiss. Hard and fast. Just enough to celebrate the discovery, not enough to cause a distraction.

Luce grinned back. Somehow, for the first time in a long time, her body hummed with excitement. Whether it was Andy himself, their adventure or their newfound something more than friend's relationship, she didn't know. And she didn't care right then and there. She was going to live in the moment for once. And she leaned in and kissed him right back.

"I don't want to leave it here. Maybe we can take it with us and hide it, then bring it tomorrow night when we come back? Not show it to anyone?"

"Luce, this is a reality show, right? Wouldn't that be considered cheating?" Andy frowned. He didn't want to participate in anything that wasn't on the up and up.

"You're right of course," Luce sighed with disappointment. "What happens if we come back and it isn't here?"

"A chance we have to take. I know exactly how to play this, OK? Do you trust me?"

Luce sat back on her heels and pulling her head back to gaze at him, she studied his expression and nodded.

"Tell you what, just go ahead and get a few shots of it now, just in case." Andy didn't want her to stay awake all night worrying about it. Something he knew he would do himself. That is, if he didn't have other plans.

## CHAPTER THIRTY

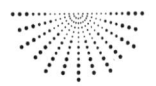

It took everything in Luce's power to hold onto their secret. The discovery of the chamber and the book had to look genuine, so it had to be an honest reaction from Chris. Andy would be edited out of the initial scene when they find it so that the audience wouldn't doubt its authenticity. There was a twinge of guilt, as Luce normally would never do this, but she had no choice. They had been exploring where they shouldn't. There'd be no hidden cameras, no hint that they'd already been there. The trick was how to rediscover the secret entrance. Andy told her he would come up with something, but she hadn't heard from him all afternoon. She'd been interviewing in the library. Mrs. Bowers, Peabody, Rodney; one after the other getting their initial stories. Andy and Chris had gone off to explore the house and would be captured on the hidden cameras. Scouting locations for additional scenes and *investigating,* according to Andy.

She'd texted him several times and ended up with nothing but frustration. She tried again to get some details.

*What's the plan?*

*Don't worry your pretty little head, all taken care of.*

Luce snickered. *Pretty little head?*

*I need to know, preferably in advance*

*Oh, you will, I guarantee it* 😊
*You know as your producer, I can have you fired...insubordination*
She didn't mean it. Totally empty threat.
*Seriously? Luce, sweetheart, don't you trust me?*
*Andy, my darling, NO!*

She gave up after that. He was impossible at times. Though she knew deep down he probably had it all figured out. No need to discuss it with her. Which riled her up even more. She had one last interview, with Lionel, then she'd go hunt him down. Or fire him.

"Can we break for a few before the last one?" Kat's voice interrupted her mental debate.

"Sure, go on and relax for a few, then get Lionel in here."

Kat smiled gratefully, as she headed out into the hall. Luce sighed. She probably should have given her a break earlier, but she'd been too preoccupied. She wouldn't let that happen again. She was made of sterner stuff than that. She couldn't let Andy get to her that way. Why he did she had no idea. Of course, that wasn't true. She knew, just didn't want to admit it.

Luce smirked knowingly when Kat returned. Hair combed, make-up freshly touched-up, she looked adorable. She'd have to pay attention when Lionel came in. Observe his reaction to her. She sensed a connection between them. Definitely some chemistry. How far that went, she couldn't know but he was certainly likable enough. The fact that in her world he was a big-time celebrity though was a drawback. Hopefully Kat was more interested in him than his fame. She was a bit star-struck, and Luce knew that feeling well. She'd been there, done that herself.

She didn't want to dampen Kat's enthusiasm, but maybe a little talk was in order. It could wait though, she thought, as the man himself entered the library. Dressed casually in ripped faded jeans and a t-shirt emblazoned with Pluto's Plan. Why wouldn't he use this to promote his band? Luce couldn't blame him. It would certainly help ratings, she thought. He nodded at Luce as he took a seat on the sofa, leaned back and swung one leg over the other in a casual pose. Then he looked over at Kat and flashed a grin causing her to flush. His eyes sparkled with a bit of mischief too. Luce chewed on her lower lip. Yep, she'd have to keep her eye on them.

The interview went smoothly with Lionel coming off interesting, charming and very intelligent. It was ideal footage and Luce was pleased. Now, if Andy would just come through with a plan for the night shoot in the chamber to find the book, it would be a perfect day. She'd find out soon enough, as they'd all gather for dinner shortly. They'd finished the shoot with just enough time for them all to shower, change and relax with a drink beforehand.

She'd met with Peabody earlier, and they'd decided that dinner would be informal that evening, out back on the patio, as there were plans for more production afterwards and formal attire wouldn't work too well. She needed everyone in casual clothes, she'd explained. He'd conferred with Mrs. Bowers, which apparently was a delicate process, and in the end it was agreed upon to allow this unusual change.

∼

ANDY WATCHED as Luce stepped outside, casually dressed in jeans and a soft light pullover. Perfect for exploring the secret passageways. Perfect for giving him ideas he needed to tuck away as well. She looked amazing no matter what, he thought to himself. But now wasn't the time. Besides, from the scowl on her face when she spotted him, she was still a bit irritated. He flashed a grin and winked as she stalked over to him. Ready to battle, he thought.

"You better have a good plan," she whispered tightly.

"Luce, you know I have a plan." He chuckled and raised an eyebrow. "If you're willing, that is," he added, leaning in to whisper in her ear.

Her whole body tingled and she was furious. More at her own reaction than at him.

Taking his elbow, she led him off to the side where they could chat privately.

"Start talking, detective," she said, then realized she was still holding his arm and let go quickly.

"OK. We'll talk now, then maybe later we can…"

Luce stomped her foot and huffed out a breath.

"Andy, please, we've only got a few minutes. Just tell me."

"All right, I'm sorry. I just like the way you heat up when you're frustrated," he replied. Then shook his head and laughed. "Okay! I'll stop. Here's the plan."

He laid out his idea quickly, and Luce had to admit, it was a good plan. After dinner, it would still be light for a bit, and he would point over toward the jetty and wonder aloud if that's where he played as a youngster... and start walking over. Chris would follow hopefully, naturally, then everyone else. Once at the jetty Andy would notice something reflecting light and somehow play with the lever while getting Chris to lean against the stone. If all went well, it would mysteriously open, and Andy would lead Chris inside.

"How are we going to keep everyone else out?" Luce asked.

"Do we need to? I don't think it matters. Let's just allow it to play out."

Luce hesitated, then nodded in agreement. "Alright. Let's hope it works."

"No worries, Luce, we got this." Andy smiled then, a genuine smile that hit Luce in the gut.

∼

IT PLAYED OUT PERFECTLY. Luce knew it couldn't have gone any better. They'd found the entrance, Andy and Chris had gone in first, with Rodney and the crew following at a safe distance behind. Once inside the chamber, the two men began their investigation of the items, with everyone else standing back and craning their necks to see. Everyone but Kat. Luce realized she wouldn't attempt entry in her chair. Frowning, she debated going back out for her. Then she saw Lionel frowning as well and smiled softly as she watched him quickly exit the way they came, then sighed as he returned carrying Kat in his arms a few minutes later. She was petite, but Luce realized that as a drummer, his upper body strength had to be pretty amazing. But it was his thoughtfulness that impressed her most. And the beaming smile on Kat's face was priceless. She decided to get that scene on film since she was recording on her phone anyway. Just in case. It was a moment Kat would never forget, but Luce wanted her to have the ability to see it for herself.

She turned back to see Andy spot them and watched as the tense look on his face softened. He was worried about Kat, true, but he could see for himself how special this was. She had a flashback then. The day she found herself in Andy's arms, being cradled, comforted. The day she'd learned Annie had almost lost her life and she'd broken down. Andy had been there for her. And she could still feel the strength in him as he held her. Let her tears fall. Giving her the ability to let go, if only for a little while. It was the first time she saw through his alpha male persona. The first time she knew Andy Holman was different. The first time she knew that keeping him at a distance would be far more difficult than she thought. And now for the first time, she wondered why she did. Maybe it was time to let someone erase those scars Jack had left on her heart.

"Andy, I've got something here." The shout from Chris was expected yet startled everyone. He had been enthralled with the stack of books that naturally drew his attention. Then, shining his own phone light on the cover of one book in particular, he exhaled slowly.

"Holy shit! It's the log from the MorningStar! I'd know it anywhere. I've seen these before at the maritime museum."

Luce shook her head and rolled her eyes. "Language Chris, now we'll have to edit that out."

"Let me see," Andy said as he went to crouch next to Chris. "Good spot, Chris. Here, put these on," he said as he handed him a pair of gloves, immediately putting Chris in charge of the journal. Luce had to admit, that was a brilliant move. They'd succeeded. The surprise discovery was captured on film. Now the real work would begin.

## CHAPTER THIRTY-ONE

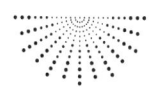

It was a dilemma. How to open the journal and capture the amazing discovery using a key she'd received prior to filming. They sat in the library, contemplating the star attraction. It was decided that this would be a perfect scene for the show, the review of evidence. The book lay on the table in the center of the room, on display. The ultimate temptation.

"This is the finale; you all know that." Luce said quietly from her perch on the window seat, in the background. Jamie was filming, and she could be edited out easily.

"This means the ship never went down." Chris looked at Andy for confirmation.

"Maybe, if this is for real. Could also mean the journal survived to be used again. Maybe it was a spare and used on another ship. We have to review the entries carefully. But the date stamped on the cover is kind of a giveaway."

"Well, it's hard to read, but clearly it's 18 something, not 1780, that's for sure."

"Here's what we know," Chris stood and began pacing. "It's a captain's journal, presumably old, but well-preserved. And the front emblem clearly reads MorningStar."

"And it's locked. We either find the key to open it, or risk damaging it to pick the lock," Andy added. "Question is, where is that key?"

Luce smiled, that was a fabulous way to set things up. She nodded to Jamie and gave him the signal to stop filming. Candid discussions didn't need to be on camera and that was a good stopping point.

"Sadly, as good condition as it's in, we can't risk damaging it," Chris said. "We need to open it carefully, and then it needs to be scanned. Can't leaf through it, the paper is too fragile. It's a major undertaking." Chris was right about that, but Luce was frustrated. If it were authentic, it may hold all the secrets needed to solve the mystery. If it were a fake, designed specifically to steer the investigation and the TV show, they'd be played big time.

"We have to know what we're dealing with." Andy thought for a moment, then looked over at Chris. "Chris you have a scanner at the house, right?"

"Affirmative," Chris chuckled.

"Assuming we find the key, can Annie get to work scanning it? Then we'll really be able to comb through for clues. To its authenticity and to the ship's disappearance."

"That's perfect." Chris smiled in gratitude. "Thanks. Annie knows being on set, especially in the basement area is a bad idea. Not just because she'd be at risk of falling, but probably mold and all kinds of things bad for pregnant women."

Annie rolled her eyes and laughed. "Hello, I'm right here! And I'm not a china doll. You all act like I'm accident prone or something."

"More like an accident magnet," Luce laughed. "Now, detective, perhaps you can lend Annie a pair of those gloves you've always got tucked away?"

"Got a whole box of them. Figured we'd need them. I'm like a boy scout, Luce, always prepared. You should see what else I brought!"

With that, they all laughed, tension broken, leaving Luce grateful she wouldn't have to edit that particular remark out of the footage. She also wondered exactly what he meant by it.

It was a question that would go unanswered however, as the week flew by in a flurry of activity. They returned to the chamber several times, to examine and collect different pieces, opening various boxes and investigating their origins. They decided to reinterview Mrs. Bowers too, trying to get any hint of family lore about underground tunnels.

"I've mentioned before, that there was a lot of activity along the shores here during the revolution. I'm sure they were used in some capacity by the colonial soldiers." Mrs. Bowers seemed quite certain of that.

"Is there a chance that perhaps the British used them?" Kat posed the question.

"I'm sure that's possible. I do know that Lionel Bowers himself was a staunch patriot, and I have no doubt the tunnels were used in a positive manner." Her tone was a bit defensive, Luce noted. As if she wanted answers, but only if they proved her own narrative.

Ultimately, solving the mystery would put to bed any misguided rumors or myths about Execution Rocks. Luce was certain of it. Whether or not it portrayed the Bowers family in a positive light, couldn't be guaranteed. What if the tunnels were used by the British with permission? What if the Bowers were slave owners who left them to die on the rocks? Luce knew it was essential to keep Adeline believing the Bowers would end up heroic, not a source of family shame.

"Mrs. Bowers, is there anything you remember, growing up here perhaps, about the tunnels or about the family ship business that might shed any light? Any odd stories?" Luce tried to sound as if this were just the next question on the list.

"You know I didn't actually grow up here. I lost my parents at a young age, went to live with relatives. I didn't return until I 20." Her tone was wistful now. Relaxed.

"I had no idea, I'm so sorry," Luce replied. "Forgive my intrusion."

"Not at all young lady, I was fortunate in many ways. You know, something I haven't mentioned, perhaps now's the time."

Luce and Kat both leaned forward. Something about her tone let them know she was about to reveal something important.

"When I came back I arrived here at night; I still remember it vividly. It was a warm June evening in 1960. I spent the first night out on my balcony, just watching the peacefulness of it all. My aunt had arranged for me to come stay for a visit. The house was owned at that time by a trust, I wasn't aware, but it seems that my father, in his infinite wisdom, had left it in his will that way. I could not inherit until adulthood. Anyway, I was out there, watching the water, the light from the lighthouse as it circled around. And there it was."

"The ship," Luce murmured.

Adeline smiled. "Yes."

"You saw it too, didn't you?" She looked pointedly at Luce.

"Not in 1960," Luce chuckled. "But yes, when I was young. How do you know that?" Luce was sure she hadn't mentioned it.

"Your father. He attended one or two of our society meetings. I had a long talk with him."

Luce didn't know what to say at that point. She'd had no idea.

"So, you see, when Mrs. Holman approached about the dinner invitation, I was thrilled. She mentioned your name, you see. I knew. This was meant to be."

∼

AS SHE STOOD, hands on the railing, eyes unfocused, she knew everything had changed. It wasn't just her and Andy sharing weird experiences. Adeline Bowers shared them too. Her whole perspective was now changing. And so would Andy's when she told him. She hadn't seen him yet. He and Chris had gone off exploring something or other and she'd been busy with the interview. They hadn't returned by dinner, which made her a bit nervous, but she'd occupied her time studying the footage and video chatting with Annie.

She heard the door open from the other side of the balcony.

"You look lost in thought, there, Luce," Andy's voice was low, husky and sent shivers over her bare arms. It was a warm night, and her shorts and tank were just enough to keep her comfortable.

"I have news," she said quietly as he came up behind her.

"Do tell," he whispered. She could feel his breath on her neck as he leaned in, placing his hands on her shoulders. She debated shrugging him off and decided against it. For once, she'd accept what was being offered, and leaned back into him.

It was time to let him in, all the way. She just hoped it wouldn't end in disaster.

"Adeline Bowers has seen the ship too."

"I know," he whispered, causing her to turn suddenly, palm on his chest, she looked up in surprise.

"You know?"

He smiled. "I do. Because I have news too."

## CHAPTER THIRTY-TWO

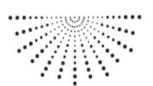

"Tell me," Luce demanded. "Where have you guys been? You found something didn't you?"

Andy smiled and shook his head. "Patience, woman," he chuckled.

"Don't you *patience woman* me, Neanderthal." Luce pulled back and glared. "Out with it."

Chuckling, Andy took his time, tipped his head and studied her. He knew he'd tell her everything, but he enjoyed watching her torture herself trying to be patient. One of the few times Luce let go of her self-control.

"Might as well sit, then, since I've got a story to tell." Andy smirked, then grabbed the nearest lounge chair, and getting comfortable, reached over for Luce's hand pulling her down to sit with him. With an exaggerated sigh, Luce gave in and leaned her back against his chest and got comfortable. As comfortable as she could with his arms around her waist, palms splayed on her ribcage, fingers tapping softy, and the air sizzling with something she hadn't felt in a very long time. She licked her lips nervously, then took a breath.

"Spill it detective," she said quietly, wanting to know everything but not wanting to disturb the moment. And they were definitely having a moment.

"We went back into the chamber," he said quietly, then felt her stiffen.

"Don't worry, Lionel came with us, and we all took turns with our phones, so all of it's on film," he quickly added.

"Good boys, go on," Luce laughed softly as she relaxed once more.

"First, Lionel started rattling on about his grandmother's fixation with the ghost ship, which he said began when she saw it herself years ago. Why nobody provided this information from the beginning is bothering me a bit. And as startling as that is, it's not the big news."

"Are you saying my news isn't as important as yours?" Luce smiled as she asked.

"Sweetheart, all your news is important to me," Andy chuckled, knowing it wasn't the time to rile her up. "But what if I told you we discovered another way in and out of the chamber?" He paused, waiting for her reaction. For once she'd surprised him by remaining quiet.

"Go on."

"On the left side of the chamber, there was an odd shaped stone in the center of the wall. We all pushed on it but nothing happened. We checked around it for a hinge or a lever, but there was nothing. We almost gave up."

"Clearly you didn't, though," Luce huffed out. "What happened?"

"Chris began feeling along the sides of the stone, and he realized there was a carved out niche on the left side. Most doors open on the right. But not this one. And it didn't push in, it pulled out. Lionel managed to get his hand completely in the niche and pulled while we pulled him."

"And?"

" It opened."

"Wait. The hinge was on the other side?" Luce was trying to sort through it. Envision it in her head.

"Exactly. If you came from the other side, you could probably push in. It led us into another passageway just like the entry from the beach, damp stone, no lighting. But when we came to a fork in the road, as it were, Lionel suddenly recalled something." Andy paused, sensing her anticipation.

"He said as a boy, he'd been playing in the basement, and one day discovered a tunnel. At least in his mind it was a tunnel. He'd gone exploring and had discovered something on the wall. An arrow scratched faintly into the stone. Chris shone his light on the wall in front of us as Lionel searched for it. And found it, pointing to the right. We followed it and discovered more markings; directional signs. Those arrows were there for a purpose, Luce."

He stopped then, and his arms tightened around her.

"They led us to the basement, just under the library."

"And then?" Luce knew a bombshell was about to be dropped.

"We went up the stairs, and through the secret door, where we found Mrs. Bowers, napping in a chair. She had a book in her lap."

"Wait, is that like, the end? Because I was expecting something more. Like you found the secret." Luce's voice rang with disappointment.

"May I continue?" Andy grinned.

"But of course, Detective, pardon my interruption," Luce grinned and tipped her head back to look up at him. "Do go on!"

"We tried to be quiet, you know sneak by her, not wake her, but just as we approached the door to the hallway, she called out, said something nonsensical," he kept his voice hushed and suspenseful. "We all turned at once," Andy continued. "She looked frightened. Lionel went over to her first and kneeled in front of her. She was so upset, he picked up the book from her lap and looked at it curiously. Then holding it up he nodded to us to come get it."

"What was it?"

"A reference book on slave ships. The chapter she'd been reading was about the MorningStar."

"So, it was a slave ship? For real?" Luce wasn't ready to settle for that. Not yet.

"Well Adeline certainly thinks so. I'm not so sure and neither is Chris."

"We need to read the Captain's journal. It's the only way." Luce sat up and leaned forward then, staying close enough for Andy's arms to remain around her though as she turned toward him.

"I hope that's not the answer, Andy."

"There's one more thing," Andy spoke softly as he gazed at Luce. Wondering how she'd react to his next bit of information. "Something I've known but not mentioned."

"You're keeping things from me?" Luce wanted to be annoyed, but the look on his face was genuine and nervous.

"I am," he nodded slowly, uncertainly.

"Out with it." Luce demanded gently. "Rip it off like a band aid."

"My fourth great grandfather owned a slave. My mother found it in a census record."

Luce waited, knowing there was much more to the story, and gave him time to find the words.

"It was on my dad's side. Edward Holman. Everyone likes to talk about how the North hated slavery, but I guess not all of them did. My mom stumbled upon a family bible at the historical society. She has a theory, based on the inscriptions inside. Maybe you and she can have a talk tomorrow. She'll be at Mrs. Bowers little shindig tomorrow to celebrate the 4$^{th}$ of July. I'd rather let her tell you the rest."

"Maybe I'd rather hear it from you," Luce said softly.

"I don't know if I can face your reaction Luce."

"What does that even mean?"

Andy sighed, and knew she was right. He had to tell her.

"I'm going to tell you, but please, allow my mother to fill in the blanks. I don't know all the details. Deal?"

"Deal."

"Edward Holman was married to Christiana Broch. They were childless. One day, Edward came home with a young black woman. A slave he'd bought at a nearby auction. Within a year, his son, Jonathan Holman, was born."

"And?"

"What do you mean, and? It's kind of obvious isn't it?"

"No, explain it to me."

"I'm descended from a slave... and her owner." There, he'd said it. "I'm not who everyone thinks I am."

Luce studied his face. Saw the worry lines above his brow. His eyes locked on hers, as if asking for something, she just didn't know what.

"Are you a murderer? Rapist? Pedophile? Embezzler? Grifter?" Luce exhausted her list.

"No, of course not," he shook his head and frowned.

"How long have you known?" Luce asked.

"About 15 years I guess."

"So far longer than I've known you, then." Luce prompted.

"Yeah."

"Then for me, it's part of who you are, the Andy I know and..."

"Know and what?"

Luce's eyes widened and she regrouped immediately. "And since this isn't new for you, you're not stewing over it or shocked by it. Nor am I. And it's time for me to get some rest," Luce spoke quietly as she stood to go, Andy quickly following suit, grabbing her wrist lightly.

"Talk to my mom tomorrow, would you?"

Luce smiled. "Of course." She gave him a quick kiss on the cheek before slipping back into her suite. She knew staying out there any longer would lead to things they couldn't take back. She also needed to consider what was bothering Andy about her knowing his ancestry. He thought it would affect her. That it would make a difference to her. But why? It was the why that would reveal how he truly felt. Either he thought she'd be put off by his black ancestry, or, the slave ownership. Hopefully, it was the latter. She could handle that. But if he thought it was race, then he didn't know her at all.

## CHAPTER THIRTY-THREE

"You asked to see me, Mrs. Bowers?" Luce tapped lightly on the doorframe, uncertain about what could be so urgent she'd been dragged out of bed at this ungodly hour. Especially on a holiday, where for once she could sleep in.

"Come in, Luce, and please, call me Adeline."

"Adeline, of course, what can I do for you?" Luce asked as she stepped into the room. A sudden sense of doom seemed to wash over her. This couldn't be good.

"I'm afraid I've changed my mind. I don't want to continue with this project any longer."

"With all due respect, Adeline, we're just about ready to produce the pilot! Only a few days left and we'll be out of your hair, I promise."

"Have a seat, Luce, let me explain." Luce promptly did as she was asked, though she couldn't get comfortable, perched at the edge of her seat, waiting for the other shoe to drop.

"It isn't all the commotion of the film crew; you've all been perfectly wonderful. And helpful. So helpful, I think I'm much closer to the answer to the mystery and I don't like it, and I certainly don't want it revealed on television." She sighed and shook her head. "I've waited years to learn the secret. I had hoped it would simply satisfy my curiosity, maybe even allow me to free myself of whatever was haunting this area."

"I totally understand Adeline, that's my hope as well. And you are right we are very close to getting answers. Maybe if we could have just one or two more days?"

"The answers aren't what I'd hoped for Luce, not at all. I no longer want them."

"What is it you don't want to reveal, we can always edit it out? Would that help?"

Adeline picked up the book on the end table next to the sofa and reached over to give it to Luce.

"I've marked the page. See for yourself," she said, quite sadly Luce thought.

Taking the book, she skimmed the pages, realizing immediately it was the book on slave ships Andy had told her about. She needed to convince Adeline it wasn't fact; it was simply an assumption by the author. A supposed renowned maritime scholar, but nonetheless, a writer who didn't have all the facts.

She knew she'd have to think fast and come up with something.

"Adeline, the author wrote this knowing only that the ship was reported to carry slaves. We have something more; we have the journal. Just give us a chance to read it and determine whether it's true or not. If it is, and you want us to cancel, we will. And where did this book come from? I mean, have you had this the whole time?" Luce wondered if someone was trying to deceive her.

"It appeared in the mail yesterday morning. No return address."

"Someone who knew we were filming must have sent it. Probably the author." Luce was simply trying to dissuade Adeline from getting sucked into the easy answers. "You know we've done our research, and this book never appeared in any reference material. Yet suddenly it arrives?" Maybe Luce could plant some doubt, she sure had a few of her own.

"There's something I haven't told you, and this is off the record, if you don't mind." Adeline looked up nervously at the remote camera that had been placed by the crew.

"Understood, Adeline, you have my word. You can tell me anything."

Luce was accustomed to this, had no problem keeping the conversation confidential. It was often the best way to learn things.

"I'm not a Bowers by marriage. I am a Bowers by blood." Adeline straightened up as she spoke, taking pride in her words. "I am Mrs. Bowers because as a young woman, I made a mistake, one I will never regret mind you, but one I needed to keep to myself."

"I totally hear you, I've made plenty of my own," Luce smiled softly, and nodded for her to continue.

"When I was a young woman, things were different. Times were changing. You may not believe this, but I was a bit of a flower child." Adeline grinned, surprising Luce. It was unexpected.

"You? I can't picture it," Luce spoke before she could filter herself. "I mean, sorry, but you seem, well, so," she faltered then.

"Buttoned up? Stiff as a board? Inflexible? Yes, I know," she sighed. "That's my cover. It was necessary. You see, when I returned here to settle down, I wasn't alone."

Luce sensed what was coming next but needed to remain surprised.

"My son, George. I knew people would ask questions, judge me. Not accept me, no matter how much money I had. And George deserved acceptance. So, I stretched the truth. George's father and I never married. We never had a chance. He disappeared during one of our protests in Georgia. There were rumors of course, about what happened, but I know the truth. He was murdered." She paused, pursed her lips then took a deep breath. "We'd been staging a peaceful sit-in, following the assassination of Martin Luther King." Adeline's voice drifted off as she remembered things. Things it appeared she didn't want to voice.

"What was his name?" Luce asked not only as a distraction, to bring her focus back, but because she had every intention of looking into this further.

"Troy Simmons. We'd been together for a few months, was all. I didn't even know I was pregnant. He never knew about George. I never had a chance to tell him."

"You must have been heartbroken," Luce murmured softly.

"Indeed, I was. But you see this is why we have to stop what we're doing. I cannot live with myself if I confirm that my own family, my own blood, is tainted with this kind of evil. I gave up protesting and speaking out, I became what I detested in order to raise my son in peace. I don't know how to atone for that. For any of this."

"But you didn't do any of this. You lived a good and decent life." Luce was more concerned now with Adeline's well-being than her show. "You can't blame yourself for your ancestor's sins."

"I lived a life of privilege. White privilege as they say now. I could wake up every day and look in the mirror and tell myself I was doing the right thing. Living a lie. Look around us! Nothing has changed. Nothing. Because people like me retreated from the fight."

Luce honestly had no answer for her. Everything she said held a ring of truth she couldn't deny. Luce had been raised in a home where tolerance and equality were emphasized, but how could she ever understand what that truly meant. She'd always tended to live her life as best she could, but maybe that wasn't enough.

"You've given me a lot to think about, Adeline. Not just about your situation, but for me. I've always thought that being outraged for others was enough. Living a decent life was enough. Your story shakes me up a bit."

"I'm glad. I'm an old lady, Luce, but you're still young enough to make a difference."

"Maybe we both can. Maybe this show is how we do that. I'm not sure what the outcome will be, Adeline, but I do know we can try to make a difference regardless. Will you give me that chance? Give us that chance to transform reality tv into something important?"

## CHAPTER THIRTY-FOUR

"All done," Annie sighed as she handed the journal back to Luce, along with a jump drive containing all the images. "I hope we find the answers, cause it took everything I had not to read as I scanned. I mean I know I promised, but that was asking a lot sis," Annie grinned and shook her head.

"Yeah, well, try going to sleep every night knowing the answers were right there and you had them, not me." Luce was grateful to have the book back.

"Too bad we can't go pop this in your laptop right now, eh?"

"I know, but with all these people around, it would be kind of obvious. As much as I hate this, we'll have to wait until after the fireworks." Luce was resigned to be patient about it, but so many questions were in her head now it was hard to focus. And the biggest one of all was why her? She now understood perhaps, why Andy and Adeline had seen the ghost ship. What she didn't understand was why she had seen it too. She had no ties to anything that she knew of. Though she knew little about her family history. They were Irish. She knew that much. Her dad had done some research, but Luce hadn't paid much attention to it.

"Annie?" Luce said suddenly.

"What?"

"Remember the family tree dad was working on? Do you have that?"

"Somewhere, buried in all his books, yeah. I think so." Annie looked at Luce curiously. "Why? What's up?"

"Andy and Adeline both saw the ship. Just like me. And I think I know why they saw it, what I don't know is why I did. And the answer may lie in that tree."

"Well, I'll bring it by tomorrow if I can find it." Annie smiled. "Right now, we have a party to attend!"

"Right now, we have to lock this book up!" Luce replied quickly. "I'll take care of it; you go find your fabulous husband-to-be and relax."

Luce scoped out the patio, looking for Kat. She'd had her bring a portable safe, which is where they were storing many of the pieces found in the chamber. Spotting her talking to Lionel, she smiled as she approached them. Lionel was seated on a stone bench, putting him at eye level with Kat.

"Am I interrupting?" Luce spoke quietly, hiding the book behind her purse so nobody would notice it.

"Not at all boss lady!" Kat grinned.

"I'll get out of your way," Lionel said, looking at Kat, "but I'll see you later!"

"Hope so," Kat whispered as he walked away. "So, what do you need? It is my day off, right?"

"Yep, but," Luce grinned back, and brought the journal out just far enough for Kat to see it.

"We need to put this away." Handing it to Kat, who slipped it into her tote discreetly. "Want me to push?"

"Nah, I got it," Kat said as she began wheeling her chair towards the doorway. "Just get the door for me."

Heading inside, they quickly made their way to Kat's suite, where the journal was placed in the safe. Luce kept hold of the jump drive, so she could slip away later and review it.

"There. Now, I think we could both use some downtime." Luce sighed. "At least I can!"

"Me too. Say how's the wedding planning going? Annie letting you help at all?" Kat asked her casually. "Must be frustrating not getting to control it all for her."

"Ha. As if. I did help her pick out the dress, and maybe offered some advice on the catering, and maybe the flowers, but she wanted to do this herself and I'm staying out of it." Luce grinned.

"And I call bullshit. I heard you on the phone with that caterer, giving him all your *suggestions*."

"If we leave it all to Annie, we'll end up in bibs, slobbering over barbecued ribs."

"I'm pretty sure that's not going to happen, Luce. She wants you to focus on your show. Besides, she told you you'll get your chance to be bossy at your own wedding." Kat laughed remembering how ticked off Luce had been at that remark.

"Whatever," Luce waved her hand in the air. "My wedding will be totally different, trust me."

"Yeah? How so?" Kat was pretty sure Luce's wedding would be as close to perfect as they come.

"If and when I find my prince charming? I won't plan a thing. He'll whisk me away and everything will be taken care of. I won't have to lift a finger."

"Really, Luce?" Kat was amused now. "Whisk you away to where, might I ask?"

"Someplace incredibly romantic. Someplace worth waiting 37 years for," Luce laughed. "I mean if I'm going to wait this long, it better be good, no?"

"Definitely agree, Luce, though I don't know, I'll probably never get married. My longest dating streak was 3 dates. And two were accidental meet-ups."

"Shut the front door. You? I'm not buying it."

"Really. My roommate? She's had three girlfriends since I've known her. Never has any trouble finding a date. Maybe I need to rethink my social life. I think men are too complicated."

"You know what they say? Men. Can't live with 'em, can't shoot 'em," Luce said with a laugh, shaking her head.

"No, you can't," the voice from the doorway made Luce jump. *Crap!* She turned slowly, hoping her face wasn't too red.

"Ladies," Andy grinned as he entered the room. "What did I miss? Other than the typical gender-bashing conversation you're all so prone to."

"Uncle Andrew," Kat sighed for emphasis. "Is there something you needed?"

"Nope. Just passing by. Why aren't you two outside?"

"We were just putting the journal away," Luce pointed toward the safe. "Annie finished the scanning and I've got the jump drive," she said, patting her bag. She paused, wondering if she should mention her conversation with Mrs. Bowers, then decided it could wait.

∾

It wasn't easy to find a good spot, Luce thought, when the fireworks were about to begin and everyone else was looking for the perfect vantage point to view them from. Slipping off her sandals, she decided to head down to the jetty, find a vacant boulder. She needed some alone time to ponder all that had happened in one day. Adeline had been a wealthy unwed mother, a civil rights activist, who it seemed descended from a slave trading boat builder. Maybe. Andy too, had some distinct stains on his ancestry; one being slave owners. But on the other hand, he was also descended from a slave. The MorningStar appeared to be the common thread through it all.

But it was her own past that haunted her now. Why did she see the ghost ship? What was her tie to it all? Would her family tree reveal something unexpected, something evil, as well? If all that weren't enough to make her brain explode, there was the pull between her and Andy. More than a pull. She was as certain as she could ever be that he was meant for her. Inexplicable as it seemed, as long as they'd known each other, there had been chemistry, sure. But now it appeared this was their moment. The question she couldn't seem to answer, though, was whether she would seize it. Or let it go.

She sensed his approach just as the first set of fireworks rose up in the distance. Climbing up next to her, he sat down and casually threw his arm about her shoulders. Neither of them spoke, as they watched the colorful display light up over the water. It was a comfortable silence.

When the fireworks began to go off in rapid sequence, and giant circular bursts of color exploded above signaling the end of the big show, a quiet settled around them. Andy was the first to break the silence.

"You're awfully quiet tonight, Luce. What's on your mind?"

"Only a million and one things, I'm afraid," Luce replied with a soft smile. "Where do you want me to start?"

"Well, now you have me curious, so how about the beginning?" Andy murmured softly. "Only first…" he leaned in, kissed her softly, and pulled back. Waiting to see her reaction. Hoping she wouldn't disappoint. When she leaned in and returned the kiss, he knew they were good.

"OK, now." He chuckled.

Luce began with Adeline's story of the MorningStar being a slave ship, and Andy simply nodded in acknowledgement. "Go on," he prompted her.

"Turns out Adeline was a civil rights activist in the 60's. And her son George was the product of a relationship with a fellow activist. One who died mysteriously. Or disappeared. She wants us to stop production. She doesn't want to know the answers, Andy."

"I'm guessing you have an idea about changing her mind?" He knew she did.

"If we can prove somehow that the MorningStar was not a slave ship, well that would fix it all wouldn't it?"

"No, Luce, it wouldn't. We aren't here to rewrite history. Maybe our purpose is to expose it. And find a way forward from it."

"Why are you always so damn right?" Luce shook her head and laughed. "There's something else though. If the vision or apparition were some sort of clue or sign from the great beyond… why did I see it? What's my role in all this? Annie's going to bring me dad's family tree tomorrow. I guess I'm worried about what I'll find."

"All right then. Tomorrow, you dive into your own family history while I go exploring the caves one more time. One of us is bound to find something that will help our cause."

"I hope so. And Andy? One more thing I guess while we're having an actual conversation…"

He studied her expression then, sensing her hesitation. Tucking a wayward strand of hair behind her ear, he spoke softly. "Anything, Luce, ask me anything."

"Were you worried about how I'd react after learning your ancestor owned a slave? Or worried how I'd react to the news that your ancestor *was* a slave?" Luce sucked in a breath and held it.

"There are those who would judge me either way, I suppose. There is so much that is wrong with all of it. Being connected to it in any way is something I've struggled with since finding out. You know I spent a lot of time concocting logical, reasonable stories to account for it all. Ridiculous as they might seem."

"Such as?" Luce wondered aloud. "What kind of ridiculous scenarios did you invent?"

"Well, there was the 'He wasn't really a slave owner he bought her to save her, fell in love' and so on. Then there was the one where she was a runaway and he took her in and fell in love. The one where she wasn't a slave, they actually paid her a salary but couldn't tell anyone. And again, he was in love."

"There's a common theme here isn't there?" Luce said dryly.

"Luce, I'm a cop. I protect and serve. Having a fucking racist rapist ancestor does not work for me."

"One of the things I love about you Detective, you really are the real deal." Luce laughed. Then quickly looked away, realizing she might have said too much.

Andy reached out and placed his hand on her cheek, pulling her back to face him. "And you Luce Porter, are one of a kind…" Leaning in, this time his kiss was harder, more determined. He was making a statement. One that would resonate in her head the rest of the night.

## CHAPTER THIRTY-FIVE

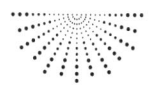

"This makes no sense." Luce mumbled aloud. She'd been reading through the journal for hours. Mostly weather related complaints about illness, as best she could tell. Some of the language was difficult to understand. So far all she had was a basic route. They'd travelled from South Carolina up the coast. Each entry was either how many sails were up, the direction of the wind, the nastiness of the humidity or even the food. But nothing to explain the very existence of a ship that had allegedly gone down years before. The journal was from 1840. That was clear.

Picking up the book she'd retrieved from the library, the one Adeline had been reading, she looked for reference information in the back. Anything to source the information presented. She'd already researched some of it through the new reparations project. Shipping companies were tasked with going back in time and reporting whether or not their ships were used in the slave trade. Not a pleasant task by any means, but necessary and filled with revelations. Even though she hated admitting it, she agreed with Andy wholeheartedly that the only way forward was an honest confrontation with history. But this particular book was too simplistic in its evidence. The author took too many shortcuts and made too many assumptions. She read the short final passage again, trying to focus not on what it presented, but what was left unsaid.

> *The MorningStar; 1780-1790 Captain R S Sturgiss*
> *Bowers Shipping Company*
> *In the spring of 1790, traveling through the narrow waters between Connecticut and Long Island, the insurrection of the slaves on board The MorningStar was violent and swift. The lack of seamanship however meant they were unable to control the vessel once under their own rule. While they managed to free themselves from bondage, they perished in the darkness of the unforgiving seas.*

If the ship went down in 1790, the journal they found was a fraud. But looking at the entries, Luce knew it wasn't. The entries were telling her something much different. She just needed to understand. And mid-19th century English was as difficult to understand as the handwriting.

Glancing at the clock, she realized she hadn't heard a peep from Andy's suite next door. She knew he'd gone off to explore a bit down in the tunnels but he should have returned already. Tucking the worry away, he was a cop after all, he could protect himself, she scrutinized the image in front of her once more. It was a strange diagram. The drawings featured long tubes, several circles and arrows, along with a compass indicating direction. There was a small x mirroring itself in the upper corners, but no indication of what they were for. It reminded her of a pirate's treasure map. X marks the spot. She scrolled to the next image, and there were two notations in particular that caught her eye; the first was a notation about a crew member, that much she could understand.

> *10 June 1841 Mate duties now to Jones. H\*\*\* abandoned. NorEstr left but 2 cloths. One F lost. Search ended without success.*

It was the second name that was gnawing at her. She closed one eye, hoping to get a better angle on it. She squinted. Blurred. Until it finally was recognizable. And shocking. But it was the second notation that finally made sense of it all.

*12 June 1841 Safe passage found. Arrows left. Liberty for all leave one. Godspeed.*

She grabbed her phone and frantically typed.
**Where are you, come now. Like as in now!!!!**
She waited, holding her breath. No response. This wasn't like him. Maybe he'd snuck in and fell asleep.
**Andy, wake up, come quick...**
When she again got no response, Luce quietly slipped into the hallway, and headed towards his suite. The door was open a crack, so she pushed it gently. Empty. The bed was made. Everything in its place. As if he hadn't yet returned. She turned to leave, when it caught her eye. His phone. On the dresser. Flashing rapidly. She went over and looked at the screen, at the series of notifications that had gone unchecked. *Where are you Andy Holman?*

THE JACKHAMMERS in his head were incessant. He tried to open his eyes but failed. Even the light sound of a water drip was painful. Shifting his leg, a pain shot up through his body. *Shit. What happened?* He'd been in the chamber. Packing up a small collection of bone fragments that had been concealed. Then he'd followed the arrows only this time, he deliberately went in an opposite direction. The next thing he remembered, he'd awoken on the cold damp stone. In immense pain.

He couldn't get up. That was for certain. He could try and drag himself but to where? He felt in his pocket for his phone, but it was gone. Did it drop? He must have had it in his hand. Yes, it must have dropped. He felt around the ground with his fingers and tried to move his head and look, but the pain was overwhelming. Reaching up, he felt around his scalp, and immediately hit upon the sticky evidence of blood. Did he fall? Was he hit? He probably should have waited for Chris. Not probably. Should have. That was his own arrogant mistake. He knew better than to explore without backup. How long he'd been out he had no idea, but hopefully, someone realized he was gone. He felt himself drifting off again, somewhere where pain didn't exist.

~

"Oh my god you have got to stop eating like you're twenty," Luce huffed out in frustration. She put both of her arms under Andy's limp shoulders and placed his head on her lap. "And you are so lucky I chose to wear a bra, or this tourniquet wouldn't be happening," she went on talking to herself mostly as Andy was barely conscious and she was bordering on a nervous breakdown.

If she hadn't printed out the drawing from the journal she'd never have found him. She had realized in a flash that it was a map of the underground passageways, and it had led her to another chamber; one that was very different from the one they'd found originally. The walls had an array of drawings carved on them. She only caught a glimpse of them before she spotted Andy on the ground. Shining her light, she saw the blood next to his head. And her world spun upside down. It felt like minutes but it was only seconds before adrenaline kicked in.

She'd ripped off her tank top and wrapped it around his head, not too tightly in case his skull was fractured. All her obsessive training came back in a flood of memories. She checked his breathing. Shallow but regular. Checked his pupils. Checked his pulse. She had no bars on her phone. There was only one thing she could do, and that was find the exit. She had to call for help. She hesitated to leave him but she had to. There was no other way.

"Don't you dare die on me, Andy," Luce whispered, her voice wavering. "Don't you dare."

She knew there was an exit somewhere above her, the other x. But whether it would still be there? She couldn't know for sure. Gently placing his head down on the ground, she stood, and gazed down for a moment. There was no time, she knew that. Turning, she headed at a rapid walk back through the passageways until she was back under the Library. Taking the stairs 2 at a time and hoping she didn't fall and break her own skull, she hit the button on the panel, only nothing happened.

"For fucks sake, not now." She pushed it again, and again, and nothing. "Damn it all." So she did the only thing she could. She pounded on the door and called out. She still had no bars on her phone. She yelled louder.

And then she heard them. Voices, faint but clear. Somebody was there.

"Thank God," she breathed out. "We need help! An ambulance!" She hoped that even if they couldn't get the door open, they'd hear her.

## CHAPTER THIRTY-SIX

*L*uce awoke with a sense of déjà vu, and dread. The distinct odor of disinfectant, the tense atmosphere. People sprawled across hard back chairs, waiting for news. It was a scene she knew too well and fought too long to forget.

She looked across the room, saw Andy's parents. Molly seated quietly, frozen in place while Gil paced back and forth. She knew she should leave. She was suddenly despondent. This was all her fault. All her idea. She should be the one lying in some sterile triage bay, not him. She stood and headed quietly over to the exit. She could slip out and disappear. She stopped as the automatic doors slid open. She couldn't leave. Not until she knew he was OK. What if he wasn't? What if moving him, even slightly, had left him paralyzed? What if she'd done more harm than good? What if she lost him? She turned back, and keeping her head down, slid back into her chair, hoping to disappear.

∼

"LUCE, HONEY, WAKE UP DEAR."

Luce opened her eyes, trying to orient herself. A hand gently tapped her shoulder. Looking up, she saw Molly Holman, smiling softly.

"He's OK, right?" Luce said quickly, her voice trembling.

"He will be dear, he will be. Do you want to see him?"

"Do you think they'll let me? Is he still in ICU?" Luce had no idea how long she'd slept. But it felt like forever. "I'm so sorry Mrs. Holman, this was all my fault." She blurted it out without thinking.

Molly sat down then, next to Luce, and took both her hands, clasping them in hers.

"Call me Molly, and none of this is your fault, sweetheart. You saved his life."

Luce sobbed softly as tears welled up in her eyes. "I can't lose him Molly. I just can't."

The older woman smiled knowingly and letting go of her hands, reached around and took her in her arms and held her. She knew enough about Luce from Andy to know she probably hadn't had a mother's hug in a very long time.

Patting her on the back, Molly pulled back and brushed a tear from Luce's cheek.

"Come on, let's go pay him a visit. He's still in ICU, but we'll sneak you in," she winked. Luce managed a weak smile and sniffed. Then with a deep breath, she nodded.

"OK, I'm ready. Say where's Kat?"

"We sent her to get some rest. She'll be back tomorrow. Lionel gave her a ride. Imagine a stuffy old bird like Adeline having such a charming grandson. Who knew?"

Luce smiled ruefully and shook her head. Funny how life moves on no matter what it throws at you.

"Maybe you can tell me if they know what happened?" Luce still had no idea. It had all been so fast and frenetic.

"We don't know much, but I'll try to fill you in as we walk. Gil? She's ready, let's go," Molly called out. "Now when we get to the nurse's station, you just follow my lead."

As they headed up to the ICU, Molly gave Luce an abbreviated version of what she knew from speaking with the officers on the scene and the doctors attending Andy.

He'd been struck from behind, suffering a severe concussion, and then in the leg, fracturing a tibia. Possibly a baseball bat or a metal pipe, they weren't sure yet. The police forensics unit was gathering as much evidence as they could, but clearly Andy was not alone in that chamber. Whoever it was got out before Luce arrived.

"And Luce, I don't know where you learned your first aid, but the doctors all agreed, your quick actions were what saved him." Molly squeezed Luce's hand, while Gil placed a hand on her shoulder and squeezed. He hadn't said much along the way.

"I took a few classes after my parent's accident. They never stood a chance, but I vowed that if I ever had an opportunity to be there for someone else's parents? I would. I briefly considered becoming an EMT, but I found I have an aversion to blood."

"Well, looks like you did get that chance to be there for someone, Luce."

"Maybe, but it was for selfish reasons you know."

Molly smiled knowingly and gave Luce a quick hug. "I know."

~

HE WAS ASLEEP. Of course he was. He'd been asleep the first time she'd come with his parents. And again a few hours later. This was her third attempt. Clearly the universe was conspiring against her. Well, she'd just stay until they kicked her out. She sat and simply watched him sleep. His broad chest rose and fell steadily. Her eyes took in the tufts of blond hair poking out of the gauze wrapped around his head. The minor scrapes along his jaw where he'd hit the ground. She swallowed hard, trying to remain composed.

"I'm sorry, I'm afraid we'll need some privacy." The nurse was polite, but he was clear in his meaning. Time to go. Luce nodded, and stood.

"Ok, I'll come back later," she murmured under a sigh. Turning to go, she stopped at the sound of his voice.

"Luce?"

No way she was leaving now. Her heart was beating a mile a minute as she turned back to him.

"I'm so sorry. I'm so so sorry." Her voice broke as she sobbed uncontrollably. The dam bursting at the sound of his voice.

"Sorry. OK. Next time, could you not…" his voice tapered off.

"What? Not what?" Luce whispered as she anxiously leaned closer to hear him.

"Not… bash me… with pipe… leave me for dead?"

"What, no, I didn't! Oh my god, I didn't!" Horrified, the tears gave way to anger. "How could you think that?"

He smiled crookedly, the sedatives apparently hard at work.

"Andrew Holman, that is not funny. Not at all." Luce turned to see Molly in the doorway, and sighed with relief. Her smile meant he was joking, assurance he was going to be ok.

"OK, folks, I'm going to need some privacy for a few minutes and then we're going to move your comedian friend here to a room downstairs. He's been cleared to leave the ICU."

Luce sighed but did what was asked, leaning over to give a now sleeping Andy a quick kiss on the cheek before accompanying Molly down the hall and into the elevator.

"Listen, Luce, you've been here for over 48 hours. You've barely eaten, barely slept. Why don't you go back to your sister's and get some rest, a shower, a decent cup of coffee?" Molly took Luce's hand and patted it. "Gil will drive you. I'll stay here and see that Andy gets settled in."

"I don't want to leave, Molly. I can't explain it, but I feel like I need to stay."

"No sweetie, you don't. You're no good to him if you don't take care of yourself. And believe me, he's going to need all of us at full strength when he gets out of here."

There was no use arguing, so Luce took the offer allowing Gil to drop her at Annie's. Maybe they were right. Maybe she did need some downtime. There was just so much to sort through, but her mind wouldn't let her focus on anything other than Andy. The scene she'd witnessed. It was burned in her mind.

She may have reacted quickly, sure, but now the adrenaline was gone. All that was left was the memory of the numbing fear that almost paralyzed her. The image of blood pooled around his head. The sound of his shallow breathing. The silent prayers she sent up begging not to take him just yet.

She'd fought so hard to keep him at arm's length, for so long, she knew somewhere in the universe the gods must be looking after her to give her one more chance. One she was determined to make the most of.

## CHAPTER THIRTY-SEVEN

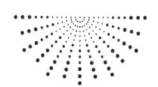

"What's this?"

Stuart looked up at Luce, his brows crinkled, scowling.

"My resignation, Stuart. I fucked up. Big time. Broke the rules, and was careless. This is all on me. If he were anyone else he'd be suing our asses. I take full responsibility."

"Good. You should. But it doesn't get you off the hook."

Luce bit her lip, knowing this could get a lot uglier than she'd thought. If the station owners wanted to, they could make it so she'd never work again. At least in Broadcast. Or Cable. Probably not even Satellite.

"I understand. I'll go ahead and clear my desk, but I'd appreciate it if you'd at least consider keeping my intern for the rest of the summer. This isn't on her."

"Luce, sit down. Please."

Luce took a seat, and waited for the other shoe to drop. She'd only come in today because Andy was being brought home, and settled in and everyone was busy getting back to their lives. Except her.

"Did they get the guy?" Stuart's question was matter-of-fact.

"No, not yet."

"Good, you find him, you get the exclusive, our ratings will be through the roof." Stuart leaned back in his chair and nodded as if it was all obvious.

"But nobody knows about that part of it, heck we haven't even produced the first episode."

"You saved a life, Luce, and possibly solved a mystery. Now go find the detective's attacker, and it's golden. Make it work." Stuart nodded toward the door. "Now go, I've got work to do."

~

"Kat, that's a brilliant idea!" Luce jumped up off the sofa in The Holman's living room and started pacing. "We'll have a war room there, film it all as we dig into this. We'll interview everyone who attended both the barbecue, and the opening night dinner." She looked over at Molly who'd been listening, a bemused expression on her face. "If that's OK with you and Gil, of course," she added.

Molly laughed, and shook her head. "Anything to get him out of our hair and back into the world again. That boy is driving me crazy."

Kat smiled, satisfied that everything was working out and grateful to be included in this discussion at all. She had thought it was all over as well, and when Luce texted her to get back to work she was over the moon. And she immediately thought about using her Uncle's clubhouse as their headquarters for the project.

"I have an idea, Luce, since Kat is going to stay here with us, why don't you stay here as well."

"I couldn't impose, Molly, though thanks for the offer. Annie has plenty of room," Luce replied.

"Don't I get a say in any of this?"

They all looked over in surprise as Andy joined them, hobbling in on his crutches, excruciatingly slowly. Luce immediately went over to help him.

"What are you doing up? They said bed rest for the first week. You have to heal." Luce sighed in exasperation.

"I'm a grown ass man and I know my limits," Andy mumbled, causing Luce to scowl.

"Fine!" She stomped back over to the couch and sat down, arms crossed. "It's your leg. Your life. Whatever." Luce looked over at Molly then for support. "Is he always like this?"

"24/7 Luce, I'm afraid he's not a good patient."

"Not surprised. I think I'll stay at Annie's for sure."

"No, you'll stay here." Andy had finally made it over to the recliner and realizing he couldn't reach the lever to lift the foot rest, just stood leaning on his crutches. "Some help over here, please?" He looked at Luce, brows raised.

"Seriously? Mr. Grown Ass Man now wants help?" Luce huffed out.

"Please?" It was his smirk that did it. It lit up his whole face.

Sighing, Luce got up and went to help, grumbling the whole time. Once she had him settled in the chair, he reached up and pulled her down.

"Thanks," he whispered, leaning in to kiss her. Pulling back, she shook her head, trying to hide her smile. She couldn't deny the chemistry. Or the fact that even in his current state he was irresistible.

"So it's settled, then, right?" Andy looked around grinning. "Luce can stay up in the room next to mine. You know, just in case I need something."

"I'm not a nursemaid, Andy," Luce frowned.

"Trust me Luce, that much I know." He wiggled his eyebrows then, and Luce realized she'd been set up.

Again.

∼

Luce had to admit, the cottage was ideal for their needs. They'd converted the sitting area into an interview set, and it was perfect. The large game table was a good place to gather around for brainstorming. Now all they needed, she thought looking about the room, were answers.

"Who's on tap this morning, Kat?"

"Rodney Court and his wife, then Jackson and Cherise Tulley." Kat tried to keep her tone impartial, though she knew Luce was going to throw out a dig.

"Oh yay, slut time."

"Luce, really. She's not all that bad. She's kind of nice." Kat was trying not to laugh. She'd actually spent a little time with Cherise at the 4th of July party and found her to be friendly. She even admitted to having a bit too much to drink that first night.

"You know her boyfriend had dumped her that day. She was just letting loose."

"Really?" Luce wondered if Cherise were just playing to Kat's sympathies.

"Yeah, he told her he only went out with her because her brother was famous."

Luce sighed. She'd been quick to judge, and that wasn't like her. Well it was, but she'd been trying to lose that habit.

"Ok, I'll be nice," Luce smiled at Kat. "I'll give her a chance but if she goes anywhere near your Uncle..."

Kat laughed out loud. "I know, all bets are off."

Luce looked over and grinned, just as her phone buzzed. "Well well, look who it is," she murmured, seeing the text pop up. She laughed seeing the newly edited contact name.

*Grown Ass Man: What time are you starting? I need help getting over there.*

*10 am. And your dad built you a ramp. You'll be fine.*

*I have something for you.*

She smiled at his obvious innuendo and fired off a quick retort.

*I'll bet you do.*

*You owe me though.*

She had no idea what he meant by that. But knowing Andy, he was trying to rile her up.

"I think your uncle is overmedicating," Luce smirked, letting Kat know she was kidding. "Oh now what," she muttered, as the phone buzzed again.

"Holy shit, Kat," she looked up from her phone, shock on her face.

"What? Please don't keep me in suspense!"

"It's from Annie. She said Mark called, Jen just got a query on a manuscript. For a book on the MorningStar."

"What the fuck?" Kat swore loudly.

"Yeah. They all signed NDA's, right?"

"Absolutely Luce. I had everyone sign. Anything discovered during filming was the property of the station and can't be disclosed to anyone."

"Why do I feel like whoever is pitching this book has something to do with the attack on Andy?" Luce wondered aloud. "Whatever he found, they wanted to silence him. So they could profit."

"You're right. If they were to discover it, after the show was suspended, the NDA wouldn't apply, would it?" Kat didn't know enough about contracts. Clearly there was a loophole.

"Andy is still in danger," Luce murmured, biting her lip. A shiver went through her at the thought.

"We all are." The women both looked up to see Andy in the doorway, leaning on his crutches and scowling.

"Chris texted me. We've got work to do."

## CHAPTER THIRTY-EIGHT

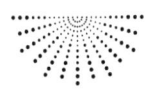

Andy looked around the table. They'd postponed all interviews until the next day and everyone had gathered at the cottage. Mark and Julie, Chris and Annie, Jen and Bill, along with himself and Luce. *The gang of 8* back together again he mused. Kat was over at the house, collecting and uploading footage in the editing bay they'd hastily re-set up.

"Once Kat gets here with the jump drive, we'll play it back on the TV and see if we can detect anything out of the ordinary." Andy was in full-on detective mode.

"If I might suggest something?" Chris leaned in and pointed to the map Luce had printed out. "Andy, you've got a camera posted outside this place right? According to this map, the other entrance to the tunnels, is right about," he waved hands around, "here!"

Andy smacked the table with his hand. "God damnit, how could I miss that? Stupid meds. Yeah, right above the entryway, on the side eaves, and the back patio."

"You have security cameras for your clubhouse?" Luce tried not to laugh. "Isn't that over the top?"

"Maybe, but we had a break-in a few years ago. It made my mom feel better," Andy mused. "And it sure is coming in handy now, isn't it?" He picked his phone up off the table, then thinking better of it, put it down. "Too small. Luce, grab my laptop will you? Over there by the door."

Luce didn't move, just pursed her lips and glared.

"Let me rephrase that. Luce, my darling, would you be so kind as to *please* grab my laptop?" Andy grinned and winked.

"Better, Detective." Luce shook her head as she headed over and unzipped the bag, grabbed the laptop and brought it to him, laying it on the table. Placing one hand on his shoulder, she leaned in and kissed his cheek softly, then whispered. "You're a fast learner." Sitting back down, she smiled at him, reassuring him that all was well. The last few days, while hectic, had also helped her make a decision. They'd yet to cross that line into a relationship, but Luce was hopeful it would happen. And this time, she was ready.

Andy quickly pulled up the app with the footage they needed. Thankfully it had been a clear night, but even so, it wasn't exactly high resolution. With a few clicks, he had it playing back on the flat screen TV so they could all watch. They ran through the first clip with no signs of anything. The second had only a few scurrying animals. Putting the third on, Andy sighed.

"Last one," he said as it flashed on the screen. They watched for a few minutes, the atmosphere in the room became frustrated.

"Stop it there, would ya?" Bill called out suddenly. "There. See it? Left corner."

"Son of a bitch," Andy swore softly. "No way we can see who, but there is someone there for sure."

"Forward it to me. I have a friend. Might be able to work some magic."

Everyone sat silent for a moment, watching the interchange between Andy and Bill. Luce especially. Who would Bill, the guy who seemed to be everyone's handyman, know that could help in a criminal investigation? Though of course it wasn't an official investigation, as Andy was on medical leave and all of them had been instructed to leave it to local law enforcement.

"What?" Bill looked around. "I have friends, ya know." He grinned then, sitting back and returning everyone's look of astonishment. The only one not appearing to be surprised was Jen. Luce tucked that away. She'd have some questions for her friend later.

∼

"Thank you Mr. Court, I appreciate your time." Luce nodded to the historian as he stood to leave.

She watched as he slowly made his way to the door. "Say hello to your wife for me," she added as he stepped out the door.

She sighed and leaned back. It was the last interview of the day. Andy and Kat had stayed up in the main house, sitting through each one, listening and watching through a feed that Bill had somehow managed to have set up. They'd compiled a list of questions, designed to figure out if any of the dinner guests had more knowledge of the ghost ship than they'd let on. Designed, Luce thought, to trick them. But so far she didn't think they'd been successful. They'd have to review each conversation. Closing her eyes, she tried to clear her head, and almost succeeded until a knock interrupted her meditative state.

The door opened before she could respond.

"Just me, Luce. Everyone gone?" Andy's voice was quiet, thankfully.

"Yes." Luce nodded. "Come sit, get off your feet, would you?" The last thing she needed was Andy in pain. He was grumpy enough.

"I'm afraid I didn't get much today." She said, as she got up and, taking his crutches, helped situate him on the couch, lengthwise, his leg resting on a throw pillow.

"Here, there's plenty of room," he said, pulling her down to sit next to him. Keeping one arm around her, he pulled her back so she was reclining with him, leaning back into his chest.

They sat that way for a few minutes, neither saying a word. She could feel his heartbeat thumping steadily, keeping her in an odd state of nervous relaxation. She felt connected in a way she never thought possible. Luce's mind drifted back to that night. And the sudden recollection of what happened before the chaos.

"Andy, I have to tell you what I learned. In all that's happened, I didn't get a chance to tell you. You know, what I wanted to tell you. The reason I went to look for you that night."

The words tumbled out of her mouth, but she was feeling so calm she didn't move. Just continued to talk.

"I found the secret to the MorningStar. At least I think I did." Luce paused.

"Tell me,"Andy murmured quietly.

Luce began by explaining what she'd read in the journal, and the image of the map, and how she'd found him. It was at least a half hour later when she stopped, and tipped her head to look at him. His eyes were closed, a small smile on his face.

"Are you even listening?" She asked, wondering if she'd been talking to herself all that time.

"Sorry, you were saying?" He asked, his smile broadening.

"Andy!" She cried in exasperation. "I am not repeating all of that."

"No need, Luce, I heard it all." Andy opened one eye and peered at her. "I think we've solved the mystery."

Lifting his head and leaning in, he tightened his arms around her as his lips crashed into hers. This time, his kiss wasn't tentative or sweet, it was as if it consumed him. Luce reacted the only way she could, by returning it with as much fervency and heat as she could, then pulling back quickly.

"You're not cleared for landing yet, are you?" Luce whispered, watching his face go from fierce to frustrated. "No. But soon, so hold that thought," he smiled then, and relaxed his hold. She laid her head back down on his chest and waited for their racing hearts to slow down. It was several minutes later she felt him tense back up.

"Luce?"

"Yeah," she murmured.

"I know who attacked me. Time to gather the troops. Let's wrap this up."

## CHAPTER THIRTY-NINE

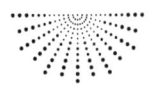

"Who? I'm not calling a single soul if you don't tell me instantly!" Luce was still stunned that Andy had figured it out.

"No can do."

"Excuuuse me?"

"Luce, we don't have evidence. We're going to need to lay a trap."

"And I'm happy to help if you tell me who we're trapping."

"See that's the thing. We need everyone to be taken by surprise. This is how we'll catch them."

"Them? So, it's more than one?"

"We'll have to wait and see."

"I have a great poker face, just so you know."

"Yeah, the one you've been using to ward me off." Andy smiled broadly. "Didn't work, though, did it," he whispered, leaning in for a kiss that was sure to silence her.

"There. That'll hold you. Now gather the troops, would ya?"

"What about the police? Don't you have to call them too? Isn't it part of your code?"

"No, not yet. We don't have enough for them to even issue a traffic ticket. We need to have some pretty solid stuff. Ergo, we set a trap."

"So, it's decided, then." Andy looked around the table, waiting for them all to agree. "Questions?"

"Just one bud," Bill spoke first. "How the hell did you figure it out?"

"Well, actually, Luce did."

"Me? I still haven't figured it out," Luce looked at him scowling. "Since you refused to tell me," she added with huff.

Andy smiled then. "All in good time, love, all in good time."

The group seated around the table grew quiet as they turned to stare at Andy, then Luce. *Love?*

"Is there something we all missed?" Annie chuckled out loud. "Last I knew you were still known as Satan's Spawn in her contacts."

Luce frowned at Annie, glaring at her. "Don't you dare," she hissed.

"Satan's Spawn?" Andy tipped his head back and laughed.

"That was a long time ago," Luce muttered.

"Really. What's it say now?" he reached over and grabbed her phone. Unlocked it with a few swipes.

"Hey! How did you get in there?" Luce demanded.

"Really?" Andy shook his head and laughed.

"Grown Ass Man? I don't think so."

With a few taps, and a roar of laughter, he handed her phone back.

"Okay! Any more questions before we get to planning?"

Luce looked down at her phone and felt the flush creep up her face. But she couldn't prevent the smile that broke out either. They'd have much to talk about later, she realized.

"I know you won't tell us who, but can you tell us why you think you were attacked?" Jen asked.

"I think whoever did this was trying to sabotage the show."

"But why?" Mark wondered. "Why would someone *not* want you to solve the mystery?"

"Money," Chris offered. "It's always about money. Maybe there's a treasure buried beneath the sand…."

"Shame. Maybe somebody really doesn't want the truth to come out."

Kat spoke quietly. "Or what they think is the truth. I mean, we're the only ones that know the true story at this point."

"Maybe not, you know I've requested the full manuscript from that mysterious query I got," Jen added. "That might tell us everything too."

"True, it could be someone outside of the show. Or, maybe it's one of the Bowers." Luce pursed her lips in thought. "Protecting the family. Not wanting anyone to discover what they think are nasty secrets."

"I promise, you'll all know soon enough. I'm going to meet with the local PD. Now that we've got a plan, we'll need them on standby." Andy leaned back and relaxed. "We need to set this up precisely as it was the first night. Invite everyone back for the finale. Only this time, we'll have one thing out of sync. The centerpiece will be a model of the Morning-Star, just like before, only this time an exact replica. Where the truth will be clearly on display."

"Do we have everything we need in place?" Bill asked.

"Yeah, you, Jen, Mark and Julie can all hang here and watch as it all goes down," Andy replied. "I know you'd rather be in the room, but we've got to keep this looking legit."

"How will we do that?" Mark asked curiously.

Andy looked at Bill and nodded.

"We posted a few more cameras. The feed will run right into the TV in here," Bill explained. Again, as before when Bill mentioned his *friend* who could help them out, they all looked at him curiously. His only reaction was to shrug and chuckle.

∼

THE NEXT FEW days went by in a whirlwind of activity. Persuading Mrs. Bowers to host another dinner was in fact a challenge. Surprisingly, it was Lionel who convinced her to go along with it. Peabody seemed to be quite annoyed but Kat was able to smooth his feathers a bit. Luce had to admit that Kat and Lionel made a pretty good team.

Andy was recovering well, and the more able he was to move around, the more control he began to take of the situation. Leaving Luce to step into the background once again. They'd hadn't had much time together with all the commotion of shooting a finale and catching a suspect, and as it all came to a head, Luce was more than ready for it all to be over. She had relocated, staying with Chris and Annie and hadn't slept in days. Everyone had agreed that it would be best not to let whoever was behind all this know how close she was to Andy. Her mind flitting from one topic to another like a speeding train. Who attacked Andy? Would they catch them? Would they get it all on film? Would she finally achieve the success she'd worked so hard for? Would she finally get the guy she'd lost her heart to?

Slipping downstairs and out to the patio with a trashy novel and a glass of wine, Luce sat down and watched the waves lap at the shore and wondered just where life would take her next. She heard the door slide open and turned to see Annie approach carrying a plate.

Luce smiled. "Late night snack?"

"Hey, you have your wine, I have my chocolate chip pecan blondies," Annie laughed as she plopped into the chair next to Luce.

"As long as you're not dipping the corn chips in the butter sauce again, we're good."

"Corn, butter. What's the problem?"

Luce laughed and shook her head. "Annie, you're my sister and I love you and I'm thrilled I'm going to be an aunt. But your eating habits lately are just too much."

"Well, I came out here because you've been quite frazzled lately, and you're not the frazzled type. What's going on in that head of yours?"

"What's *not* going on? I mean yeah, the show, the mystery, all of that. I need to get my act together but that's not it. I'm terrified Annie. He almost died. Now I know how Chris felt last summer when you were run off the road. I mean I was terrified for you, and traumatized, but I'm your sister. Chris? He was literally shattered. And I wondered then, what that's like to have someone love you that deeply." Luce sighed and looked out across the water.

"You don't need to wonder anymore, do you?" Annie said quietly.

"If what I feel for Andy is any indication? No, I don't." Luce whispered now.

"Take it as it comes, Luce. Just don't wait like we did. Don't make the same mistakes Chris and I did."

"No, I won't. I promise you that."

"What are you reading anyway?" Annie leaned over to read the cover. "Hot Detectives on Ice? Wow you're dipping into the bottom of the barrel there aren't you?"

"Nope! I'm learning how to seduce one stubborn alpha male. There are some pretty good tips in here."

Grabbing the book, Annie examined the cover. "You're going to dress like a hooker on ice?"

Luce wiggled her eyebrows and laughed. "Chapter three. I'm going to dress like frozen hot chocolate! With extra whipped cream."

## CHAPTER FORTY

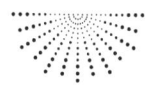

"Stuart? What are you doing here? I mean obviously you're welcome to be here, but it's unexpected." Luce turned to her boss, a questioning look on her face. He wasn't known to go on location unless it was due to a presidential visit or the Queen of England was in town.

"You think I'd miss this?" Stuart smiled. "We're doing something important here Luce. And yeah, we're going to open up some pretty large and gaping wounds in our history, but the rewards justify it. And it's all thanks to you," Stuart placed an arm around Luce's shoulder and gave it a squeeze. "I gave you an impossible task Luce and you rose magnificently to the challenge."

"I appreciate that, you know I do. I am worried about those wounds though. Andy won't tell me who the suspect is, but clearly someone feels victimized by what we're doing." Luce chewed on her bottom lip, suddenly struck by a thought.

"Stuart, do you think when we wrap this up, we could do a follow-up? Take what we've learned, bring in some influential people to talk about it?"

"I think that's brilliant. Let's talk about it next week. In fact, I've got some documents from my grandmother, you know my great great grandfather was born in the south, as a slave..."

Luce inhaled sharply. "You never mentioned that, this whole time!"

"No, because I didn't want my story to interfere with yours. Objectivity is key, Luce, you know that. If there were any correlation I would have mentioned it. At the time, I didn't think it was relevant to the mystery ship. Now I'm not so sure. But first things first, let's get this wrapped up," he said, patting her shoulder once more. He then headed off to take a seat and watch the taping from a safe distance.

Luce exhaled the breath she'd been holding. She knew Stuart had a keen interest in the story, and rightly so. As a prominent Black journalist he'd risen in the ranks at the network. He'd mentored her now for several years. And in all that time, she'd never considered his roots. His genealogy. His family. This story had taken so many turns on her, but ultimately, it was the way in which she was faced with her own story that was a wake-up call. Annie hadn't located their father's research yet, but as they came closer to the end of this journey, Luce had a strange feeling that their family history was entwined in all of this, too. That was still the final missing piece for her. And the reason for requesting the follow-up.

∽

"GOOD EVENING. Welcome to what we believe will be the final Ghost Ship dinner. I'm so glad you all could join me. It is my sincere hope that tonight will be the night we finally solve this centuries-old mystery." She paused for a moment, letting the silence permeate the room before continuing. "I'd like for us to share a lovely meal, then we can all retire to the library, where our fearless leader, Detective Holman, will share with us all what he's learned."

In full aristocratic mode, Adeline Bowers stood at the head of the table, looking at each guest, one at a time, assessing them. Luce cued Jamie to make sure he panned out and caught everyone's expressions. She was in fine form, Luce thought. So different from the Adeline she'd met that day when they'd had their private chat.

Thankfully, Cherise was careful to keep her hands off Andy, Luce thought. Jackson and Lionel were more subdued, she noted. And Rodney looked as ghostly as ever. In fact, she wondered what was causing him to twitch nervously. She had Jamie focus on him for a minute. There was something odd there she thought.

Most of the participants had not been told the details of Andy's injuries, only that he'd had an accident that had suspended filming for several weeks. So much of the chatter during dinner was Andy warding off questions about his injuries, focusing on how well he was doing rather than how it had happened.

He did give them just enough to keep it interesting. Said he'd gotten lost in the tunnels and tried to climb out of the chamber and had fallen. Quite plausible. He actually made a joke out of the fact that he'd totally forgotten to bring his phone with him. He still hadn't sufficiently explained that one to Luce. Who goes exploring without their phone?

When it was time to move to the library, Peabody removed the centerpiece carefully, carrying it with him as he led the guests out of the room. Luce paid careful attention to which guests seemed to notice the curious action. Cherise and Jackson certainly raised an eyebrow. Lionel paid little attention. Rodney seemed to be looking down though his wife glanced about a time or two. Nothing significant, Luce thought, but she took note of it.

Peabody placed the model ship centerpiece on the mantel for all to see, while Andy took the chair that had been placed in front of it, as standing was still painful for him.

Everyone else took their places, seating themselves around the large table in the center. When everyone was settled in, Luce signaled Andy to begin.

"Well, my friends, here we are back again at the Estate of Adeline Bowers. It's been an exciting summer of discoveries for all of us. With a dose of adventure and not just a small bit of mystery. Our purpose was to solve the mystery of the Execution Rocks Ghost Ship. And I'm pleased to say, mission accomplished."

A soft murmur went about the room, as nobody had been informed of the success of the show. Not everything would need to be said at this point, as the plan was to insert clips from the opening episode to fill in for viewers who had missed it.

"Every few years, around June 10$^{th}$, many claim to see an old schooner sailing around the lighthouse in the middle of the Long Island Sound. The lighthouse built upon an island known as Execution Rocks."

"There are many theories," Andy went on, "but there were three that intrigued us most. The boat crashed against the rocks in the dark of night during a storm. According to sold weather records, certainly a summer storm could have blown them off course. Perhaps it was a British ship carrying prisoners of war, as they were known to leave them out on the deserted island to die. Or it was a slave ship, delivering its human cargo to a New York drop off."

Andy paused and looked at each guest, registering their expressions.

"It's said that Execution Rocks was also the site of many a bootlegger's mishaps during prohibition. There's no shortage of myths and legends surrounding that little island. But regrettably, all signs seemed to indicate the MorningStar was in fact, a Slave Ship."

"But this was Yankee territory," Jackson commented, a bit defensively Luce thought. "People around here didn't have slaves."

"I'm afraid you are quite wrong, young man," Rodney huffed out. "Of course they did. Servitude did not limit itself to the southern colonies. In fact, several landowners right here in Port Newton were known to keep slaves, some were quite abusive in fact." He looked over at Adeline then, practically sneering. Luce sensed some serious animosity emanating from him. The question was why.

Andy went on to detail how the clues all led him to that simple conclusion, then as everyone nodded in agreement, he suddenly nodded over at Jamie, who turned the camera on Luce.

Luce frowned and shook her head. Slicing her hand across her neck, the universal symbol for *stop filming right now*, Andy smiled at her instead, and started talking once more.

"Our producer had other ideas though. You see the secret lay in the ship's log, where she discovered the truth."

Luce tried to remain relaxed though she wanted to crawl out of her skin. She hadn't been on camera in a long time, and she wasn't ready. She breathed a sigh of relief as Jamie swung the camera back to Andy.

"The MorningStar was not a slave trader's ship at all. In fact, it was just the opposite. The MorningStar freed hundreds if not thousands of men, women and children using the maritime route of the underground railroad. You see Lionel Bowers was an abolitionist."

## CHAPTER FORTY-ONE

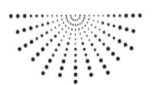

They all sat in stunned silence. This quite possibly was the most unexpected news any of them could have imagined. Except Luce. She'd discovered it the night Andy was attacked.

"But the underground railroad didn't exist then, did it?" Cherise leaned forward, curious. Didn't the ship sink in the late 1700s?"

"There was a ship, and it did sink in 1790, and it was reported to be the MorningStar. Yes." Andy waited a moment, looking around, making sure everyone was paying attention. "But the ship log that Ms. Porter discovered? It was from the mid-1800s." Luce was in awe. Andy had convinced Luce to edit out the footage of the journal's discovery, he said he had an idea. Luce had agreed, but never imagined he'd drag her into it. Letting the world know who really found it.

"So not the MorningStar?" Adeline breathed out slowly.

"Yes, the MorningStar." Andy smiled at her, reassuringly. "You see Lionel Bowers, your ancestor? He built two ships, and sank one."

"Deliberately?" Lionel jumped in. "You mean it was a ruse?"

"Yes. According to the map and journal, the MorningStar couldn't have gone down, but according to all public records, including the national registry, it did. For years, whenever it was spotted, which was rarely, it was deemed a ghost ship."

"But sightings of it continue to this day," Adeline insisted. "How do you explain that? What eventually happened to it?"

"I think some mysteries are better left unexplained, don't you?" Peabody spoke up for the first time.

"Perhaps, Mr. Peabody, you're right," Andy responded. "But there is so much more to this story. If I may continue. My own ancestor, to my dismay, appears by all accounts to have been a slave owner. I can't change that nor can I understand it. The slave in question was also my ancestor. I've yet to find her name recorded anywhere. And I've known about her for a long time."

"How do you know? If there's no record with her name, I mean?" Annie was curious about that.

"Family history, a little DNA," Andy offered. "But there's more to this. I myself have seen the ghost ship."

He let that sink in before going on.

"I believe I have seen it because it relates to me. The ship's log may in fact prove that. Because it details how a sailor named Holman abandoned ship along with a female during a massive storm. I believe they were my ancestors. Whether Edward Holman knew that the slaves were on their way to freedom I can't say. Whether he wanted to save her or own her, I'll never know."

"I'm afraid your theory has far too many discrepancies, detective. In fact, the MorningStar was indeed a slave ship, built by Lionel Bowers," he sneered with disdain as he said it. "If I may?" Rodney nodded to the center of the room, as if asking permission to speak.

"By all means, Mr. Court, proceed," Andy bit back a smile and nodded.

The historian suddenly shot up out of his chair, showing more energy than he'd had in months, and began pacing as he spoke.

"I've researched this extensively, as you know. In fact several publishers are after me for my work. So I can't reveal too much."

Luce eyes widened as she stifled a gasp. The pieces were rapidly falling into place.

Adeline interrupted then, and Luce cued Jamie to have his assistant close in on her as well.

"I believe we all signed contracts, my good sir, that you cannot divulge or discuss any of what is learned here. I don't believe anyone has given you permission to publish it." Her tone was angry. Betrayed even.

"Ah, but I am not publishing anything learned here at all, it's my own work, and it disproves everything you've all found. I've been at it for years! You can't stop me." Luce quietly snickered knowing all this was on film, and he was digging a very big hole for himself.

"What do you have that wasn't discovered during our time here?" Andy asked, his voice relaxed, inquisitive.

"The Bowers have owned this community for far too long. They've wielded their money and power around, all built on the backs of slaves. And when there were no slaves to be had? They imported fresh labor. Taking advantage of those who came to find a better life."

"Go on, please," Andy said quietly.

Rodney's face was red now, and he was sputtering it all out. Andy clasped his hands behind his head, waiting for the other shoe to drop. Clearly there was an element of jealous rage over his own family history, but that wouldn't seal the deal.

"My own family came from Ireland you know. During the famine. They needed just a bit of money to get here. Took an advance on working for Bowers shipping company. Ended up working it off the rest of their lives. I have proof."

"What kind of proof?"

"Letters. Documents. And no, you won't be getting your hands on any of it. Your family is just as bad, isn't it *detective?* Those tunnels connect to your property too. The slaves were led off the ship, into the tunnels and then dispersed to the various homes along the shore. In total secrecy. Well, the secret's out."

Suddenly he barked out a laugh and pointed a finger at Andy.

"And if you hadn't been so careless in your tunnel exploration, you would have known there was an exit from the chamber leading right to it. You didn't need to try to climb out at all. Could have saved yourself the trouble."

And there it was, Luce thought. He couldn't have known which chamber Andy had been found in. He shouldn't have known there was a second chamber until tonight.

It was only seconds later that the uniformed officers burst into the library taking Mr. Court into custody. They'd been waiting, she realized, for him to place the proverbial nail in his own coffin. His knowledge of the tunnel system, and his knowledge of how to get in and out of the secret chamber was enough. The big question remained why? But there would be plenty of time to sort out his motive later. The chaos was far from over. There would be witness interviews for all of them, again, and then turning in all their treasures as well, as evidence. But right at that moment, all Luce wanted to do was crawl into a safe space and clear her head.

∼

"Luce?"

Luce turned to see Adeline approaching her, a warm smile on her face.

"I want to thank you. I cannot tell you what it means to know the truth behind The MorningStar. Someday you and your detective can share with me how you figured it all out. It seems awfully complex. But knowing my life wasn't built on the backs of slaves is a monumental relief. At the same time, I realize I haven't done enough to continue the work my ancestor's started, if that makes sense."

"How so, Adeline?" Luce took the hand Adeline was holding out, and led her to the sofa nearby, where they sat for a while.

"The thought that my family, our wealth, our status, was derived from such evil has haunted me. Knowing it didn't isn't enough. Besides investigating the Ghost Ship, what have I done to contribute as Lionel Bowers did?"

"You participated in the movement to give equal rights to all. You were an advocate for change, Adeline. You didn't sit back and accept things. That's something right there."

"Kat told me about her first meeting with you," Adeline said suddenly. "How you immediately jumped to fix the door. You didn't just voice your displeasure to support her, you acted. For years, I've simply voiced my support. Written checks and tried to stay out of the limelight."

"You were protecting your son, shielding him."

"Maybe. But I'm an old lady now, nobody needs that kind of protection. I want this show to make a difference. I want to use it as a call to action. I don't want viewers to think just because their hands are clean, that they can turn away from injustice. There's plenty of it now to be dealt with, too much to be done. I want to be a part of it."

"I agree. There is still an unanswered question, Adeline. Why me? Why did I see the ship all those years ago? Annie never did. It can't relate to our family. It has to be something else."

Adeline smiled at Luce then, and looked over at Andy, deep in conversation with one of the local detectives.

"I think your answer is sitting right there."

## CHAPTER FORTY-TWO

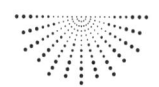

"How did the ship, the original MorningStar or its decoy, go down?" Chris posed the question out loud. "I mean if Lionel Bowers sunk his own ship, how did he accomplish it without being caught?"

Andy glanced at Luce, who'd been quiet for the last few minutes. They'd yet to tell anyone about the explosion they'd seen. That they'd mysteriously shared a vision and ended up face down in the sand.

"Probably set off some explosion of some sort, and I'm guessing nobody was aboard." Andy tossed out whatever he could on that. This was still his and Luce's secret.

"Last question for a while, then I'll stop," Chris said, leaning forward in his chair. "Now that everyone else is gone, tell us. How did you figure out they were hiding slaves and not selling them?"

Andy looked over at Luce, who was curled up on the window seat. "I didn't, Luce did."

Hearing her name, Luce looked up. She was exhausted. The local police had been coming and going like worker ants. Everything seemed to be a crime scene. The Bowers Estate. The Holman's. The entire stretch of beach front in between. Now that they'd cleared out, everyone had settled in comfortably, discussing all they'd learned.

"Tell them Luce, how you figured it out." Andy grinned knowing she'd prefer to let him tell it.

Luce smiled back, wondering how she'd finally found a guy who could let her shine without feeling like it diminished him. He'd given her all the credit, and some she didn't even deserve. She pointed to the ship on the mantle, the one that had been used as a centerpiece.

"I was studying the map. The Log entries. The drawing of the ship. And I realized that if I closed my eyes and imagined the ship, there weren't cannons jutting out from the lower deck. When I looked closely at the drawing, and at the model? There were no cannons. There were people. At first, I cringed, thinking they were slaves being hauled off to be sold. The sheer inhumanity of it made me ill. But something kept bothering me. The arrows in the passageways. The notation in the log that said *Liberty for all, leave one.*"

"According to the notes in the log, Holman absconded with one female." Chris got up and began pacing. "Which meant if they were carrying slaves, then all were freed, leave one. Holman took her, and then the ship anchored, led their passengers to the tunnels, where the arrows led them to freedom."

Andy interjected then. "The arrows all pointed here. To Lionel Bowers' manor house. The other passageway led to Edward Holman's house." He sighed. "Take a right, go to heaven take a left.... "

"You don't know that, Andy. Maybe if we keep searching we'll find more answers." Luce got up, went to sit on the arm of Andy's chair, leaned in and in front of them all, kissed him softly. "You're a good man, detective. This doesn't change that."

"No, it certainly doesn't," Adeline chimed in. "Now it's late, and I think we ought to call it a night. I don't want anyone having to drive back to the city at this late hour, so anyone who needs to stay, Peabody will get you settled in."

∽

THE NEXT MONTH FLEW BY. While Andy recovered, Luce and Kat went to work producing the final cuts for all 6 episodes of what would be titled

Phantom of Execution Rocks. It would be billed as a reality/documentary series on the deeply held secrets of the gold coast of Long Island. Hopefully, if the ratings were good, it would continue to explore other secrets and legends of Long Island.

It was tedious work. Long hours, with no free time, which left Luce with little ability to help Annie with her wedding. Her big day — and Luce felt like an outsider.

Finally having a few minutes to spare, she put her feet up on her desk, and called.

The minute Annie answered, Luce broke down sobbing.

"Luce, please don't cry. Please. It's fine."

"No, it's not. It's your big day and it's two weeks away and I should be there with you right now making sure it all goes perfectly." The words sputtered out of her mouth. Very unlike her normally unruffled demeanor, and at that moment, she just didn't care.

"No, you shouldn't. Luce, it'll be a wonderful day I promise. But you know me. It's not about the day it's about me and Chris. I don't care if we get married in a corner deli, well, as long as there's cheesecake. You helped me pick the dress Luce. You took care of the invites. You approved the venue, though who wouldn't? You haven't slept in weeks, I know you. Now relax, it's all good."

Luce sighed. "But you're pregnant and exhausted."

"Chris is more than pitching in, Luce. Just relax. Though yes, I would love it if you could come out a few days early. But I know you've got to get things wrapped up on the show. Your whole career is riding on it. I get it."

"You know I'll be there early. That much I promise. Maybe we'll finish up sooner than expected. Kat's been amazing and the post-production team is zipping along."

"Knock knock?" Luce looked up to see Kat in the doorway. Grinning, as she obviously overheard.

"Hang on Annie, let me see what Kat needs."

"Stuart sent me to tell you that you're officially on vacation starting tomorrow." Kat announced.

"Wait, what? We've got a show to do!" Luce shook her head.

"He said we've got it covered, and you can work remotely as needed." Kat said, a bit emphatically.

"Luce that's fabulous!" Annie screamed into the phone. "Come to the house tomorrow. Bring everything, you're staying here until the wedding. No wait, bring more, you can house sit while we're on our honeymoon! This is awesome, see you tomorrow!" With that, Annie hung up, leaving Luce glancing between the phone and Kat, still sitting in the doorway grinning.

"What just happened?"

"You got your life back!" Kat looked smug.

"You did this, didn't you?"

"Maybe only a little, Luce, Stuart really does want you to take some time. Promise."

Something in her voice made Luce a bit suspicious, but it was too late to fix. Annie was ecstatic. And if Luce were being honest, she desperately wanted to do this. Truthfully, Luce was feeling left out. This was after all, All About Annie. Her big beautiful day. And Luce needed to be involved as much as she needed to breathe.

## CHAPTER FORTY-THREE

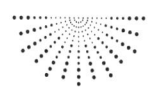

It was a perfect day for a wedding. Luce had to admit, Annie really had planned it perfectly. Even though it was a holiday weekend, she'd managed to book one of the most coveted venues around... a chartered schooner sunset cruise wedding. They would sail from a port on the south shore of the Island, and the ceremony would be held just as the sun started to set.

The private harbor had a small clubhouse, where cocktails would be served prior. Afterwards, dinner and dancing. It was a small wedding party, Luce and Jen, Andy and Mark. Julie and Bill were going to usher everyone to their seats. The guests were limited to close friends and family. No more than about fifty people. Annie was starting to show, her small baby bump barely visible under the beautiful chiffon gown she'd chosen.

As Luce buttoned what seemed like hundreds of tiny closures up the back, she smiled. "You know if you weren't sure I'd be here to do this, you probably would have gone with a pullover dress!"

"Maybe, but you're here and I knew you would be. You always have been. Now it's my turn to be there for you Luce." Annie smiled as she watched their reflection in the mirror. Luce was wearing an emerald green that complemented Annie's gown. "We need a selfie, quick."

"Buttons, then selfie Annie."

"OK. Seriously, Luce, you've been my rock, and now I'll be yours."

"Thanks Annie. I love you to pieces you know that, but you'll always be my baby sister. Can't help it."

"Well, turnabout is fair play, sis," Annie said with a wink.

∽

THE CAPTAIN STOOD at the helm of the ship, offering a spectacular backdrop sunset view. The bands of yellow, orange and red hovering above the horizon. He nodded as a cellist began the sweeping, melodic notes of a popular wedding canon.

Mark and Jen took the lead down the small aisle separating the few rows of white folding chairs laced with flowers and garland. Luce and Andy were next, taking their places. Luce watched as Annie began coming down the aisle alone, and her eyes immediately welled up with tears. She was as radiant and stunning as any bride, ever. The floor length gown with its subtle sheen and specks of gold in the champagne-colored fabric reflected the setting sun. The sweetheart neckline and empire waist allowed the material to flow creating the perfect silhouette.

Annie insisted that she could enter alone, though Luce thought she should have walked with her. So she let out a grateful sigh when Chris quickly left his spot next to the Captain and went back down the aisle to take Annie's arm and escort her. It was as perfect a moment as anyone could wish for, Luce thought. He couldn't bear for her to walk alone. Glancing at Andy, she found his eyes on her, a curious look on his face. Luce briefly wondered what he was thinking, but was soon focusing once again on Annie and Chris as they took their place under the floral archway. The Captain cleared his throat and began.

"Normally I'd give a little spiel about marriage, but Annie and Chris have chosen to recite their own personal vows, so Annie, if you'd like to begin?"

Annie gnawed her lip nervously. "Chris. I spent the last 24 hours agonizing over what to say and how to say it. I even thumbed through some of my favorite novels looking for the perfect phrase. Only there isn't one. Because nothing could be more perfect than you and I, here today, finally starting our lives together. You're my perfect. I loved you then, I love you now, and I'll love you for all our tomorrows." Slipping the simple gold band she'd chosen on his finger, she looked up and smiled softly, her eyes locking on his,

The Captain nodded at Chris.

Taking a breath, Chris smiled. "Annie. You've always been the one. The one who could fill my heart with joy. The one who could shatter it into a million pieces. The one meant for me and only me. The universe gave us another chance to get this right. And we will. I'm eternally yours. I too loved you then, I love you now, and will love you for all our tomorrows." Slipping the diamond and sapphire band he'd had designed for her on her finger, he reached over and wiped an errant tear from her cheek.

"Go on, kiss your bride, Chris," the Captain said, grinning as Chris hadn't waited at all. He'd scooped her into his arms, and dipping her back as if they were dancing, kissed her as if he were starving, not coming up for air until the captain tapped his shoulder.

Cheers rang out, muffled only slightly by the breeze and the flapping of the sails.

Luce hugged Annie tight, and reached out to hug her new brother equally tightly. "Take care of her, Chris."

"Always, Luce."

∼

DINNER WAS BUFFET STYLE, outdoors at the marina, followed by the customary champagne toasts, though it was cider for Annie, and then the traditional cake ritual. It was a small reception, intimate, yet as full of joy as any large wedding Luce had ever been to.

The small live band Annie had hired was perfect. Playing all the typical wedding favorites from different decades and genres of music. Something for everyone. When they hit the intro for everyone's favorite Al Green hit, Andy jumped up and looked down at Luce with a fire in his eyes she couldn't ignore.

"They're playing our song, Luce," Andy smiled and winked as he reached for her hand, pulling her into his embrace.

"Are you cleared to dance?" Luce asked, knowing it had been barely six weeks.

"In fact I am. Have I told you how stunning you look?" Andy stared at Luce earnestly.

"You have now, handsome," Luce fired back with a grin. "You wear a tux well."

They danced, swayed, and held onto each other for the rest of the night. Pausing only occasionally for another glass of champagne or to say hello to someone. The dance floor sparkled under the twinkling white lights dangling from the eaves and twined around the outdoor porch railing. It was magical, and Luce sighed as she breathed in the night air and rested her head against Andy's chest. This was a perfect night she thought to herself, smiling.

"Care to share," Andy whispered looking down at her upturned face.

"Nope." Her smile grew wide. "Some things are better left unsaid," she whispered back.

Finally, it was time for the Bride and Groom to leave. Luce knew eventually it would end this way, but she wasn't ready for it.

∾

ANNIE THREW her arms around Luce and squeezed as hard as she could. Pulling back slightly, she whispered in her ear.

"Sleep with him."

"What?" Luce pulled back and stared at her sister.

Annie laughed and leaned in to hug her again. "You and Andy are meant for each other and you've wasted enough time. Just go for it." Squeezing Luce once more, she stepped back and grinned, then held her hand out to Chris who'd been waiting a few steps away.

Watching them head to their Limo, Luce wiped a tear from her cheek and turned back to head inside, only to find Andy blocking her path.

He stepped toward her and grabbed her hand, pulling her in for a hug.

"They'll be back in a few weeks, Luce." He said softly, as he placed a hand behind her head pulling it to his chest, letting her rest it there while she regrouped.

He took a breath then, and plunged in.

"We're not going back to the way things were, Luce. You know that, right?" He said suddenly, pulling back a bit. Luce tipped her head up, bit her lip and nodded.

"All in?" Andy asked with a soft smile.

She smiled back, still nodding, another tear slipping down her cheek, which he gently brushed away.

"Starting now?" His voice was low, husky. When she nodded again, his eyes blazing, he swept her up in his arms, cradling her, and headed to the waiting car.

"Andy, your leg. This is a bad idea," Luce said, wriggling and pushing for him to let her go.

Setting her down, he took a breath. "Can't a guy have some fun?"

"I think there are other ways to have fun, detective, that won't involve you collapsing in a heap."

Taking her hand, he pulled her into his side. "We'll have to try those out then," he whispered.

"I'm game if you are," Luce laughed.

"You sure?" he asked, his tone a bit more serious.

"As I'll ever be." Luce whispered softly. But her smile said it all as he slid into the back of the waiting car next to her.

## CHAPTER FORTY-FOUR

"Maybe you can just have the driver drop me at Annie's?" Luce spoke softly, she'd woken up suddenly after falling asleep on the ride back with her head nestled on Andy's lap, his arm wrapped around her.

"I think that's doable," Andy replied, smiling. "Just need to stop at my folks' place and grab my things."

That got Luce's attention, and she quickly sat up and pulled away. "What are you saying, Detective?"

"Ah, back to detective now, are we." Andy laughed then. "Chris asked me to house sit while they're away."

"Annie asked me to house sit while they're away." Luce widened her eyes and then burst into laughter. "Did Chris tell you to take the Master?"

"I believe he did," Andy shook his head grinning. "Annie told you to take the Master, didn't she? I'm on board if you are, Luce," he said, almost defiantly. His eyes blazed, daring Luce to refuse.

Luce took a deep breath, her green eyes flaring just as brilliantly. "All in," she whispered.

They sat locked in the moment, as the car slowed to a stop.

"Come on, we'll get my stuff and take my car over so we have a ride."

Andy opened the door and took hold of Luce's hand to help her out. "You're parked at Annie's, right?"

Luce nodded as she carefully stepped out. "You sober?" She asked, brows raised.

"Yeah, I stopped drinking a few hours ago. One of us needed to maintain control," he grinned and winked.

"Oh I'm plenty in control, detective." She laughed.

They were at his parent's house, and Luce turned as the outside front lights suddenly came on and the door opened. She smiled as they approached the house, seeing Molly step outside in her Robe and fuzzy slippers. They had left the reception earlier, Gil claiming exhaustion from Molly's insistence they dance every dance.

"You two looked quite the pair out there tonight," Molly was grinning. "Come on, have a nightcap before heading out. Except you Andy, you have coffee. Luce, I want to show you something anyway."

Now that made Luce curious. She was tired, but could feel a second wind coming on. She followed Molly into an office just off the entry.

"Sit, please." Molly went over to the solid mahogany hutch in the corner and opened the door, retrieving a decanter and two glasses.

"What do we have there, Molly?" Luce grinned.

"A personal favorite, which I think you'll enjoy. Frangelico."

"Oh, the hazelnut liqueur? I love it!"

"See so much in common," Molly sighed. "We're going to get along famously."

Luce looked at her curiously but brushed it aside.

"I was talking to Annie at the reception tonight. And she told me how all of this local history you've dug up has made you both curious about your own family history. But she wasn't able to find your dad's research. I was discussing it with Gil on the way home, and I suddenly remembered something. Years ago, the historical society had a request for records from a historian up in Westchester somewhere."

"Wow, no kidding? You probably still don't have it I'm guessing." Luce tried not to sound too disappointed.

"That's where you're wrong. It was an email, and I still have that email address so I located it right away. His name was Stephen Porter."

"That's my dad."

"I thought as much, so I printed out the entire thread. Including the answers he was looking for. I've put it all together for you." Molly set her glass down and went over to the bookshelf and retrieved a large manila folder. Handing it to Luce, she smiled.

"I think this will answer some of your questions. Not all, but maybe it will give us all a starting point."

∼

THE PAIR RODE BACK to Chris and Annie's in relative silence. Both seemingly lost in thought. Andy, thinking toward his future. Luce toward her past. Both nervously contemplating the next move they would make.

Setting their bags down in the foyer, they turned to face each other. Andy reached over, tucking a strand of loose hair behind her ear, and brushed a finger softly down her cheek.

Taking her hand, he laid her palm against his chest, then raised his to lay against hers. "You feel that Luce? My heart racing? I feel yours." He paused. "This is right, Luce. Us. It's meant to be. Whatever happens, it's not just a hookup you can chalk up to wedding delirium."

Luce locked her gaze with Andy's and took a deep breath.

"You think I don't know that? I do."

He leaned down and kissed her, slowly and thoroughly. Then taking her hand, led her up the stairs toward the Master.

"Wait." Luce said quickly, causing him to stop suddenly.

"Is the house on fire?"

"Um, no," Luce giggled. She couldn't remember the last time she giggled.

"Did you leave your car lights on?"

"No."

"Wrong time of the month?"

"Definitely not."

Andy sighed dramatically.

"I don't think we should sleep in there." Luce whispered, as if it were a secret.

"I don't intend to do any sleeping, Luce." He raised a brow and smirked.

"I mean it's their room, you know? Where they..." Luce let her voice trail off.

"Say no more," Andy laughed loudly and swung around to head towards the guest rooms pulling her along. Since his was the first one they came to, that's the room he entered. Turning her to face him, he began walking forward, forcing her backwards until she felt herself bump up against the bed.

He looked down at her, his expression a bit pained. "Here's the thing, Luce, I'm just too old for this shit."

"What?" Luce stared at him, horrified. "You are so not backing out now."

"Not a chance. I'm just not waiting another moment." With that, he shook off his jacket, ripped off his tie and practically shoved her onto the bed, using his elbows to keep him from crushing her small frame.

"Now where were we," he said, lowering his head and crashing his lips into hers.

"Where's the zipper," he murmured, his hands wandering aimlessly.

"No. Zipper," Luce gasped. "There's a few little buttons on the back though."

"Ok then." He paused, took her hand, and flipped her so her back faced him.

Andy sat motionless, glaring at the long line of beadlike fasteners running down her back. "Are you kidding me?"

"Eh, no?" Luce tried not to laugh.

"Let's get one thing clear, Luce Skye Porter," he muttered. "No more buttons. Ever."

With that he began gnashing his teeth and grumbling as he unbuttoned every single round little bead on the back of her gown. It was agonizing, for both of them. When he'd finally undone the last one, he slowly pushed the gown off her shoulders, letting it drop. Turning her back around, he swore softly.

"Damn I'm glad I skipped dessert."

"Me too," Luce whispered.

"Detective?" Luce murmured softly as she stretched her arms above her head.

"Yeah, right here," Andy spoke from the doorway, where he stood holding two mugs. The sunlight streamed in, creating a halo around him.

"Coffee?"

"Uh huh. A little sweet, a little cream."

"How did you know?"

"I texted Kat," Andy laughed.

"Well points for that then. You can set it down though I'm not quite ready to get up. I think you gave me a hell of a workout last night. It's been awhile," Luce grinned.

"And I'm glad for that at least." Andy set both cups down and slipped back into bed with her, wrapping his arm around her. Pulling her close.

"It was the best night of my life, Luce. I mean it."

"Mine too." Luce whispered softly.

"Luce?" He smiled softly.

"Andy?" she smiled in return.

"There's something you need to know," he smiled as he felt her stiffen.

"I'm almost certain I'm in love with you."

"Almost?" Luce's eyes widened. "You did not just say that!"

"Well, the thing is, it's something Annie said. I don't know if I can get past it."

Luce huffed out a breath and pulled her arms across her chest.

"Spill it, detective."

"You like ketchup on your eggs."

"You will so pay for that," Luce laughed, slapping him lightly on the chest.

"What do you think, you love me too?" Andy smiled hesitantly.

Luce looked over at Andy, then looked away, gathering her thoughts.

"I think I might." She answered, equally hesitant.

"You think?"

Luce sighed and her expression sobered as she reached over to smooth a lock of hair off his forehead.

"I thought I'd lost you. That night, in the chamber. And it was as if someone ripped my heart out. Is that love Andy? Is this how much it can hurt? When Jack ghosted me, I hurt, but it was out of anger, not sorrow. The thought of losing you, even for a moment, isn't something I can deal with. If you go back to work? What will I do? Is it wrong for me to want you not to?"

"So you do love me." He grinned and leaned over and kissed her softly. Then pulled back and looked at her seriously. His lips pursed, he tipped his head as if in thought.

"How about I hang up that shingle instead. Andrew Holman, Attorney at Law."

Luce widened her eyes in surprise. "Would you?" She was almost afraid to hope.

"I would, on one condition."

Luce frowned. "What kind of condition,"

"The kind where you marry me?"

"What?"

"Marry me." Andy's voice was husky, and nervous. He couldn't imagine this not going as planned.

"It's too soon," Luce whispered, eyes remaining wide.

"Ten years Luce, do you need another decade to decide?" He didn't mean to snap, but there was no way he would back down.

She took a deep breath, searched his face, looking for something, anything, to hold her back.

"No, I mean, yes... I mean..."

"You know I love you right? And I gotta say, I'm pretty sure the feeling's mutual." He smirked then, causing her to laugh out loud.

"It probably is, but Andy, it really is too soon. I'm not saying no, but I'm not saying yes. I'm saying let's see where this takes us. OK?"

"You will eventually say yes though, right?" Andy practically growled then, wrapping his arms around her and squeezing her tight.

Luce sighed. "I probably will, but right now you have a whole new career to launch, my sister's on her honeymoon and pregnant with my first niece and I've got a show to finish up."

"But we'll take all this on together, right?"

"Yeah. I think together sounds perfect."

## CHAPTER FORTY-FIVE

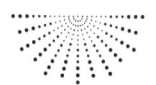

Luce fingered the envelope closure nervously. Molly hadn't seemed too concerned about what was in her father's research, but she was. The mystery of the ship may have been solved, but not the mystery of her sighting it years ago. Adeline Bowers had a reason. So did Andy. But Luce didn't see any connection to her own life. Yet.

She'd waited until the afternoon to settle in and look through the emailed information. Admittedly that had nothing to do with nerves, and everything to do with her not being able to keep her hands off a really hot detective. When he went off with his dad to look at office spaces, she heaved a sigh of relief. She was still trying to process everything that had happened between them.

They'd made love three times the night before, and twice already that day. She shook her head realizing she might just be insatiable. Perhaps ten years of fighting it off finally drove them to the brink. Their connection wasn't just physical either. It was as if they were meant to be together. They completed each other, she thought with a smile. Sappy, maybe. But true.

Sighing, she tried to focus on the matter at hand. Her family history. Sliding the papers out and laying them out on the kitchen table, she flipped through the first through looking for anything significant. Page one had her father's original email and she paused, resting her fingers on his name in the signature line. Feeling a moment of sadness that he wasn't here to be part of all of this.

He'd been asking, it appeared, about Execution Rocks and the Lighthouse that was built upon it. As she flipped through the pages, she began to notice a name that popped up frequently. He seemed to be looking into a Porter ancestor, Luke Porter, who was allegedly a spy in the revolution and an expert in explosives. Her father had been asking about a legendary ship that sank in 1790. He thought maybe Luke Porter was behind its demise.

"I'll be damned," Luce whispered, then jumped as she felt Andy's hands on her shoulders. Leaning in for a kiss, he chuckled.

"What's got you so nervous, babe," he asked.

"Babe? Babe? Oh no, no no no. You will not ever call me babe." Luce shook her head, laughing.

"Princess?"

"Nope," Luce grinned.

"OK, then give me a minute. Honeybun?"

Luce turned around and swatted him on the chest.

"Then how about I just call you Sunshine."

"It'll do, detective. Now look at this. My dad thought his ancestor blew up the MorningStar. That somehow my great great great, well I don't know how many greats, grandfather, Luke Porter, was connected to Lionel Bowers. And he hired him to sink the decoy ship. My father couldn't have known it was a decoy."

"May I?" he looked down at the papers she was holding, and she handed them over.

"You know this means my dad, at some point, believed me. He must have." Luce contemplated that. She'd always thought he'd dismissed her as being highly imaginative. But somewhere along the way, he must have realized there was some truth to her story. Or did he see it as well?

"Look here," Andy said, and laid one of the papers down, pointing his finger in the middle of the page. "He says that he believes Luke posed as a trader to purchase a female slave, and while on board the vessel, planted the explosives. And that he left with the woman, who stayed with him until she died."

"As a slave?" Luce narrowed her eyes. "I hope not."

"There's one way to know, Luce, and that's your family tree. Let's get you a DNA test, upload it to a genealogy site and see what comes up."

"Do I want to know?" Luce wondered aloud.

"Yes you do," Andy said as he took a seat next to her. "You need to know."

Luce nodded. "Ok. I'll do it. Soon. I just need a little time to digest this. On the one hand, thinking my ancestor saved a young woman from slavery. On the other hand, finding out that maybe it was much more nefarious than that? That he took her and kept her in servitude? That's a lot to process."

"I kind of get that," Andy chuckled. "I'm processing it too. You know, however it turns out, I have an idea you should start journaling all this. I think it has the makings of an important book."

"Maybe someday. For now, I still have to figure it all out. The irony of it all is our society is so defined by race, when in reality, it's all kind of a lie, isn't it? I'm no more white than you are black. Neither of us would be considered a person of color, and neither of us understands what it is to live in their skin. I feel as if the North was no better than the South. And our history books make a mockery of the truth in some respects."

"Not completely, but they do tell a story that perhaps is unique to one group of Americans. Certainly not all. Like Columbus discovering America. Except the indigenous people already had."

"Or how about Kamala Harris being the first woman of color to run for VP?"

"How about it?"

"She wasn't. Charlotta Bass was."

"What?"

"Yep, 1952 Progressive Party."

"Well damn, I didn't know we had one back then. See Luce, that's why you should write a book, once you know what really happened. These stories need to be told."

Luce sighed. "OK, maybe someday. For now we've got a TV show to produce. One thing at a time. Now, moving on. Did you find an office?"

"Yes." He leaned in and kissed her, impulsively.

"Spill it detective," Luce grinned.

"Over on Main Street. Next to that Italian bakery. I signed a lease and now it just needs a few touches. I thought you could help."

"OK. I can do that. When will you let them know you're retiring?"

"I'm headed in tomorrow to meet with the Captain. He'll understand."

"As long as it's truly what you want, Andy. Please don't do this just for me, I couldn't live with that."

"It's for me too. And Kat, and others like her Luce. It's the right time." He leaned in and kissed her again, this time lingering a bit longer.

"This means we'll need to relocate, won't we? I suppose I won't mind commuting," Luce sighed. "Plus I'll be closer to Annie."

"Or I can commute from the city if you prefer. Plenty of time to decide. And I like the way you said we." Andy grinned.

Luce took a breath and studied his expression. She knew she loved him. With every fiber of her being. And while she wasn't ready to start planning a wedding, part of her did want her fairy tale to come true. Like Annie, she had dreams too. She just hadn't imagined they'd ever come true. Grinning back, she leaned into him and kissed him until they were both breathless.

"Come on lawyer man, let's go christen that office of yours!"

"Anything for you Luce," he whispered. "Anything."

# EPILOGUE

Luce sat comfortably ensconced in her reading chair, a wide, plush recliner built for two. It had been a gift from Andy. They'd temporarily relocated to his former clubhouse, now dubbed MorningStar Cottage. With Thanksgiving around the corner, she knew she had some decisions to make.

First and foremost, whether or not to renew her contract at KNNY. Andy's idea of her becoming an author at first seemed silly, but now it was taking hold. She looked down at the letter she'd received from the New England Historical Society and sighed.

*Dear Ms. Porter:*
*In response to your inquiry, we do have a significant amount of information in our archives relating to Luke Porter. Unfortunately, it has yet to all be digitized. I can tell you that he was certainly an interesting character, and there is much to be learned from his activities. It seems he was quite a mischief maker, particularly during the Revolution. Locals dubbed him the Cow Neck Rebel, in fact.*
*We do invite you to come to the NEHGS Library in Boston at your convenience, where we will be happy to assist your efforts.*

Luce had read it over and over. Clearly she knew what she needed to do. It was a big step. One she'd need to discuss with Andy. But she knew he'd support her decision whatever it was. At least she hoped. It was his idea after all. The Porter family history was intertwined with American History, and she was destined to document it. The truth. The whole truth. Whether that would be to her benefit or detriment was yet to be seen. And ultimately, she knew, it wasn't about her at all. There was a bigger cause in play. Stories that needed to be told.

As she settled it in her mind, her phone rang. Seeing it was Stuart, she answered.

"Hey boss, working on a Sunday, are you?"

"Actually, no, well, a bit." Stuart chuckled. "Alright, you caught me. I just spoke to Arnie over in Sales. We've been working on a project. One you might have an interest in. Didn't want to tell you until we had a firm go."

"I'm all ears," Luce laughed. "But I should warn you I've got news, too. I've made up my mind."

"Well, you might want to hear me out first," Stuart replied with a friendly warning. "The newly formed Bowers Historical Foundation has offered to sponsor a new documentary series focusing on the history of the Gold Coast of Long Island. In particular on Cow Neck Peninsula and its role in the slave trade as well as the abolitionist movement."

MAYBE HER MIND wasn't made up after all…

ALSO BY MJ MILLER

All About Annie

The Christoph Curse

Holiday Homecoming

Coming 2021
from Scarsdale Publishing:
The Luckland Ladies Mysteries

# ACKNOWLEDGMENTS

None of this would be possible without the unwavering support of my family. Putting up with my ridiculous tales and encouraging me to write them all down. And none of this would be worthwhile without the tremendous support of my readers.

*THANK YOU!*

## ABOUT THE AUTHOR

A lifelong teller of tales, MJ Miller grew up inspired and mentored by an entertaining collection of master storytelling matriarchs. Women who could spin a yarn better than anyone. A native New Yorker and mother of two amazing women, MJ and her fabulously supportive husband share their Tucson home with their resident feline genius, Darwin. A hopeless romantic, MJ loves to tell tales filled with romance, mystery and mayhem that keep the reader turning pages long into the night.

Made in the USA
Columbia, SC
04 December 2020